LUNAR ASSAULT

LUNAR ASSAULT

METAL LEGION™ BOOK FOUR

CH GIDEON   CALEB WACHTER   CRAIG MARTELLE

LMBPN

DISRUPTIVE IMAGINATION

LMBPN Publishing
PMB 196, 2540 South Maryland Pkwy
Las Vegas, NV 89109

First US edition, January 2019
Version 1.01, February 2019
Print ISBN: 978-1-64202-439-5

LUNAR ASSAULT TEAM

Thanks to our Beta Readers

Micky Cocker, James Caplan, Kelly O'Donnell, and John Ashmore

Thanks to the JIT Readers

James Caplan
Misty Roa
John Ashmore
Kelly O'Donnell
Micky Cocker
Jeff Eaton
Crystal Wren
Peter Manis
Paul Westman
Tim Adams

If I've missed anyone, please let me know!

Editing services provided by LKJ Bookmakers www. lkjbooks.com

PROLOGUE: A MATTER OF PRIORITY

"I say again, *Bonhoeffer* Actual," Admiral Wallace's light-delayed voice said in an unyielding, nearly hostile tone. "You are ordered to join the *King Solomon* and assume a defensive posture under Commodore Maeda's command. Acknowledge your orders."

Wallace was the commander of the Terran Armed Forces' 8th Fleet elements, which consisted of eight corvettes, four cruisers, two carriers, and, most importantly, two Republican-class dreadnoughts. The heavily armed force had the critical mission of guarding the New America 2-Nexus gate.

"Admiral Wallace, this is Colonel Li. My ship is essential to an ongoing Code Black priority mission authorized by General Benjamin Akinouye," Li argued. Lieutenant Colonel Leeroy Jenkins braced himself for the end of the dialog with Admiral Wallace. "For reasons of extreme importance to Terran security, I cannot deviate from my mission directives."

Several long, tense seconds passed before Wallace's reply came. "*Bonhoeffer* Actual, let me be blunt. General Akinouye is dead. As the Terran high commander present in this star system under Candlelight conditions, my authority supersedes even

Code Black. Comply with your orders or Terran forces will consider you hostile."

"Candlelight" was the code used by TAF personnel to indicate that, as had occurred once before in the Republic's history, the wormholes had gone dark. Under such conditions, Fleet flag officers were given command of Terran military assets in order to secure Terran interests. Li had argued that Operation Antivenom was of such vital importance that it overrode Candlelight conditions, but Admiral Wallace wasn't buying it. He was ordering the *Bonhoeffer*, even in its badly-damaged state, to rendezvous with the 8th Fleet elements under his command to address the newly-arrived Zeen worldship.

The Zeen moonlet was five hundred kilometers in diameter, and different from anything humanity had seen. Jenkins didn't envy Wallace, and he could well imagine the man's current pucker factor, although, if a warrior had to face a potentially hostile force, there were few better platforms from which to do so than a Terran dreadnought.

The *Marcus Aurelius* was Admiral Wallace's flagship, and few sights could inspire awe and fear like a Republican-class dreadnought. With a keel measuring ten kilometers from bow to stern, the titanic Terran warship was the product of intensive decade-long mining operations that slowly converted mineral-rich asteroids into heavily-armored mobile mass drivers.

Although the "mobile" part was a matter of some debate. It was true that the Republican-class warships were capable of moving under their own power, but to do so at anything approaching tactical speeds required the ship's mass driver to be employed as an engine.

"Tactical assessment?" Jenkins asked.

"They don't have anything close enough to hit us," Li replied matter of factly. "But that could change if he gets a bug up his ass between now and our rendezvous with the Zeen.

Those Sleipnir-class corvettes can run down anything in Terran space," he gestured to two pairs of 8th Fleet corvettes, "and they pack more than enough punch to put us down in our current state."

Jenkins nodded knowingly. Sleipnir-class corvettes were, uniquely in the Terran Armed Forces, exclusively crewed by cybernetically-augmented voiders (the update to the archaic "sailor" label). Every member of a Sleipnir's thirty-nine crew had been radically modified to deal with the extreme gravitational forces of high-speed acceleration. The enhancements were extensive and, ultimately, life-shortening in the extreme. A Sleipnir voider had a life expectancy of just twenty-two years following installation of the implants, but despite the cost, there was no shortage of applicants for the job.

"Those things can pull thirty-five gees during combat." Jenkins scowled.

Li scowled as well. "Those are just the official numbers. I've seen classified testing records verifying closer to fifty."

"They're sprinters, but the speed comes at the cost of stamina," Jenkins mused as all four corvettes broke formation and assumed an intercept trajectory that would bring them into missile range of the *Bonhoeffer* a full half-hour before it rendezvoused with the Zeen worldship.

"We need more time." Jenkins grimaced, meeting Li's gaze and holding it. "Break it down for him."

Li's scowl deepened. "We're already facing mutiny and dereliction of duty charges. What's a little treason sprinkled on top for revealing classified intel?" He sighed shortly before keying up the mic. "Admiral Wallace, this is *Bonhoeffer* Actual requesting a secure P2P link."

Seconds ticked by at a torturous pace before the telltale blue light pulsed on the priority comm station. The *Bonhoeffer* was down to a skeleton crew, which meant that only one in four of her bridge stations was manned. With no one to handle the priority comm console, Li moved to authenticate and accept the inbound connection.

"Li, what the fuck are you doing?" Admiral Wallace veritably snarled. "For over a century, every member of the TAF has trained for Candlelight conditions. There is no single greater threat to the Terran Republic than the one we currently face with the wormholes down. And not only that, but a fucking moon-sized unidentified battlestation just arrived on New America's doorstep. I need answers, and I need them *now*!"

"Admiral, I understand your frustration," Li said heavily. "Let me put it as bluntly as I can: my mission, code-named 'Operation Antivenom,' is more vital to Terran security than erecting a defense against that moon base. Incidentally, that moon base is here to facilitate Operation Antivenom. I'm transmitting operational details previously kept from the rest of my branch, and even from the rest of the TAF, by General Akinouye and General Pushkin. The only active Terran Armed Forces personnel who have full access to this operation's intel are the men and women presently aboard the *Bonhoeffer*, although Admiral Zhao should be apprised of it within the hour."

Li's transmission contained everything except Jem's existence. Wallace was in a position to deny them the opportunity to carry out their mission—which meant they had no choice but to deal with him on his terms—but to reveal Jem's existence was to reveal the most sensitive aspect of their operation, which was simply too great a risk for them to take. If Wallace's command was compromised by Jemmin collaborators, and if they revealed Jem's existence to the Jemmin, there was no way for Operation Antivenom to be successful.

Their trust could go only so far.

Seconds passed before Wallace scoffed, then said, "Your

story's got more holes than a Vorr sexbot. How could you get a message off to Admiral Zhao with the wormhole down? As far as I'm concerned, your data packet is just another in a long string of attempts to push me off while you rendezvous with that moon base. Heave to, Colonel Li, and await my inspection teams."

"Admiral Wallace." Jenkins raised his voice as the four Sleipnir-class corvettes surged forward, accelerating at nearly thirty gees. "This is Lieutenant Colonel Lee Jenkins. It was my team that conducted the secret diplomatic mission on Shiva's Wrath where we first contacted the species aboard that moon base. That mission was carried out under the direct supervision of General Benjamin Akinouye, who was killed during Operation Brick Top a few weeks ago. That operation produced tangible evidence in support of my mission. General Akinouye died so that we could safely extract that evidence, sir."

"Why am I not surprised to find a ship-jumping drunk at the heart of this mess?" Wallace sneered. A "ship-jumper" was what Fleet personnel disdainfully called someone who transferred from Fleet to another branch of the TAF, and the drunk bit was a well-known fact of Jenkins' personal life. "Your careers are over, gentlemen. Enough with the hand-waving; I'm dispatching inspection teams. Heave to and await them or suffer the consequences."

"Admiral," Jenkins pressed, ignoring the digs about his personal history, "I respectfully request that you do not reveal any of what I'm about to tell you, not even to your command staff." He waited for several seconds, giving Wallace a chance to isolate the inbound data stream if he chose to. Eventually, Jenkins continued, "That moon base was built by a species known as the Zeen, who were introduced to us by the Vorr back on Shiva's Wrath. They used an alien FTL transit system to come to New America 2, which is a sparsely-inhabited star system. If they meant the Terran Republic harm, they could have dropped into orbit over Terra Americana, or even Terra Han. They came here to rendezvous with the *Bonhoeffer*, Admiral, not to antagonize Terran interests."

The pregnant pause stretched on before Wallace replied, "All you're doing is admitting to collaborating with an alien species, Colonel, under circumstances that clearly make such collaborations treasonous. You're not a diplomat, Jenkins, you're a serviceman...or at least that's what you're *supposed* to be. You may have forgotten your duty, Colonels, but I most certainly have not forgotten mine. We are at Candlelight, gentlemen. This is the most dangerous moment in the Republic's history, and I will not suffer mutiny under such conditions. Your careers are over, but you might be able to save your lives if you comply with my orders."

"Admiral," Colonel Li interjected, "I urge you to review the packet I sent over. We already have an officer aboard the Zeen moon base, and our operational timetable is set. Operation Antivenom is go, and we must complete it as quickly as possible."

"You have your orders," Wallace snarled. "8th Fleet, out."

Jenkins and Li watched as the Sleipnirs continued their sprint to intercept the relatively sluggish *Bonhoeffer*. Li cocked his head grimly before raising his voice. "Set Condition One throughout the ship. Everyone to their couches."

The crew did as bidden, with the bridge stations requiring little in the way of adjustment to convert workstation chairs into couches capable of supporting their occupants at up to twelve gees for sustained intervals.

But anyone with a decent grasp of mathematics could see that the Sleipnirs would easily intercept them long before they reached the moon base. In fact, at the Sleipnirs' present forty gees of acceleration, they would do so just as the *Bonhoeffer* began braking for final approach to the moon base.

Jenkins strapped into the XO's couch, since she was no longer aboard the ship following Li's decision not to include her in the mission. Concerns about her Fleet affiliations had ultimately caused him to reject her, and Jenkins wasn't about to second-guess Li's personnel decisions in such a critical hour.

The *Bonhoeffer* began its max-burn, and the couches supported their occupants up to the *Bonhoeffer*'s maximum twelve gees of acceleration. For several long, agonizing minutes, it seemed as though the Sleipnirs would intercept the *Bonhoeffer* precisely as Wallace had declared.

Then they slowed. Forty gees fell to thirty, down to twenty, and ultimately they stabilized at fifteen gees of acceleration. At that rate, they would be unable to intercept the *Bonhoeffer* in time to prevent it from linking up with the Zeen worldship.

But no sighs of relief were breathed aboard the *Dietrich Bonhoeffer* as the battered Assault Carrier continued its max-burn approach to the Zeen worldship. Admiral Wallace had given them a grudging reprieve, and they needed to take full advantage of it if they were to complete their mission.

Jenkins blacked out several times during the burn, as he generally did during such conditions, but his focus on the objective never wavered for a second.

He had a job to do, and by God, he was going to get it done.

1

PREP FOR LAUNCH

Captain Xi Bao, aboard the courier ship *DC03*, finally docked with the *Dietrich Bonhoeffer* as the aged warship took up station near the Zeen worldship. She was one of a handful of humans who were allowed on board the massive Zeen ship. The *Bonhoeffer* wasn't even authorized to dock with the worldship.

Xi was greeted at the airlock by Lieutenant Colonel Jenkins, to whom she offered a salute.

"Maybe we should have gone to headquarters to get promoted," Xi suggested.

"Nah. They would have expected too much from us then. It would have sucked to get there and have General Kavanaugh tear up the promotion orders in front of us." Jenkins shrugged.

"I'm sure you're right. Easy come, easy go."

Jenkins nodded and returned Xi's salute.

"Good work, Captain. Report."

"The Zeen will need some time to recharge their FTL system, sir," Xi replied promptly. "It's difficult to get details out of them, but I don't think they even know how long it will take for them to calibrate the system for us."

Jenkins' brow lowered darkly. "Admiral Wallace has put

four warships just beyond engagement range. Every minute that ticks by gives him another chance to change his mind."

"Understood, sir," Xi replied grimly. "But even if the FTL system was charged and ready to go, the Vorr ambassador suggests that we make certain...modifications to the *Bonhoeffer* before transiting to Sol."

Jenkins cocked his head. "I don't think Colonel Li is going to like that."

"No, sir," she agreed. "But Deep Currents has shown me tactical simulations that convince me there's something to the idea. The whole process should only take a few hours to complete."

"Hours?" Jenkins repeated darkly. "We don't have hours, Captain. We might not even have minutes."

"Colonel," Xi explained, "I believe the Zeen encountered unexpected difficulties with their first use of the FTL system. I don't think there's anything we can do to hurry things along. I gave it my best effort, sir."

Jenkins seemed to relax. "All right. You'd better make your report to Colonel Li. The sooner we get these 'modifications' moving forward, the sooner we can go."

"Yes, sir," Xi acknowledged, and the two of them made their way to the *Bonhoeffer*'s CAC where Colonel Li oversaw the disembarkation of the *Bonhoeffer*'s last crew.

But some of those crew were less willing than others to follow Li's orders.

"We're not finished with repairs to four of the mechs, Colonel," Chief Rimmer insisted. "We're not leaving until those mechs' systems are green across the board."

"Your people have done their jobs, Ace," Li said irritably. "Your orders were to make them combat-ready, not parade-worthy. You've done your bit."

"Respectfully, sir," Rimmer jutted his chin defiantly, "one of us has never worked a drop-deck before, and the other has spent his entire career running them. If anyone is going to provide a lecture on the subject—"

Li held up a hand to stop the tirade. "Arnie, I appreciate the support, as I'm sure our Metalheads do." He tilted his chin toward the approaching Xi and Jenkins. "But what you're talking about amounts to several hours' work just to tighten a few bolts and run a series of diagnostics on mechs that, just ten hours ago, were down-checked for damage sustained during Brick Top. You've surpassed even *your* lofty standards, Chief, just by getting them field-ready. It's time to call it a day. The general's yacht is ready to leave, and I think it's time for your people to board it."

"Colonel, with respect," Rimmer reiterated, although this time his voice was suffused with genuine deference. "This is probably the most technically difficult drop in the Metal Legion's history. It can't be done via remote, and it can't be done without a full drop-deck team." His visage softened, but his eyes remained diamond hard as he finished, "Our entire careers... hell, our entire *lives,* have prepared us for this moment, sir. We absolutely will not step back. So, if you'll excuse me, sir, I've got a drop-deck to run."

He turned smartly on his heel, making brief eye contact with Xi before stopping to address her.

"Captain Xi," Rimmer said officiously, producing one of many data slates from his multi-pouched belt. "*Elvira*'s repairs were completed forty minutes ago, and her systems are green across the board. She's ready for your inspection, and my people will make whatever additional adjustments you deem necessary."

Xi was moved by the longtime veteran's determination and resolve, and nodded approvingly while accepting the slate. "Thank you, Chief."

"Ma'am." Rimmer saluted before exiting the CAC, causing Li to chuckle.

"He's a good man," Li said, and Xi thought she saw a slight glisten in the colonel's eyes as he turned to face her. His expression darkened almost instantly. "Something tells me I'm not going to like what you've got to say."

Xi tucked the data slate Rimmer had given her into her pocket. "The Vorr and the Zeen have several modifications they're prepared to make to the *Bonhoeffer*, Colonel."

Li snorted. "If those squids and crabs think they'll set foot... or claw or tentacle on my ship..." he stammered.

"No, sir," Xi replied promptly. "Not a single Zeen or Vorr will need access to the *Bonhoeffer*'s interior to make these modifications."

Li and Jenkins shared looks of mutual uncertainty before Li grunted. "Now I *know* I'm not going to like it."

***

"They want to cover the entire ship in a meter of...nanotech resin?" Li blurted after Xi completed her report on the proposed modifications. "You can't be serious."

"I field-tested the material myself, Colonel," Xi reiterated. "Using a sidearm from the DCo3, I checked the integrity of the stuff, and it confirmed the Vorr's schematics. It would take dozens of railguns strikes or a direct hit from a Republican mass driver to punch through a meter-thick shell of it applied to the *Bonhoeffer*'s forward hull. As robust as Luna One's defensive grid is, it *doesn't* include a Republican mass driver."

"Not to our knowledge." Li scowled.

"Colonel," Jenkins put in, "we've got a narrowing window here. Surviving final approach was a concern from the outset of this operation's planning phase. Even with Jem's proposed virtual takeover of Luna One's sensor grid, we're still looking at no better than a coin-flip chance of the *Bonhoeffer* reaching the drop point. This stuff might just push the numbers far enough in our favor to put Legion tracks in virgin regolith."

Li rubbed his forehead irritably but eventually relented. "Fine. Tell them to get started. But I need all the technical data regarding this stuff. We'll need to adapt to our new mass profile, and also shut down the rotating compartments so they can worm this...*stuff* into every exterior nook and cranny. That means zero-gee aboard this vessel for the duration of this operation...and probably for the rest of the *Bonhoeffer*'s service."

Xi winced, knowing he was right. Once the Zeen coated the *Bonhoeffer* with the nano-resin, it would turn the ship into a mobile brick with just engine ports, sensor arrays, and drop bays exposed. Not even the *Bonhoeffer*'s weapons could be left exposed since doing so would compromise the ship's ability to deploy its mechs. Besides, if they got into a shooting war with Luna One before they were treads down on the Moon's surface, the operation was already a failure.

One way or another, the *Dietrich Bonhoeffer* was about to end its storied service to the Terran Republic. Even though Xi had briefly bounced back and forth between *Elvira* and *Devil Crab* earlier in her career, she had still formed a profound attachment to the Scorpion-class—and she had only been with the Legion for a couple of years. Colonel Li had served the Terran Armor Corps with distinction for half a century, the vast majority of which had been aboard the *Dietrich Bonhoeffer*.

Xi shuddered to think of the emotional turmoil he must have been going through. "Thank you, Colonel." Xi nodded, handing him the data slate she had prepared. "Tight-beam your acknowledgment on the indicated channel and the Zeen will commence the work."

Li reviewed the slate's contents before affixing his signature to it and transmitting as Xi had suggested. He turned to her. "I think it's time you filled us in on what you saw aboard that... base, Captain Xi."

Jenkins nodded in agreement, and Xi felt the eyes of Sergeant Major Trapper and also those of Colonel Moon, the *Bonhoeffer*'s Commander Intercept Group, the CIG, as she prepared to deliver her report...which contained some undeniably disturbing news.

"They only let me see a little bit of the structure's interior, but every single compartment I saw was *filled* with Zeen insectaurs," she explained. "They let me tour what they called a 'small sub-hive,' that contained no fewer than fifty warships."

"When you say 'warships...'" Trapper said leadingly.

Xi nodded direly. "Most were between one hundred fifty and two hundred meters from bow to stern, but they were nowhere near as uniform as the vehicles we saw back on Shiva's Wrath. I asked why that was, but got a stonewall in reply. One thing I did manage to get out of them is that they claim not to have an extensive ground force. They developed the vehicles we encountered on Shiva's Wrath primarily because the Vorr requested them to, but it seems there's some hesitation on the Zeen's part to give that particular project maximum support."

Li cocked his head dubiously. "You're saying that the majority of the Zeen military assets are spacecraft and that their worldship is stuffed full of them?"

"That's the impression I got, sir," Xi agreed. "But again, I was only exposed to what they wanted me to see, and they weren't exactly forthcoming on my lines of inquiry."

"You make it sound like they're distrustful of us," Jenkins mused.

"That's one way to look at it." Xi nodded grimly. "Another way would be to say they were ready to declare humanity was subservient to Jemmin and worthy of being 'eaten' for supporting Jemmin, knowingly or otherwise. They might have made good on that threat if I hadn't presented the 'credentials' I received from the Zeen back on Shiva's Wrath."

A pin drop would have been deafening in the seconds that followed. Xi knew it wasn't what anyone wanted to hear, but her job was to report events to the best of her ability so that her superiors could make the most informed decisions possible.

"That's," Colonel Moon mused, "not exactly encouraging."

"It's what we've got." Jenkins shrugged. "And it's more than we had. A *lot* more. Good work, Captain," he said with feeling. "Is there anything else of note you'd like to report?"

Xi shook her head confidently. "Only to say that the Zeen really, *really* dislike Jemmin. I think their entire preoccupation with symmetry and asymmetry stems from the fact that the Jem'un were biologically asymmetrical, and given the history between the Jem'un and the Zeen, asymmetry was elevated from an ugly or discordant feature to one worthy of eradication. Their hatred of the Jem'un, and Jemmin, over the destruction of their homeworld is so driving...so all-consuming that even if I *did* understand it fully, I'd have no way to express it with words. Destroying Jemmin might be the fundamental purpose of their existence. It seems to inform every facet of Zeen society to one degree or another."

Trapper turned to Moon and Li. "Hatred like that is irrational. It doesn't just pop up and persist without a whole lot of help."

"Agreed," Li nodded. "Someone is manipulating them against Jemmin."

"Are the Vorr behind it?" Moon asked, prompting Xi to shake her head.

"I don't think so," she said firmly. "They say they didn't even know about the Vorr until a few decades ago, which tracks with the Vorr's account and with Jem's. It's possible they're all in on some major deception, but—"

"Occam's Razor," Jenkins interrupted, agreeing with Xi. "The most likely scenario here is the simplest one: they're all telling the truth to a significant degree, or at least that they're not actively conspiring to mislead us."

"For all their social peculiarities," Xi nodded deferentially to her CO, "the Zeen are remarkably forthright about most things. I guess you could consider some of my rebuffed inquiries to have related to their equivalent of national security."

"We've all got to keep *those* cards close to the chest," Trapper grudgingly allowed.

Colonel Li turned to Sergeant Major Trapper. "Sergeant Major, I would be remiss in my duties if I did not formally request that you board the general's yacht. Your name and reputation hold a lot of weight in the TAF, and I can think of no one better to debrief the Joint Chiefs than you."

"Fat fucking chance, Li." Trapper scoffed. "There's a very good reason I stuck at sergeant major, and it had nothing to do with my aptitude or lack of opportunity for advancement. The pay bump wasn't worth the cost of shaking hands with those bastards on a monthly basis. I've avoided debriefings of that type for fifty-two years, and I am not about to surrender that particular patch of high ground."

"Luna One is the most heavily-fortified installation in human history," Li argued.

"Which is why we're sneaking in the back door," Trapper countered. "Only a fool would go head-on against the Moon after Luna One knocked the Canary Islands out with mass drivers and wiped out the entire eastern seaboard of North America. Even a century and a half ago, facing literally everything the Yanks could throw at it, Luna One didn't suffer so much as a single scratch before that tsunami erased half of the

American civilization. The next day, Luna One pummeled half of California into the ocean, bringing the death toll to nearly one out of every two men, women, and children in the Americas." His bushy brows lowered thunderously. "Fuckers made Mao's Great Leap Forward look like riot control with rubber bullets and tear gas in comparison to the hell they unleashed on the Old West."

"Which is why forty more Terran soldiers can hardly be expected to make the difference," Li pressed, and for some reason, Xi felt an unexpected twinge of shame as Trapper accurately outlined the events of America's last days as a sovereign nation. She knew she'd done nothing, said nothing, and even *thought* nothing in support of the atrocity that had secured China's victory in Earth's last World War, but for reasons not immediately clear to her, she felt a measure of guilt for those events.

"It's not about the body count, Colonel." Trapper smirked, snapping her focus back to the present. "It's about having the right soldier in the right place at the right time. My people won't break, and they won't bend. We're going down there, so cut the yacht loose and let's get to work."

"Hear, hear," Colonel Moon agreed.

"Agreed." Xi nodded, drawing a scowl from Li before the *Bonhoeffer*'s CO finally relented.

"All right." Li sighed. "Cut the yacht loose."

A few seconds later, the general's yacht disembarked, loaded with the *Bonhoeffer*'s engineers, gunners, and other personnel made unnecessary by the Zeen resin shell. Only a skeleton command crew remained to operate the warship's systems. Along with Chief Rimmer's First and Second Shifts, Colonel Moon's top twenty pilots, Trapper's forty troopers, and the Metal Legion mech crews, one hundred twenty-three Terrans remained aboard the venerable warship as the Zeen began the process of encasing the battered but still mighty vessel in a thick coat of nano-resin.

Two dozen ships, appearing like bulbous puffer-fish to Xi's eyes, slowly encircled the *Bonhoeffer* and rained a steady stream of the material onto its hull. Their application was extremely precise, leaving just drop decks, engine ports, and a few key sensor systems exposed.

The process took several hours to complete, during which time Admiral Wallace's people remained surprisingly silent while standing off just beyond the *Bonhoeffer*'s nominal engagement range.

Of course, had the quartet of Sleipnir corvettes chosen to attack, the *Bonhoeffer* would have been totally defenseless against them.

Thankfully, no one felt the need to inform Admiral Wallace of that fact.

2

FLEET COMMANDS

"This is Admiral Wallace of the Terran Republic's 8th Fleet," Wallace's commanding voice stated over all major hailing frequencies. *"Bonhoeffer* Actual is hereby ordered to disengage from the foreign planetoid and its ships. This is sovereign Terran territory, and as the local commander of Terran military assets, it is my duty to secure that sovereignty by any and all means at my disposal. Unidentified alien vessels are ordered to disengage from Terran assets and return to their moorings. Failure to comply will be met with deadly force. All Terran assets are ordered to assist 8th Fleet in securing the foreign planetoid and its attachments. Wallace out."

Li and Jenkins exchanged looks of uncertainty, and both men kept an eye on the secure comm line. When no priority message came over that line, Jenkins' confusion grew.

"Why would he broadcast a general hail?" Jenkins asked. "If he really wants us to participate, he would have transmitted direct orders via P2P."

"He might think we're too close to the Zeen worldship to risk a secure link being intercepted," Li mused. "Besides, we've still got a dozen of those spunk-throwers out there coating my hull."

"Wallace is a prick," Trapper opined, "but he's not a fool. He's working an angle."

"But what?" Colonel Moon cocked his head skeptically.

"You'd have to ask him." Trapper inclined his chin to the priority comm station.

"If he didn't initiate, we shouldn't either," Jenkins replied. "Let's just play along and see where he's going with this."

"That means answering." Li grunted, picking up the mic and keying into the hailing frequencies. "8th Fleet, this is *Bonhoeffer* Actual. We cannot comply with your orders at this time. We—"

"This is Deep Currents of Radiant Warmth." The Vorr's distinctly feminine, auto-translated voice overrode Li's on the comm, cutting him off mid-sentence. "As a duly-appointed ambassador for the Vorr government, I am authorized to contribute to this conflict in the hope of facilitating its peaceful resolution. We mean the Terran Republic no harm, and in fact seek to forge an alliance with your government so that our nations might navigate this perilous time to a mutually beneficial conclusion. I am willing to come aboard one of your ships as a gesture of good faith so that we might initiate a productive dialogue."

Seconds ticked by, during which time the Sleipnir-class corvettes surged toward the moon base. "Vorr ambassador, this is Admiral Wallace." The admiral's voice was full of contempt. "If the Vorr played a part in this moon base's violation of Terran sovereign space, then that is anything but an act of 'good faith.' And I can assure you that my government has authorized me to employ deadly force in defense of Terran sovereignty."

In reply to the oncoming corvettes, a swarm of Zeen warships emerged from the worldship. A dozen, then two dozen...three dozen...fifty...finally, eighty-one distinct Zeen signatures emerged from the worldship's surface.

"Admiral Wallace," Deep Currents serenely replied, "there is no need for a threat display. The Vorr make no claim that would violate Terran sovereignty. On the contrary, we seek to bolster your Republic's position against hostile agents, chief among them, the Jemmin. But if a demonstration of force is necessary to establish a productive dialogue between us..." her voice trailed off as the eighty-one Zeen warships adopted a picture-perfect offset diamond formation, "*we* can assure *you* that such a demonstration will not require what your people call an 'encore.'"

The Zeen ships accelerated even faster than the Sleipnirs as they tore across the void at greater than fifty gees of acceleration. Jenkins quickly realized that they were not aiming to intercept the four Sleipnir-class corvettes, but were instead burning straight toward the wormhole where the majority of 8th Fleet elements were presently deployed.

Including *both* Republican-class Terran dreadnoughts, which loomed just behind the gate where they could best deploy their mass drivers against enemies coming through the wormhole.

Every ship that traversed the wormholes needed to do so by precisely matching its rotation, velocity, and angle of approach so as to survive the unthinkable forces that warped the very fabric of space-time until two points practically became one.

This meant that any ship emerging through a wormhole gate would do so with a specific and predictable trajectory, making them vulnerable to carefully positioned defensive assets.

But the Illumination League's founding charter pertaining to wormhole use outlawed the emplacing fixed assets, requiring that any sentinel platforms be capable of a minimum degree of motive power. To Jenkins, the reasons for that particular limitation had only grown clearer in recent weeks as he came to accept the truth of Jemmin's hostility toward any and all non-Jemmin spacefaring races.

Jemmin used the wormhole gates like a slaughterhouse uses a chute. Younger, less technologically advanced, and frankly less intelligent species were herded into the chutes, where they blindly proceeded into the kill box. Before they understood the danger, the hammer came down, and it was lights out for the unsuspecting younger race. Nobody knew how many times Jemmin had done this, but it seemed like a fairly refined system. Refinement required practice, and in this case, each practice session required a new, unsuspecting race to test its refinements on.

Part of how Jemmin achieved this was by convincing everyone in the so-called 'Illumination League' to agree to certain ground rules in order to take advantage of FTL access via the Nexus and its myriad linked gates.

Some of these ground rules greatly limited how effectively individual nations could secure their own interests at the wormhole gates. This was why the Arh'Kel scourge had been a constant thorn in the Terran Republic's side: because IL law prevented Terrans from proactively defending themselves at the Nexus, where weapons fire was strictly forbidden, and it also limited just how heavily they could fortify their wormhole gates on the Terran side of the system.

Therefore, optimal firing angles found just behind the rim of the wormhole gates were taken up by Terran dreadnoughts and their support ships standing sentinel. When Arh'Kel invasion fleets came through a gate, ninety percent of their ships were destroyed outright by Terran fire before they could adopt anything approaching a coordinated battle-ready posture. The rest would generally try to slip through and hit Terran interests as hard as possible, and those few survivors had wrought sheer havoc on the Terran Republic in the years leading up to Jenkins' transfer to Armor Corps.

And with eighty-one Zeen warships on an intercept course with the 8th Fleet elements standing guard at the wormhole gate, it seemed the Terran dreadnoughts were about to prove their worth yet again.

The Sleipnir corvettes faltered just as they crossed into engagement range of the *Bonhoeffer*, and to Jenkins' mild surprise they banked and assumed a flanking trajectory on the Zeen formation. They were already in firing range, but their weapons remained silent as they carefully maneuvered for an advantageous arc. Their course would loop them wide of the Zeen formation before dropping them into a slot on the Zeen's stern quarter precisely as the Zeen warships were scheduled to reach engagement range of the 8th Fleet dreadnoughts.

"This isn't good," Jenkins muttered.

"We can't give away anything more than we already have," Li said darkly, and the Terran Armor Corps' most senior officers watched in grim anticipation of what seemed inevitable: live fire exchanged by Zeen and Terran forces.

Xi was busily scrambling through *Elvira*'s exterior, with her Wrench following close behind to update her on the mech's various systems.

"We've still got some issues around Five Leg," Gordon explained as she came to inspect that particular limb's hull joint. The welds were ragged, heavy, and downright ugly. "Not only does it look like ass, but we're also at fifty percent integrity on the armor there," Gordon continued as she ducked beneath the joint to visually inspect the chassis. "The joint itself is spotless, though. She'll sprint just fine."

"Normally I'd be worried about these gaps," Xi pointed to a few centimeter-wide openings in the hastily-welded casing, "especially on the Lunar surface where the regolith will destroy anything it works its way into." She slid out from beneath the mech and nimbly regained her feet before finishing, "But there's nothing normal about this deployment. You did good work, Gordon. I'm just sorry you had to do it alone."

Gordon smirked. "Oh, I wasn't completely alone. *Some* of Rimmer's people aren't total bastards."

She snickered. "He must be slipping, then."

"Well played, Captain." Gordon laughed.

"How are the fifteens?" she asked, deftly clambering up Five Leg and standing atop *Elvira*'s roof. To her eyes, they looked well-greased, which was the single best indicator that they'd been gone over by a competent crew.

"Ready to shred," Gordon assured her. "I've already updated the targeting computer with Lunar variables and tested those figures in a few thousand simulations run on the *Bonhoeffer*'s computer. But the SRMs have got me a little worried," he admitted as he hauled himself up beside where she crouched next to the port missile launcher. "I've already put the thickest grease I can muster on the main bearing's exterior, but there's no way it will last more than a few full rotations before that moon dust gets in there."

"And the polymers in the servos will get ground to powder by the regolith once it works its way in," Xi agreed sourly, having hoped he would come up with some kind of brilliant solution to the problem. "Damn!"

"Oh, come on, Captain," Gordon said, sounding legitimately offended. "You don't think I'd stop *there*, do you?"

She gave him an expectant look. "Go on. Impress me."

He grinned before reaching into his pocket and producing what looked like a giant black garbage bag. "With any kind of atmo," he explained, unfurling the bag and flapping it full of air, revealing it to be just large enough to envelop the entire SRM launcher, "this thing would come apart in the breeze of a rough fart. But with no atmospheric drag, it should last indefinitely... until you fire through it, of course."

She returned his grin and breathed a sigh of relief. "A garbage bag—I'll be damned. Good work, Chief."

"I'll have to replace them after every firing," he explained, "which means I've got to perfect my moonwalking technique, and we'll need to keep your cockpit continually isolated to protect against the regolith. You'll also need to deactivate the auto-cycles to prevent unnecessary movement. But these should give us at least three, maybe four full uses before the regolith wrecks the alignment system. I've already gone over the process with the other crews whose launchers are of this design. We're ready."

"We are," Xi agreed before going about her last-minute preparations, mercifully unaware of the firestorm about to erupt at the wormhole gate.

"8th Fleet is adopting a defensive posture," Colonel Moon reported from the Sensor section. "The *Martin Luther* and *Crimson Monsoon* are scrambling fighters. I'm reading four hundred interceptors."

"That's both carriers' full complement." Li grimaced. "And Admiral Wallace seems uninterested in discussing the matter further. He has denied our attempts to initiate a private uplink and ignores our open hails. Even the Vorr isn't getting anywhere with him."

To Jenkins, it was like watching an asteroid impact in slow-motion. There was nothing he could do to stop what was about to happen, and he knew that on some level he was responsible for the blood that would soon be shed.

The bitch of it was, he couldn't see a viable alternative to the path he and his fellow Metalheads had chosen. Rather than reassuring or comforting him, that particular realization fueled his frustration and the glimmer of despair he felt while watching his fellow TAF servicemen prepare to engage the Zeen.

Colonel Moon nearly leapt out of his chair in Sensors, declaring, "Wormhole is online. I say again: NA2-Nexus wormhole is online."

A Jemmin warship emerged a few moments later over the gate's event horizon.

Jenkins said what they all thought. "Oh, shit."

3

A JEMMIN GATE-CRASHER

The first seconds, as with any engagement, were absolutely crucial to determining its outcome.

If Admiral Wallace disbelieved Jenkins and Li, his focus would be centered on the approaching Zeen fleet and he would miss the chance to react appropriately to the Jemmin threat. After all, Terran humanity was not officially at war with Jemmin, and it was unlikely that details of the engagement on Shiva's Wrath had been widely-disseminated among the TAF. As such, it would be nearly unthinkable for a Terran dreadnought to open fire on a newly-arrived Jemmin warship.

If, however, Admiral Wallace *did* believe the Metal Legion's report regarding the Jemmin threat, he would have kept his biggest guns focused on the kill box at the gate's event horizon. Those opening seconds, as the Terrans had learned in the Arh'Kel conflict, were critical to determining victory or defeat in the face of a newly-arrived aggressor.

When both the *Marcus Aurelius* and the *Socrates* unleashed their terrifying arsenals upon that warship, utterly annihilating it zero-point-four-six seconds after it had emerged from the event horizon, Jenkins realized that some of the previous posturing had been just that.

Posturing.

Jenkins' respect for Admiral Wallace grew by leaps and bounds as the first Jemmin ship was followed by a second, then a third, a fourth, a fifth, and a sixth. Terran fighters swooped out of concealment behind the wormhole gate, stabbing railgun bolts into the Jemmin hulls before ducking back behind the safety of the wormhole's superstructure and event horizon.

Jemmin reactors failed in those opening seconds as the debris cloud unfurled in a glittering cone that sprang forth from the wormhole gate. Republican mass drivers fired again, and again, and again. With each delivered projectile, a dozen counter-thrusters fired in perfect unison to prevent the mighty warship from falling out of orientation, since the recoil of each shot increased the dreadnought's acceleration in the direction opposite the target. These stabilizing jets, firing at equidistant points around the cylindrical dreadnought's forward hull, gave the appearance of a ten-kilometer-long rifle's muzzle suppressor flashing with each bolt. Several tons of gaseous plasma were ejected by the smaller mass drivers with each slug, and while they managed to keep their dreadnoughts' keels on-target, the mighty Terran warships slowly but surely began to accelerate away from the wormhole gate.

Ship after ship was scrubbed by merciless Terran fire, and a pause followed the sixth Jemmin warship's appearance. For a moment, Jenkins' mind leapt to the thought that maybe, just maybe, they had been wrong about the Jemmin conspiracy. Maybe those six ships had come on a mission of peace. Maybe Admiral Wallace had just slaughtered six ships full of Jemmin who had wanted nothing more than to help humanity.

They were irrational thoughts to be sure, but they were in

the forefront of his mind as the seventh Jemmin warship appeared.

When it did, Jenkins' fears were totally allayed.

Unlike the first six Jemmin warships, which were uniform in size and identical in design to the one the *Bonhoeffer* had engaged at Shiva's Wrath, this one was nearly as large (and apparently half-again as massive) as a Terran dreadnought. It had a bulbous, roughly egg-shaped hull and a mass profile suggesting it was almost solid. Hundreds of capital-grade weapons sprouted from its curved hull, each aimed back toward the wormhole gate's rim. To Jenkins, this previously-unseen warship looked like the images of a porcupine he had seen as a child.

And when the newcomer's guns cleared, the devastation they wrought was every bit as terrifying as what Admiral Wallace had unleashed on the enemy dreadnought's escorts.

The *Socrates* suffered the worst of the enemy's wrath, receiving hundreds of railgun strikes as dozens of laser beams carved deep rents into its nickel-iron hull. The Jemmin lasers swept across the mighty dreadnought's hull in search of capital-grade weapon placements.

Returning fire with aplomb, both the *Socrates* and *Marcus Aurelius* fired their mass drivers, sending multi-ton slugs hurtling toward the enemy ship, which they struck with terrifying force. Each strike knocked the enemy ship off-axis with enough force to turn any crew member within into pudding on the bulkheads. The shock-loads were unthinkable, and the rents the impacts tore in the Jemmin super-ship's hull were a hundred meters long and a dozen meters deep.

The Terran interceptors surged forward with a single purpose, streaking toward the enemy dreadnought with murderous intent. Jenkins felt a chill run down his spine as he considered the prospect of the Terran fighters unleashing their combined arsenals of four hundred one-megaton nukes against the enemy warship.

Especially if they did so in such proximity to the wormhole gate.

Nobody knew what would happen if a gate was destroyed. Some had theorized it would cause a rip in space-time that might destabilize any planetary bodies nearby, pulling them apart with a single 'gravity ripple' more intense than any found outside of a black hole. Others thought the gates would contain the energies of their destruction since such a failsafe would seem to be an obviously desirable design feature that should have been within the technical ability of any race capable of building the things in the first place.

Unfortunately (or fortunately, depending on one's perspective), the Terran fighters did not get the chance to test the gate's limits with their nukes.

Streaming out of the Jemmin dreadnought's hull, hundreds of void fighters leapt out to oppose their Terran counterparts. Capital-grade weapons fire flew back and forth between the titanic warships, killing a handful of both Jemmin and Terran fighters as the flights of interceptors broke off and engaged in the most chaotic, expansive, and violent interceptor firefight in Terran history.

Like most firefights, the majority of the losses occurred in the opening seconds. A hundred Terran fighters were killed in the initial exchange, and nearly as many Jemmin died in the same span. The surviving interceptors broke ever-farther apart, with each Terran pilot taking the opportunity to unleash his nuclear missile at the enemy dreadnought. Most of those missiles were sniped by Jemmin fighters, whose maneuverability and acceleration were quickly proven to be far superior to the Terrans'. Of those missiles that slipped through the interceptor screen, ninety percent were scrubbed by the dreadnought's point-defense systems. A handful of megaton-strong impacts registered across the dreadnought's hull, carving deep gashes in the enemy's flanks, but their collective energies were far from decisive and only managed to knock a dozen or so weapons offline. Weapons that had targeted the ailing *Socrates*.

The *Socrates'* wounds grew steadily worse as unrelenting fire from the Jemmin dreadnought dug deeper and deeper into the handful of precise strike points. Jemmin capital lasers continued to scour the *Socrates'* hull clear of secondary capital-grade weapons, slowly but surely weakening the mightiest war machine Terran humanity had ever constructed.

The *Socrates'* hull glowed fiery orange for a hundred meters surrounding each of its wounds, giving the appearance of blood welling up on a wounded beast's hide. It was clear that, despite the Terran dreadnoughts' game-changing mass drivers, the Jemmin warship would overcome the *Socrates'* robust defenses.

And it would happen sooner than any Terran could have thought possible.

In reply to its would-be murderer's efforts, the *Socrates* unleashed a storm of missiles from its bow-mounted heavily-armored launchers. A near-constant stream of missiles and torpedoes flew from the dying dreadnought, each one a Terran declaration every bit as clear and potent as the one written in the Republic's founding documents. Amidst the missile storm, the *Socrates* delivered a final bolt from its mass driver system before that all-important central weapon fell ominously silent.

Missiles were sniped by interceptors, but there were *thousands* of missiles against hundreds of fighters. At such close range, it was impossible for any countermeasure screen to intercept all of the inbound ordnance, which carried several *gigatons* of combined destructive force.

The enemy dreadnought continued to pour fire into the dying *Socrates*, seeming to ignore the inbound torpedoes and missiles as its interceptors steadily reduced the number of inbound platforms. Just two hundred Terran fighters remained, but they took full advantage of their counterparts' divided attention to devastating effect. Dozens of Jemmin fighters died each second, while twice as many Terran missiles were shot down by the survivors.

But this was a simple numbers game. And even as the *Socrates'* interior rippled with explosions that ejected geysers of material out its bow and stern, its dying breath fell upon the enemy dreadnought with the fury of a vengeful god.

Dozens of ten-megaton missiles slammed into the enemy's seven-kilometer-long hull in rapid succession, flashing with such intense radiance that the nearby interceptors' drive systems were temporarily knocked offline. Several of these voidcraft, both Jemmin and Terran, collided with the ever-growing cloud of debris as they fell victim to the simplest laws of physics.

But it was the twenty-five surviving fifty-megaton torpedoes that best delivered the *Socrates'* final fury.

With multiple explosions going off near-simultaneously, each torpedo's destructive energies were carefully designed to deliver maximum devastation directly ahead of the weapon rather than omnidirectionally. Terran scientists had spent decades developing the most effective fusion-based ship-killer system possible.

And those weapons dug *deep* into the Jemmin dreadnought's seemingly impregnable hull.

Carving off great shards of the enemy vessel's outer armor, the ripple of torpedo impacts blinded even the *Bonhoeffer's* sensors. When the *Bonhoeffer* was no longer blind, the wave of fire had abated, and the *Socrates* drifted backward from the wormhole gate as it gently tumbled stern-over-bow. A few dozen escape pods flew from its hull, but there was little doubt that only a tiny fraction of the *Socrates'* crew had survived the exchange.

For a moment, it seemed as though the Jemmin warship might have suffered the same fate as it, too, was tilted off-axis as it started to tumble. The *Marcus Aurelius'* mass drivers continued pouring slug after slug into the Jemmin warship's hull, but the Terran dreadnought's rate of fire had slowed to a snail's pace compared to its earlier output.

As the Jemmin weapons turned their fury upon the last remaining Terran dreadnought, it seemed as though the beleaguered *Marcus Aurelius* would be unequal to the task of ending the unthinkably durable Jemmin warship. Despite Terran fire rendering its shape no longer remotely symmetrical (the irony of which was not lost on Jenkins), the Jemmin dreadnought had lost no more than twenty percent of its firepower.

Then the Zeen entered the fray.

Eighty-one Zeen warships lashed out with perfect precision, stabbing 324 laser beams into the Jemmin dreadnought's badly-damaged flank. Jenkins had seen Jemmin capital-grade lasers in action, and they generally persisted for between two and three seconds before cutting out.

The Zeen lasers poured their energies into the Jemmin hull for *nine* seconds before, with unerring unity, cutting out as the offset diamond of Zeen warships split into three groups of twenty-seven ships apiece.

For a moment, brief though it was, Jenkins saw something akin to hesitation in the movements of the Jemmin void fighters. It was almost like a palpable chill had run throughout the Jemmin force.

A clearer example of fear sweeping through a fighting force would be difficult to imagine.

Energetic eruptions blew apart the Jemmin dreadnought's hull where the Zeen had poured their fury, sending hundred-meter-wide chunks of the warship's multi-layered hull spinning off into the void. The *Marcus Aurelius* hammered its mass driver slugs into the Jemmin dreadnought from the other side of the devastating pincer, while the mixed interceptors split off into dogfights and other increasingly broken and frantic engagements.

Some Terran pilots survived the maelstrom, but Jemmin interceptor superiority was now on full display as they seemed to abandon their guard duties in support of the Jemmin dreadnought. The Jemmin super-ship focused its fire on the *Marcus Aurelius'* mass driver ports, which remained shut between shots and were comprised of hundreds of layers of interlocking reactive armor. The Jemmin behemoth seemed focused as it ponderously reoriented to put as many guns on Wallace's flagship as possible. To Jenkins, it almost seemed like a desperate move.

With a killer instinct rarely matched in human history, Admiral Wallace unleashed a storm of missiles similar to that which preceded the *Socrates'* death throes. Counterfire sniped dozens of them from the void, but dozens subtracted from hundreds made little difference to the outcome.

One after another, digging into the deep rents in the Jemmin dreadnought's hull, multi-megaton explosions tore into the guts of what had been the most impregnable warship ever to visit Terran space. With each successive strike, more energy was delivered *into* the enemy ship than was wasted into the dead of space. And then, like dynamite set off inside a slab of granite, the *Marcus Aurelius'* storm of ordnance blew the enemy vessel apart.

Dozens of explosions rippled across the Jemmin hull as the nukes touched off like a string of firecrackers under a pot. Each eruption spewed hundreds of tons of molten minerals and armor fragments into the void, and then Jenkins was greeted with the most satisfying sight of his entire life.

Like an egg cracked on the lip of a bowl, the Jemmin warship split apart in two roughly equal halves, with its flaming entrails belching into the blackness as the last of the Terran missiles finished the job of cleaving the mighty warship. Improbably, the Jemmin guns of both halves continued pouring fire into the *Marcus Aurelius*, as well as striking out at the Zeen warships as they approached at flank speed.

A dozen Zeen warships were destroyed in the ensuing seconds, succumbing to the extraordinary arsenal of the dying warship. In reply, each Zeen sent railgun bolts into the dying gate-crasher's hull. Just as the Jemmin had done to *Socrates*, now the plague of Zeen warships scrubbed the surface of the broken super-ship's hull until not a single capital-grade weapon remained.

The *Marcus Aurelius* continued to pour mass driver fire into its Jemmin counterpart until, finally and without fanfare, the enemy dreadnought fell silent. At that point, Admiral Wallace conserved his ammunition and recalled his fighters.

But the Zeen were far from done.

Expending vast amounts of energy in the process, the Zeen stabbed beam after beam, bolt after bolt, and plasma ball after plasma ball into the dead Jemmin warship's hull. The wormhole gate once again fell dark as the Zeen forces tore the dead ship apart, but the Zeen seemed heedless of anything but the destruction of their nemesis' carcass.

For a full hour, they expelled ordnance at a terrifying pace while the Terrans could only look on with mixed approval and trepidation. The Zeen were certainly acting in defense of Terran interests by securing the star system against the most dangerous enemy to ever cross into Terran space, but it was clear that the Zeen's motives were just as Xi had intimated.

They *hated* the Jemmin, and it was such a profound hatred

that Jenkins sincerely hoped he never understood it...or found himself the target of it.

"This is Admiral Wallace," the now-familiar voice came over the CAC's speakers. "On behalf of everyone in 8th Fleet, I appreciate the assist. We couldn't have fought our mutual enemy without Vorr and Zeen help."

Several seconds passed before Deep Currents replied with an unmistakable hint of challenge in her synthesized voice. "We trust that this will suffice as a meaningful gesture of good faith in Admiral Wallace's estimation?"

The delay was significantly longer this time than when Deep Currents had replied, but eventually Wallace said, "Let's say it was an encouraging first date. My intelligence officer recognized your code-word 'encore,' and while I'm not used to being kept in the dark on joint military exercises of this nature, I trust you'll forgive any insult I previously offered?"

Jenkins' brow rose in surprise at hearing that bit about "joint military exercises." His mind raced as he tried to recall who the intelligence officer aboard the *Marcus Aurelius* was, but he was unable to remember the name.

"General Pushkin," Li muttered wryly as if reading Jenkins' mind. "His daughter is the *Marcus Aurelius'* intelligence officer. He must have been in contact with Deep Currents and somehow got a coded message to Wallace's flagship before things went tits-up back at HQ."

Jesus. Jenkins closed his eyes in silent reflection. *No wonder Kavanaugh pushed him out. Pushkin wasn't going to go down without a fight, and he's obviously better-connected than I thought.*

Jenkins knew a thing or two about playing with political fire, but it seemed that Pushkin was a grandmaster. He and Akinouye had made a formidable team, but Jenkins was only now realizing just *how* formidable. Either the whole "joint military exercise" line was a red herring—which meant that Pushkin's daughter was potentially throwing her career and freedom away just to back her father's play—or it was real, and Pushkin had managed to secretly secure high-level allies in Terran Military Intelligence (an agency affectionately referred to by their acronym 'TMI' by pretty much everyone).

Such allies would have been able to not only craft, push through, and disseminate fleet-wide contingency plans for situations like this, but also keep those plans secret from all but the top brass at TMI.

Jenkins found his appreciation for the ousted Pushkin growing by leaps and bounds.

"Your reticence was understandable," Deep Currents assured Wallace. "If you permit them to do so, the warships that helped neutralize the Jemmin 'gate-crasher' will now reinforce your defensive position at the gate. If you prefer not to incorporate them, they will return to their worldship at this time."

This time Wallace replied as promptly (and humbly) as he could. "We could use the help holding the gate. We'll work up a revised formation and forward the details in ten minutes."

"Very good, Admiral," Deep Currents agreed, and a few seconds later the blue icon flashed at the priority comm station.

"Colonel Jenkins," Li said after receiving a private communique at that station.

"What is it, Colonel?" Jenkins asked.

"I've got the Vorr ambassador on the line," Li replied. "She says the Zeen will need another hour or so to complete the *Bonhoeffer*'s modifications, and she's requesting permission to accompany us to Sol. This is your op, so I'll defer to your judgment."

Jenkins quirked a brow and saw both Trapper and Moon seemed as perplexed by the request as he was.

Ultimately, he wasn't about to refuse an offer to help with

what was undoubtedly the most important mission he had ever undertaken.

"Aside from my concerns about her not being present to coordinate between Wallace and the Zeen," Jenkins allowed heavily, "I've got no objections. Does anyone else?"

Not a single person voiced dissent as the rest of the CAC's occupants shook their heads in solidarity.

"She says she's not the only Vorr aboard the Zeen worldship, so Terran-Zeen coordination will proceed uninterrupted," Li replied, and although it surprised Jenkins to hear it, he knew he shouldn't have been. This was too important of an operation to entrust to any one person. "She'll arrive in thirty minutes."

"Good." Jenkins nodded approvingly, momentarily amazed that he didn't feel the least bit shaken by the epic engagement he had just witnessed.

Frankly, the stakes here were peanuts compared to what lay in store for his people on the Moon, and that particular thought managed to rattle him enough that he had to physically shake it off before re-focusing on the task of prepping for launch.

4

REFIT

"That thing was purpose-built to crash a Terran-fortified gate," Moon declared. "Nearly all of its weaponry was rear-facing and perfectly positioned to engage any Terran fleet, and it didn't seem to have any motive thrust of its own. Simple inertia carried it through, and attitude-control engines adjusted its orientation during battle."

Li nodded. "Agreed, but I have a hard time believing it could have taken down a whole Terran Fleet. What if instead of Wallace's two dreadnoughts, there had been *six* holding the NA2-Nexus gate?" He shook his head skeptically. "They could have torn it apart. They might have lost two more dreadnoughts in the process, but Jemmin victory was far from assured had they faced a full fleet."

"You seem to be operating under false assumptions," Deep Currents intoned. "Jemmin does not engage in conflicts it cannot win, nor does it engage in conflicts where victory is less than highly probable. The most important tactical variable in determining whether an engagement is to one side's favor or the other is information. Jemmin prides itself on operating with superior information at all times. It did not anticipate the Zeen presence, which is why we were able to trap it here in the New America 2 star system and halt Jemmin's advance deeper into Terran territory. It will take Jemmin quite some time to recover from this disturbance in its plans."

"Jemmin didn't count on the Zeen being here," Jenkins mused. "Moreover, it *knew* there would only be the two dreadnoughts here."

"That is probable," Deep Currents agreed.

"Do they use the gates to gather intel?" Trapper asked.

"That is also probable," Deep Currents replied. "Although, if Vorr theoreticians are correct on this point, that capability is nonfunctional whenever the gates are offline. Another point I must insist upon clarifying is that Jemmin is not as numerous as you likely think. The fleet we just defeated might have only housed twenty or thirty individuals. It is difficult to determine with certainty given Jemmin's reclusive and xenophobic nature, but the force you engaged on the world you call Shiva's Wrath likely featured a single Jemmin."

"One?" Xi blurted in surprise.

"Almost certainly," Deep Currents replied serenely. "Using a combination of limited but extremely robust adaptive intelligence systems, lone Jemmin operators are capable of conducting planetary-scale invasions."

"Like a fucking video game?" Styles shook his head in amazement. "You're saying that we were fighting *drones* back on Shiva's Wrath?"

Podsy shrugged. "Hey, *we'd* do it if we could work out the virtual architecture and security issues. Who wants to actually ride a vehicle into combat when you can do the same work from the safety of a bunker or better yet, from high orbit?"

"It makes sense," Jenkins said as he recalled how the Jemmin vehicles on Shiva's Wrath had seemed to be thrown into disarray following the destruction of the Jemmin

Poltergeist. He shook his head to clear it before addressing Deep Currents. "Why do you want to accompany us to Sol?"

"We Vorr consider the issue of Solar security to be an internal one," Deep Currents explained. "We would therefore refuse to actively intervene during that operation for philosophical reasons. But in the operation's aftermath, we believe it might be beneficial to have a representative of my people present to provide as much information to your Solar cousins as possible. If you disagree, I will recuse myself."

"No, you're probably right about that," Jenkins allowed. "But it's going to be dangerous down there."

"I am aware of the risks," Deep Currents assured him from the confines of her egg-pod, which was unquestionably superior to the unit she had been within during his first meeting with her on Durgan's mobile HQ. "Remember, Lieutenant Colonel Lee Jenkins, that we Vorr are not adventurous risk-takers by nature. That I am willing to accompany you on such a dangerous expedition is thus a more significant gesture of solidarity on behalf of my people than you likely realize. We sincerely wish for humanity to survive this conflict."

"And we appreciate that because we want to survive, too," Jenkins said earnestly, although he still didn't understand the Vorr's angle in all of this. It gave him no pride to harbor ongoing and growing suspicions about the Vorr's motives in safeguarding humanity against the Jemmin apocalypse.

"Good," the Vorr declared. "Then let us complete the preparations to your ship."

"Agreed." Jenkins nodded before turning to Podsy. "I think it's time for Jem to walk us through the plan one last time."

Podsy produced the sixty-centimeter long, five-centimeter diameter ruby-red bar of crystalline material. After some work, he and Styles had crafted a wired linkage system that permitted Jem to access devices like data slates and translators. Jem claimed to be incapable of remotely interfacing with technological devices, but this self-described limitation had done little to assuage Jenkins' concerns about the potential security risks posed by the alien entity.

"Jem?" he urged when the entity failed to speak through the translator Podsy had connected to it.

"My apologies," Jem finally replied. The device worked as they had hoped. "I am still unaccustomed to military protocol governing information transmission at gatherings such as this one."

Jenkins' eyes flicked to the Vorr ambassador, whose tentacles had splayed out from its vaguely octopus-like body in what he now knew was a display of heightened interest. He suspected that one of the main reasons the Vorr had requested to join the expedition was to more closely observe Jem. Jenkins continued to watch the Vorr watching Jem.

"Walk us through your plan, Jem," Jenkins requested, refocusing his attention on the bizarre, seemingly sentient piece of mineral.

"According to the technical schematics the Vorr have provided that pertain to Solar humanity's technology," Jem began, causing hackles to rise around the room as Jem matter-of-factly described Vorr espionage efforts, "I have deduced that this operation requires two objectives to be achieved. The first is to access a direct communication line integrated into Luna One's primary virtual systems. The second is to secure one of twelve Moon-based transmitters that has access to Earth's orbiting virtual architecture. These objectives must be simultaneously achieved in order to reduce the risk that they will discover our true objective. Using the *Dietrich Bonhoeffer*'s communications array shortly after our arrival, I should be able to transmit and infect Luna One's sensor grid with a 'blind spot' similar to the one Jemmin employed against your forces on

Shiva's Wrath. Once that is done, there is a high degree of probability we will remain undetected long enough to deliver the insertion team to the Lunar surface."

"Stupid question." Podsednik raised his hand, looking very much like the class dunce as Jenkins suspected was his intent. "Why don't we just touch down on Earth to do this? If we inserted into a heavily-populated area, the Solarian military would be limited in their response options."

"Earth-based uplinks are essentially inaccessible." Styles shook his head firmly, sounding as though he and Podsy had already gone over this point.

"And Luna One *isn't*?" Podsy retorted.

"Luna One," Deep Currents smoothly interjected, breaking the two from their pending argument, "is formidable, but its defensive systems are relatively limited. The installation relies extensively on mobile assets to provide sensor coverage and to intercept inbound threats."

Jenkins nodded grimly. "Luna One was originally developed as a veritable Sword of Damocles. With Chinese interests seizing functional control of the Moon, they were able to erect bombardment platforms that rendered all Earth-based countermeasures ineffective. And given the distance between Earth and the Lunar surface, the only weapons that could possibly engage were ground-based lasers, which humanity has *still* not perfected."

"That particular failure, like so many others in your species' recent history," Jem said bluntly, "was due to Jemmin interference. Humanity's unwitting reliance on Nexus technology has essentially made it impossible to develop military-grade direct-energy weapons like lasers. Terran laser technology is, in point of fact, already on the verge of breaking through to the development of direct-energy weapons, while Solar tech development has stalled in accordance with Jemmin's aims."

"Wait, wait, wait." Xi leaned forward intently, her eyes fixed on Jem's ruby-red cylinder. "Are you suggesting that Jemmin was secretly manipulating the Chinese as far back as the mid-twenty-first century?"

"That is probable, given the sequence of events," Jem agreed. "In fact, it would be consistent with Jemmin's protocols to intervene even earlier—possibly as early as Earth's 2020s."

"Let's keep this on track," Jenkins said, causing Xi to relax back into her chair. Jenkins swept the assemblage with a hard look. "Everyone in this room should know by now that the Jemmin conspiracy is way, *way* above our paygrades. We need to focus on the operational variables alone. Let's let the investigators, journalists, and historians deal with digging into the past once this is finished. How we got here doesn't matter compared to what we have to do right now. Our job is clear: we go in, establish the hard-link, and upload Jem's inoculation as soon as possible. Every second counts. If Jemmin beats us to the punch, it's lights out for Sol." He shook his head with grim determination. "We *cannot* let that happen."

Heads bobbed in agreement while Podsy said, "Ok, so we have to land on the Moon, and Jem thinks it can get us past the sensor suite. I'm still not clear on that point, Colonel."

"Nor am I," Jenkins allowed. "Jem?"

"Given sufficient transmitter capacity, I am capable of instantly overtaking nearly any Solar virtual system," Jem explained. "The 'back doors' Jemmin left in the quantum processor permit the upload of almost any modification I desire, but given the One Mind network's impressively complex, procedurally-generated virtual architecture, every takeover attempt radically increases our odds of discovery."

"What do the discovery chances become with each successive use?" Jenkins asked.

"The first takeover will be practically impossible to detect,"

Jem replied. "The second will have an approximately one in six thousand chance of discovery, with the third at one in three hundred. After that, operational security will be severely compromised by future takeovers. I calculate a one in ten chance of discovery with the fourth application of this method and a greater than fifty percent chance of discovery with the fifth."

"Jesus!" Lieutenant Ford shook his head solemnly, drawing a nod of agreement from Lieutenant Winters at his side.

"I require two full uses of the takeover method in order to secure both the uplink node and the transmitter array," Jem continued. "Combined with the takeover to mask the *Dietrich Bonhoeffer*'s approach, my proposed upload sequence of three distinct takeovers already features an alarmingly high possibility of detection."

"What happens if they do detect us?" Jenkins pressed.

"That is difficult to predict with precision," Jem admitted. "But my calculations suggest that, while my inoculation would affect a majority of humans connected to the One Mind system, those who are not inoculated will still be functionally vulnerable to Jemmin control since Jemmin has certainly built redundant upload systems directly into the One Mind network. And I will remind this assembly that Jemmin was able to eradicate ninety-four percent of the Jem'un by manipulating the other six percent."

Sergeant Major Trapper grunted. "If we get detected, it's the end of Solar humanity as we know it."

The somber silence that followed stretched until Jenkins finally broke it. "Let's go over the operation step by step. Any questions, no matter how minor, need to be fielded. This is our last pre-drop briefing, people," he said seriously. "Let's get it right."

Two hours later, with the last of the Zeen resin applied to the *Bonhoeffer*'s hull, the aged assault carrier stood ready.

Podsy floated down an access corridor, using the regularly-spaced handholds to propel himself through the zero-gee environment. In one hand, he gripped the crystalline shaft that housed (or was?) Jem. He had left the translation device attached per Colonel Jenkins' orders, but Jem was quiet as usual as they moved down the keel of the Metal Legion's battered flagship.

The ship seemed empty compared to its previous deployments, which he supposed was because it *was* practically empty. Hundreds of Metalheads and voiders had filled these corridors just a few weeks earlier, to say nothing of the colonists they had carried back to Terran space.

To Podsy, it felt as though the *Bonhoeffer* was a ghost ship—and that was a feeling he could not shake.

"I am impressed by your species, Lieutenant Podsednik," Jem said, breaking Podsy from his reverie.

"Oh?" Podsy asked. "Why's that?"

"Terran humanity suffered greatly during its inceptive period," Jem replied, "and much of that suffering could have easily been alleviated by a relatively minor intervention by your Solar cousins. But they did not intervene on your behalf, and the Terran Republic nearly failed to draw its first metaphorical breath as a result. Were it not for clandestine Vorr support in the form of technological gifts funneled through certain Terran corporations, it is probable that your Republic would not have survived."

"What's your point?" Podsy asked irritably. He still hadn't wrapped his mind completely around the notion that both Solar and Terran humanity had been pawns in some vast interstellar game between rival alien species. The thought angered him. No, it *infuriated* him for reasons he could not adequately express with words.

"Solar humans could have helped you, yet they did not," Jem said simply. "But now Terran humans are in a position to help Solar humans, and not once during the pre-drop briefing did a single Terran ask if this great risk was worthwhile. Successfully accomplishing this mission's objectives is considerably less than a certainty, and surviving the experience is even less probable. Most warrior castes are reluctant to take such risks if reciprocity is unlikely."

Podsy smirked. "We don't have a 'warrior caste,' Jem. Terran Armed Forces personnel are volunteers to the last. Self-selection for military service produces a caste-like culture. Many of us were given the choice to clear our records by joining the Armor Corps, so we did. It was self-serving, but once we got here, we found that we were drawn to the life of a warrior. Serving the Terran Federation is what we do. We call it freedom of choice, and it's the fundamental tenet of Terran society."

"But you are not serving your fellow Terrans in this mission," Jem observed. "You are knowingly sacrificing many, if not all, of your lives in service of Solar humans. Solar humans do not respect your freedoms in the same way Terrans do."

"They're still human," Podsy said firmly. "We might disagree on some pretty fundamental things, but disagreement is a feature of freedom, not a glitch to be fixed."

"Solar humans are brutal collectivists by any standard," Jem pressed. "Dissent is dealt with via punishment, reprogramming, or exile. Their forebears mercilessly bombarded North America from the very base we will now use to save them from self-destruction. Many of my Jem'un forebears would have argued that Solar humanity does not deserve to be saved."

Podsy shook his head adamantly. "That's not our call to

make, Jem. There are a hundred billion lives in Sol, and none of them understand the danger hanging over their heads. That's *unacceptable*," he declared, feeling his resolve strengthen with each word that passed his lips. "Besides, in some ways, the Solarians have been victimized by Jemmin even worse than us Terrans. Humanity isn't a Jemmin plaything. We're not a Vorr plaything. And we're going to prove it."

"And that is why you impress me," Jem said approvingly as Podsy finally came to the drop-deck where Sergeant Major Trapper and his people had assembled for pre-drop inspection. "As individuals, you arrived at a collective conclusion faster than even my Jem'un forebears could have done. We deeply believed in something similar to what you call freedom of choice that allowed self-sacrifice, but despite the Jem'un's superior intellect, we lacked the clarity and unity you have repeatedly demonstrated. I hope that I am able to learn more about your species and its cultures."

"I'll be your tour guide," Podsy quipped as he put his magboots down on the drop-deck and clomped his way over to Trapper's assemblage. He had been assigned to the sergeant major's insertion team, which would escort Jem, Podsy, and Styles to one of Luna One's underground uplink nodes.

"Lieutenant Podsednik." Trapper smirked. "Good of you to join us. Grab a rifle and field kit." He gestured to a neatly-arranged row of supplies. "Word is the Zeen have finished coating the hull and that we'll get shot out of that 'gravity cannon' within the hour."

Podsy felt a thrill of anticipation as he joined the group and went through the final pre-drop preparations.

It was almost time.

5

PREP THE GRAVITY CANNON

Under Colonel Jenkins' orders (and with Colonel Li's grudging acceptance) Captain Xi Bao accompanied a trio of Zeen technicians throughout the *Bonhoeffer*'s interior. Using peculiarly-shaped scanners, they conducted an inspection of the ship with the goal of precisely measuring the assault carrier's dimensions and mass.

In fact, aside from a security contingent comprised of Sergeant Major Trapper and a dozen of his people, nearly all Terrans aboard the ship were in their grav couches during the measurements. The Zeen, in their difficult-to-understand way, had informed them that the measurements needed to be extremely precise in order for the so-called 'gravity cannon' to precisely deliver them to their destination.

The way they talked, it seemed to Xi as though even a few unaccounted kilograms might cause them to miss their destination point by thousands of kilometers.

Obviously, Colonel Li was less than enthusiastic about the prospect of allowing anyone not in the TAF aboard the *Bonhoeffer* for such a detailed inspection, but he had ultimately agreed to cooperate.

"Scan complete," declared one of the Zeen. "Ship ready. Transport soon. Terrans ride couches. No movement."

"Thank you," Xi said graciously, and the trio of insectaurs turned in unison to make their way to the airlock through which they had arrived. Xi raised Colonel Jenkins on her wrist-link and reported, "Colonel, this is Captain Xi. The Zeen are finished with their scans. They suggest we get in the couches and try not to move."

"Copy that, Captain," Jenkins acknowledged. "It's time for you to get in your couch. As soon as the Zeen are off the ship, the sergeant major's security detail will follow your lead."

"Yes, sir," Xi replied as she made her way, using a combination of mag-boots and zero-gee handrails to propel herself through the *Bonhoeffer*'s corridors en route to her assigned grav couch.

A few minutes after parting company with the team of Zeen, Xi arrived at the so-called "lounge" where the majority of the *Bonhoeffer*'s one thousand grav couches were located.

Just a tiny fraction of those couches were occupied, since the various operations decks had their own grav couches to ensure ongoing shipboard operations during high-gee maneuvers. The couches in the lounge were fairly primitive by comparison, affording their occupants only the bare essentials.

"Ah, Captain Xi," Dr. Fellows greeted her, beckoning her to her couch, to which he was making some final adjustments. "I just need to dial in your current biometric profile, and you'll be set."

The doctor produced a medical scanner, which he used to gather precise measurements of her body. Dimensions, total mass, hydration status, hormone levels...everything. As he scanned, she removed the majority of her clothing, leaving her standing in just her underwear—penguin panties and a black sports bra. Fellows didn't bat an eye.

Some people hated undergoing the scans. They thought it reduced them to a series of numbers. Xi thought they were fascinating and was always curious to know what her current figures were.

"There, all done," Dr. Fellows declared, offering her the nondescript form-fitting body-glove that was necessary to maximize the couch's capabilities. Xi accepted the full-length garment, which she easily slipped into. "You'll be happy to know," he added dryly, "that your menstrual cycle won't come into play during this op, which should be more than enough time for us to either get ourselves killed or find a suitable parade float to ride in victory. Either way, you won't have to worry about the monthlies depleting your blood volume."

Xi smirked. "You should know better than anyone that *every* drop of blood counts in a crisis, Doc."

"Too true," Fellows agreed with a grin.

Xi finished slipping into her body-glove and scrunched her brow in consternation.

"I've decided I dislike that particular look," Dr. Fellows said with a smirk of his own.

"It's just..." Xi's voice trailed off, uncertain how to put her thoughts into words.

"Let me guess," Fellows deadpanned. "You think I'm considering you for the next ex-Mrs. Fellows? Not quite."

She gave him a withering look. "Well, yeah, now that you bring it up."

"Young women are the worst." He snorted. "You think everything's about you."

"Isn't it?" Xi challenged half-jokingly.

"In some sense, sure," he allowed.

"It's just..." she started again. "Well, you didn't need to come along for this mission, Doc. There are plenty of people in the Brigade who are trained on setting up the couches, and once we go wheels down—"

"What?" Fellows cocked an eyebrow challengingly. "You think I'll be dead weight down there?"

"In some sense, sure," she retorted, turning his words back on him.

He snickered. "Captain, you're not the only one who's been up to her eyeballs in the shit and lived to tell about it. Before I went to medical school, I suffered from a particularly virulent strain of patriotism and enlisted in the Terra Americana Colonial Guard. It was only an eighteen-month service term, but I was always good at fixing things, so I became a field mechanic. Worked on old Wolfhound- and Proselytizer-class mechs. You know, swapping the axles in a meter of half-frozen mud while your buddies try to keep you from getting shot before you can tighten all the lug-nuts? That kind of thing."

"Bullshit." Xi scoffed. "You're telling me you were a Wrench before you became a sawbones?"

"I was," he replied matter of factly, ignoring her incredulity.

"Why the career change?" she asked. "Why didn't you stay in the service?"

He sighed. "Some of us just aren't made for hurting people and breaking things, Captain. The thing I learned about myself during those eighteen months was that I'd rather heal people than kill them. It's not philosophical, mind you," he amended pointedly. "Some people *need* to be killed. I'd just prefer that I wasn't the one pulling the trigger. I value my ability to sleep through the night too much."

Xi shook her head in muted wonder as she climbed into the grav couch. "It seems like I learn something new about you every time we talk."

"There's a lesson there, Captain," he chided.

"Wisdom begins in wonder," Xi replied by way of agreement.

"Well, look at that!" Fellows grinned. "You know your Socrates. There might be hope for your generation after all."

"I wouldn't count on it," she said, inspecting the couch's helmet using a long-practiced checklist. "Most people my age couldn't tell Plato from Pluto, the cartoon dog."

Fellows chuckled. "That's probably normal."

"Probably," she allowed as she finished her inspection and prepared to slip the tight-fitting helmet over her head. "But that doesn't make it good."

"No, it doesn't," he agreed before helping her squeeze her head into the helmet.

A few seconds after the helmet was snug on her head, the seals around her jaw clamped down and the helmet went through a series of diagnostics. The helmet's HUD showed all systems green, so she gave the doctor a thumbs-up and laid down in the molded bed of the grav couch. When she was prone, Dr. Fellows lowered the mostly-transparent lid of the rectangular box.

The lid sealed with an audible hiss, and Dr. Fellows looked in, silently asking if she was good. She replied in the affirmative, and the doctor moved out of view. Alone in the grav couch, Xi had no choice but to wait for the countdown. That was, of course, assuming the Zeen forewarned them in such a fashion.

She felt the grav couch's molded surfaces slowly squeeze her on all sides. She didn't mind the closed space, the medical scans, or even the helmet, which restricted airflow to a very specific volume. The one thing Xi had always hated was being held in place and unable to move.

And nowhere was the sensation of being physically restrained more overpowering and nerve-wracking than within the confines of a grav couch.

"Breathe, Bao," she muttered, closing her eyes and trying to relax as the gel-filled surfaces of the grav-couch continued to press against her body. The pressure was far from crushing, but she still could not ignore the mental image of her body being crushed by the coils of a giant snake.

She tried to focus her thoughts on what little she had learned of the so-called gravity cannon FTL system. From what she could understand, the technology allowed for the temporary folding of space between two points, joining them. The amount of energy required to achieve such a feat was extraordinary, Terran scientists having long postulated that the only power sources sufficiently potent were entire stars.

The only way to harness so much energy was via a Dyson Swarm or a Dyson Sphere, mega-structures consisting of thousands upon thousands of energy-harvesting satellites. It was unclear to Xi just how that energy could be utilized, even if it were merely redirected, but the eggheads seemed confident that if one could erect a stable Dyson Sphere, then focusing the energy would be a surmountable obstacle.

The Terran Republic had never mastered the necessary technology to keep a full Dyson Swarm in a stable orbit of its parent star, and the Terran Republic's wormhole-linked star systems did not feature a star of optimal size for such a project to be considered economically viable.

Still, there were several vast solar arrays in the Republic that were primarily used to generate antimatter in a process that seemed like magic to Xi. She couldn't even pretend to understand how it worked, but the eggheads had proven worthy of their pocket protectors and secured sufficient funding to expand that particular project, much to Fleet's approval.

If the Zeen had been using Dyson Swarms of their own to create antimatter and had undertaken that project uninterrupted for as long as four thousand years, it was entirely possible that there were metric *tons* of antimatter at the heart of the Zeen worldship. Antimatter was the only source of power Xi was aware of that could fuel something like a space-folding drive without directly harvesting energy from a star.

Then again, it was possible the Zeen were using something else entirely, and Xi wasn't sure if that should be a comforting or worrying thought.

But despite the enormous power requirements inherent to a space-folding system, Xi had learned it was not power so much as computational capacity that was the most limiting factor of such a system.

The Zeen had boarded the *Bonhoeffer* to take measurements of the ship and its crew that were precise down to the nanogram. Obviously, the numbers could not be perfect, which Xi had been told increased the computational demands by an order of magnitude compared with a conduction using precise measurements.

That meant the Zeen worldship had a computer that was so powerful it outstripped every virtual system in the Terran Republic *combined* in terms of raw computational capacity.

Stellar measurements, cosmic radiation, mass and dimensionality of the transited object, mass within a given area near the destination point... Hundreds of interconnected variables needed to be calculated in real-time to keep a transited object from missing the mark by light-seconds, or even light-minutes.

"This is Colonel Li," the *Bonhoeffer*'s CO declared, his voice piped straight into Xi's helmet. "The Zeen have disembarked and informed us we have eight minutes before they conduct us to our destination. Everyone sit tight in your couches. The ship is at Condition One. I say again: we are at Condition One."

Xi forcibly relaxed as the countdown appeared on her

HUD. She silently mouthed each second as it slowly wound down to two minutes remaining.

"None of us knows how this is going to work," Colonel Li intoned at the ninety-second mark, "so all hands need to be ready for emergency couch releases. Engineering will re-fire the reactors as soon as we emerge, while everyone else will await orders. With a little luck, we'll slip through without a hitch, and the doc can pull us out at his leisure. But as a wise man once said, hope for the best but plan for the worst. One minute to transit."

Xi continued her silent countdown, feeling her heart beat anxiously in her chest as her limbs tingled from the pressure of the couch squeezing her.

"Ten seconds..." Li informed them.

Xi started to tense despite her best efforts to relax as the clock wound down to six. Knowing these might be the last six seconds of her life quickened her breathing.

"Five...four..." the *Bonhoeffer*'s CO called, "three...two... one...mark!"

A sudden jolt snapped Xi's body into the grav-couch, and her stomach began to riot as an intense wave of vertigo washed over her.

She was dimly aware of the blaring of sirens, accompanied by flashing blue emergency lights.

"Emergency couch release," Colonel Li declared, causing the pressure on Xi's body to quickly diminish until she was floating free in the tiny, form-fitting compartment.

The lid of her grav-couch popped open with a muted hiss, and she quickly doffed the couch helmet before pulling herself free.

Thanks to the lack of artificial gravity, she was spared a date with the deck as another wave of vertigo cascaded into her.

When she could once again see, she found everyone else in the compartment as disoriented as she was.

"Emergency stations," she barked, gripping a nearby rail and waving Lieutenant Ford over. "Get to the drop-deck on the double. Move! Move! Move!"

Slowly but surely, the lounge's occupants clambered out of their grav-couches and moved down the corridor that led to the drop-deck. When the last of the sixty-three people had disembarked the lounge, Xi allowed herself to check the ship's onboard status report.

Despite having expected it, and despite having gone over the science so many times she felt cross-eyed just thinking about FTL flight, Xi still felt her heart skip a beat when she saw the readout for the *Bonhoeffer*'s current location.

Sol, Earth-Luna Bi-planetary System.

They'd made it.

6

LUNAR APPROACH

Colonel Jenkins' grav couch was in the *Bonhoeffer*'s CAC, which made his vantage point one of the best aboard the TAC warship as the first sensor feedback hit the readouts.

And there it was: Earth. The cradle of humanity. A blue-green marble with lush vegetation covering the vast majority of its land mass and pristine blue waters stretching to the horizon from every shore. Centuries of climate-control systems had rendered inclement weather a thing of the past, and now a precisely-curated band of wispy white clouds maintained the planet's ecosphere under direct human guidance.

Ninety-one percent of Sol's hundred billion humans lived beneath those clouds. For a moment Jenkins had the discomforting thought that this was the best, and last, view he would ever get of humanity's birthplace with his naked eyes.

"We're fifteen thousand kilometers off-target," Colonel Li declared after running a series of numbers, confirming that the Zeen "gravity cannon" had essentially threaded the needle and dropped them almost where they needed to be. Podsy had previously brought Jem to the main comm station, where he awaited the all-important order. Li raised his voice. "I'm reading four void interceptors on patrol forty thousand kilometers out."

"Nothing closer?" Jenkins asked.

"No." Li shook his head firmly before adding, "At least nothing that shows up on our systems."

"That's *one* stroke of luck in our favor," Jenkins muttered, drawing an approving nod from Li. "Lieutenant." Jenkins turned to Podsy. "Is Jem able to initiate the sensor takeover from here?"

"I am," Jem replied before Podsy got the chance to do so. "However, it would be optimal to avoid doing so until they detect us. It is possible, albeit unlikely, that the material the Zeen applied to this ship's hull will mask our approach long enough to deliver the insertion team to the Lunar surface."

Jenkins and Li shared mutual looks of concern before Jenkins nodded. "Fine, we wait until they detect us. You understand the operational risks here as well as any of us. Probably better."

"An accurate observation," Jem replied matter of factly.

As the CAC's watch standers went through the tasks of restarting the ship's computer systems, the engineers deep in the heart of the assault carrier rekindled the mighty fusion reactors that powered the Terran warship. One by one, the reactors sprang to life.

And not a moment too soon.

"Colonel," Styles called from a nearby Sensor station, "that squadron of interceptors is altering course."

Li's eyes snapped to the CAC's central tactical plotter. "They see us." Li grimaced.

Jenkins eyed Jem's crystalline rod. "Send your first takeover, Jem."

"Transmitting," Jem replied, and the data slate connected to Jem's ruby-red surface sprang to life. Data streamed down the display faster than a human could process and corresponding icons flickered into and out of being at the sensor station where Podsy was seated.

The CAC's occupants collectively held their breath as Jem sent the all-important transmission. The Solar interceptors were less than a quarter of a light-second away, so the feedback should have been nearly instantaneous.

But seconds ticked by one by one until nearly a minute had elapsed since the Solarian interceptors had altered course.

"Podsy," Jenkins said urgently as active scanning sweeps pinged the *Bonhoeffer*. "*Podsy!*" he snapped.

Then, after the third inbound sensor ping sounded from the *Bonhoeffer's* Sensor section, the Solar interceptors adjusted course back to their original bearings.

"Takeover successful," Jem declared neutrally. "Hostile interceptors have resumed their previous course."

"That's it?" Li blurted. "They're just going to turn around and ignore us now?"

"Centralized decision-making offers many advantages, Colonel Li," Jem explained, his tone falling just short of that of a patronizing lecturer, "but it also features many disadvantages. The One Mind system, which is a direct result of Jemmin manipulation, potentially permits all of Solar humanity to focus on any given event or decision simultaneously. As a practical matter, this rarely occurs, but the confidence in such a system's product has radical and difficult-to-predict effects. One such effect is that if a sufficient number of a phenomenon's first inspectors dismiss that phenomenon for consistent reasons, that phenomenon is removed from consideration. It is considered 'solved' for a significant interval."

Styles nodded in comprehension. "You tricked the first responders with your method, infecting them with false input. And after a sufficient number of them concurred that there was nothing worthy of investigation out here, the whole system dismissed the matter."

"How is it possible," Colonel Moon growled in astonished indignation, "for the Solarians to put so much faith in their precious One Mind system? A little sensor trick and they'll let an assault carrier right through the front door?"

"My available evidence is limited, Colonel Moon," Jem said pointedly, "but in every recorded instance of Jemmin manipulation similar to what your species has undergone, no species has successfully extricated itself from this particular trap. Jemmin developed this method after centuries of refinement and testing. Put simply, humanity had no real chance to avoid its current situation."

"That doesn't make me feel any better." Moon scowled.

"As if it should?" Trapper smirked.

"Also," Jem continued, "there is nothing 'little' about the sensor trick I employed. The runtimes required to create my takeover system were far in excess of anything the Terran Republic could manage in under a century, even with full commitment to the project."

"If Sol is so vulnerable," Jenkins asked, "why hasn't Jemmin come in and wiped them out already?"

"Sol's status is likely in flux. As a compliant species, Jemmin might prefer to employ Solar assets in direct support of its future pacification efforts against the Vorr. Now, the Vorr, Zeen, Terran, and Finjou elements have drastically changed posture from Jemmin's previous assumptions, and that change has introduced what is likely an unprecedented degree of uncertainty in Jemmin's calculations," Jem explained. "As a result, Jemmin will certainly move to control those new variables prior to proceeding with its plan. However, once Jemmin realizes the magnitude of these new variables, its first move will be to eliminate potential future threats in whatever order is most efficient. Sol represents precisely such a threat."

"How long do you think that will take?" Li pressed.

"No more than three Earth days," Jem replied with chilling indifference. "Possibly as few as thirty of your standard hours."

Those who heard the declaration had no answer to humanity's frailty. The mission's importance was never clearer than at that moment.

"Helm," Li called without missing a beat, "put us on a hot-drop trajectory. All hands, prepare for maneuvering acceleration in thirty seconds."

The *Bonhoeffer*'s engines flared in short, controlled bursts, generating between three and five gees with each multi-second burn. Before the first burn, all of the crew had strapped into flight seats where they rode out the experience. After fifteen minutes of carefully-executed engine burns, the *Bonhoeffer* was on approach to the drop-zone.

As soon as the *Bonhoeffer*'s maneuvering bursts were complete, Xi jumped out of her flight seat on the drop-deck and worked to coordinate the 1st, 2nd, and 3rd Company final pre-launch efforts.

"Drop the protein bars, Fatso." Xi groaned as *Cave Troll*'s Jock lumbered toward his mech's can bearing an over-full crate of food. "Or are you really *that* hard-up for a twenty-centimeter hunk of meat to choke on?"

"Gotta watch my blood sugar, Captain," Lieutenant Yuan, callsign "Fatso," retorted unabashedly. "My reflexes fall off by at least six percent if I don't keep at a rocksteady one-one-zero on the needle."

"Try a piece of fruit, you fat bastard," Xi barked as the

thickly-built Jock hurried up the ramp into *Cave Troll's* drop-can. The ultra-heavy *Cave Troll* had been hammered several times in the last few deployments, but like a bad case of genital warts, it just wouldn't go away no matter how hard you picked at it.

One of *Generally's* crew came running by with loose hoses and connectors tucked under her arms. As Xi turned to get out of the harried-looking woman's way, the other woman tripped on a divot in the deck and nearly fell.

Xi opened her mouth to rebuke the woman, whose name was Quinn and who had quite the reputation among the Legionnaires for being a klutz, but Quinn managed to save herself from a date with the deck with some fancy mag-boot-enhanced footwork.

"What did I tell you about trying to make out with my deck, Quinn?" Xi asked in her most dire and ominous tone.

In reply, the other woman lifted her left hand as high as she could manage without losing the loose parts tucked under her arm, and Xi was unable to stifle a laugh at what she saw.

On Quinn's ring finger, precisely where a wedding ring should have been, was a hexagonal steel nut that appeared to have been custom-machined to fit the diminutive woman's hand. "We haven't set a date yet," Quinn said with a brief look at the deck, "but you're definitely invited to the wedding, Captain."

Xi shook her head and laughed, recalling the time she had told Quinn that she should produce an engagement ring the next time she tried to make out with the deck on company time.

"Get the fuck out of here, Quinn." Xi waved her hands dismissively, equally proud and amused by the other woman's spunk.

"Yes, ma'am," Quinn replied, flashing a grin before heading off toward *Generally's* drop-can. Her previous assignment had been to *Forktail* as a Monkey, but the recent roster shuffle had seen her transferred to Lieutenant Winters' mech as a Wrench. Seeing the clumsy, surprisingly spirited woman come into her own was like a breath of fresh air. Xi hadn't realized how badly she needed it.

At that moment, more than any other, Xi knew they were ready.

"Your people are resilient," Deep Currents said as her egg-pod rolled toward Xi's position. "Humanity is indeed a rare species."

Xi turned to the Vorr and schooled her features. "We should board *Elvira*, Ambassador."

"It is unfortunate," Deep Currents said with evident disappointment, "that Jem will not accompany us. I am curious about it, although I understand this mission requires a certain division of assets."

"You could request to transfer to Sergeant Major Trapper's team," Xi suggested, half-hoping that the Vorr would take her up on the offer.

"No," Deep Currents said calmly. "My place is either at your side or with Colonel Jenkins. I understand his reluctance to permit me to accompany him aboard the command vehicle, and to be blunt, I am less interested in him than I am in you."

"Me?" Xi quirked a brow in confusion.

"Of course." Deep Currents' auto-translated voice conveyed unmistakable amusement. "Your species is rare, Captain Xi Bao, but certain members of your race are even less uniform than others. You, in particular, represent an enigma that fascinates my people, who instructed me to gather as much information about you as possible during this cooperative exercise."

"You're interested in *me*?" Xi repeated disbelievingly. "Why not Colonel Jenkins or Podsy or Colonel Moon?"

Deep Currents replied, "They are uninteresting specimens

of humanity. Predictable. Expected. You, however, are not. For a sexually dimorphic species to thrive, sexual specialization is essential. An essential component of optimal human male-female labor division is for males to take greater risks than females, which risks naturally include premeditated participation in combat. Men like Colonel Jenkins, Colonel Li, Colonel Moon, Sergeant Major Trapper, and Lieutenant Podsednik are typical in this regard. But you, by any objective biological metric, are prime breeding stock whose genes and lived experiences would be immensely beneficial to future generations. Your physical geometry, psychological makeup, superior reflexes, and mental acuity make you a potential high-value node in the human genealogical tree, and it goes without saying that you are an exceptionally desirable mate."

Xi recoiled in surprise to hear the Vorr describe her as "prime breeding stock" and "an exceptionally desirable mate," but in truth, it was a pretty tame jab considering the circles Xi ran in. Besides, coming from the asexual Vorr, she chose to take the remarks as compliments rather than insults.

"So," Xi mused, "you're interested in why a woman like me would choose a risky life instead of a safer one as a kept woman with a litter of puppies?"

"That is one interest, yes," Deep Currents agreed. "Another is your ability to flex your decision-making during the high stress of combat. There are multiple reasons why this might be, but my people operate under a principle we refer to as 'the stream effect.' Essentially, we do not believe it is appropriate to permit our thoughts to be governed by simple probability equations. We prefer to ride the stream of reality as far as it can safely be ridden rather than to predict where the voyage will end, and simply trust in those predictions. To deprive ourselves of the opportunity to experience is to submit to fear, and as a prey species, fear is something we constantly seek to master. It is only by navigating treacherous situations that we can learn how to better navigate them in the future. Seeking safety for safety's sake is ultimately self-defeating and, indeed, the behavior of prey."

"The journey is more important than the destination." Xi nodded in agreement. "You have to learn how to be safe by putting yourself in jeopardy rather than building taller and thicker walls around yourself to create the illusion of safety. So in order to safeguard yourselves, you have to constantly expose yourselves to danger, creating an endless journey with the ultimate destination being safety which, practically speaking, is impossible to attain." She snickered softly. "It's a self-defeating directive that spurs your people in a certain direction, sort of like the concept of original sin."

"Precisely," Deep Currents replied. "In accordance with that directive, we wish to understand you specifically rather than to trust in simple logic to deduce what makes you, Captain Xi Bao, so very different from your fellow humans."

Xi flashed a lopsided grin. "Usually a girl's got to pull a few teeth to get someone interested in what makes her tick."

"We Vorr have no teeth," Deep Currents said sadly, apparently misunderstanding her meaning. "Historically we consumed bacterial colonies that broke off from underwater volcanoes. To remove the nutrient-rich bacterial paste from their hard castings, our mouths feature structures similar to a crab's proboscis, although Vorr proboscises vibrate to loosen the bacterial paste from its castings. I can offer one of my proboscises if the gesture is of social significance?"

Xi's grin widened as she recalled a line from an ancient two-dimensional "movie." "You know, I'd be the luckiest girl alive if that did it for me. But no, it's fine." She held up a hand haltingly as her mind's eye was filled with the horrifying image of Deep

Currents ripping its mouth apart in some sort of social gesture. "Please don't give me your proboscis."

"As you wish," Deep Currents replied serenely.

Xi suddenly cocked her head in belated realization and demanded, "Wait a minute...was that a joke?"

"Possibly," Deep Currents allowed.

Xi threw her head back and laughed.

Yeah, she thought with fiery determination, *we're ready*.

7

VIRGIN REGOLITH

1st Company's eight drop-cans drifted through the void in perfect formation en route to their Lunar landing. Consisting of the so-called brigade's lightest mechs and led by the battlefield behemoth *Roy*, this first group of eight mechs bore the insertion team centered around Styles, Podsy, and Jem.

"Thirty seconds to braking thrusters," Jenkins called over the P2P linking the eight mechs of 1st Company. Their angle of approach was gentle, and their velocity was well below standard combat-drop parameters. The Zeen worldship had dropped the *Bonhoeffer* into a near-perfect position for a relatively stealthy drop of the Metal Legion's mechs that had almost eliminated the need for braking burns.

Of course, "stealthy" and "Metal Legion" were usually anything but synonymous, but given the circumstances, Jenkins knew that his people were sneaking in as quietly as a teen coming home after curfew.

"Ten seconds," he called as his drop-can fell steadily toward the pristine Lunar surface.

After Solar humanity had consolidated under Chinese rule in the late twenty-first century, the majority of the Moon's surface had been declared a monument of unique historical significance. Colonial expansions, helium-3 mining operations, and all other forms of human activity on the Moon had been immediately curtailed. As a result, over eighty percent of the Moon's surface was untouched regolith, rich in helium-3 and never once violated by humanity.

"Five," Jenkins intoned. "Four...three...two...one...brake!"

The drop-cans' braking rockets roared to life, the sound of their fury lost to the void while the regolith beneath each can billowed outward from the steady force of the rockets' fire.

The braking thrusters cut out in perfect unison as the drop-cans touched down together, throwing outward what little Lunar dust remained beneath them as 1st Company landed with the expected jolt.

"1st Company, roll out and sound off once you're clear," Jenkins commanded, and *Roy's* drop-can fell apart as explosive charges severed the unifying brackets that held it together.

The mighty Razorback-class mech's legs unfolded from beneath it, stretching out on the thin metal deck as the vehicle's central chassis rose from the floor. The lid had broken apart in an X-shaped pattern before flopping out onto the Lunar surface and paving the way for *Roy's* disembarkation.

Roy rolled forward while the rest of 1st Company did likewise from their unfolded drop-cans. Chaps was the first to sound off as *Roy's* four omnidirectional roller-bearing feet dug into the thin layer of regolith remaining after the landing. "*Roy*, checking the kitchen."

"*Blink Dog*, in-and-out." Corporal Miles "Blinky" Staubach was next to speak as his canine-looking mech moved out.

"*Shirley Temple*, not the drink," reported the third of 1st Company's Jocks.

"*Leaf Cutter*, tending my crop."

"*Octopede*, defying classification."

"*Wet Willie*, making you squirm."

"*Forktail*, double the pleasure."

"*Anaconda*, holding tight."

"1st Company," Jenkins called as the drop-cans of 3rd Company, led by Lieutenant Winters, splashed down five kilometers behind *Roy's* position, precisely where they were supposed to land, "form up and roll on insertion point Alpha. Flank speed."

As 1st Company's mechs surged forward in a pair of offset columns, 3rd Company took up position at the formation's rear.

That left just 2nd Company in the air, and according to the plan, they would be streaming from the *Bonhoeffer's* launch tube momentarily.

"2nd Company," Xi called, "we begin our drop in sixty second—"

Elvira lurched violently beneath Xi, briefly disorienting her before she realized what must have happened.

"We're taking fire," Colonel Li declared over the ship-wide as the *Bonhoeffer* lurched again. And again. And *again*. "An orbital defensive platform has us bracketed with railguns, and we've got Reaver-class missiles inbound. I'm assuming direct control of the drop. CIG, scramble! Scramble! Scramble!"

"2nd Company," Xi barked, gripping the arms of her pilot chair, "activate links and prepare for a hot drop!"

The neural linkage flooded her body with a wave of endorphins as the now-familiar surge of coolness washed over every nerve ending in her body. Her senses blurred into the systems of the mech, and for a moment she felt as though she and the machine were no longer separate but had become a single entity.

The moment passed, as it always did, and her attention returned to her surroundings as the *Bonhoeffer* repeatedly lurched around her.

The telltale thrum of the *Bonhoeffer*'s launch tube signaled that one of Xi's mechs was away. A second launch followed, then a third. A fourth. A fifth. But the launches ceased as Colonel Li's voice came over the comm. "Brace for impact!"

Xi didn't even remember what had happened as her senses slowly returned. Apparently, she had blacked out, and a quick check of her linkage showed that *Elvira*'s automated neural-balancing systems had pumped her full of stimulants to awaken her from the stupor.

The launch tube thrummed again. Then again, leaving only *Elvira*'s can in the tube awaiting deployment.

"Brace for imp—" Li's words were cut short when once again the *Bonhoeffer* was struck by enemy ordnance and began to yaw well out of its previous alignment.

If Li launched *Elvira* now, she would sail into the dark void of interplanetary space. The drop-can would become a tomb for its trio of occupants, two human and one Vorr, and that thought filled Xi with an unexpected rage. She had not come this far and done so much to be erased from the board just like that.

Chief Rimmer's voice came over the line. "Stand by, *Elvira*. I'm accessing the...emergency attitude control systems. CAC's dark...hold..."

"Roger, Drop Control," Xi acknowledged as her heart rate skyrocketed.

Fortunately, it seemed that Rimmer's efforts met with success since the *Bonhoeffer* slowly re-oriented to its previous attitude. "Adjusting," Rimmer said as he made minute changes to the ship's orientation. Those changes were less than a hundredth of a degree, which could result in landing on top of another mech or even missing the drop-zone entirely. "Launch!"

Rimmer declared, and Xi once again braced herself as *Elvira's* drop-can was hurtled forward by the *Bonhoeffer's* launch rails.

The drop-can cleared the *Bonhoeffer's* launch tube less than a second before a hail of railgun strikes tore into the beleaguered warship's resin-coated hull. *Elvira's* sensor display, plumbed into the can's external feeds, lit up as the damage to the *Bonhoeffer* became apparent.

Xi's throat tightened when she saw just how bad the damage was.

The forward third of the mighty Terran warship had been blown completely off and was now a cloud of expanding debris, which *Elvira's* drop-can was moving through.

Clatters and clangs sounded across the drop-can's thin hull, but nothing larger than a human body impacted. Thankfully, the can's braking and attitude-control thrusters were unaffected by debris leaving dents and scratches.

In *Elvira's* wake, the *Dietrich Bonhoeffer* took round after round of railgun fire as no fewer than three separate orbital platforms pummeled the once-mighty assault carrier. Flashes enveloped the *Bonhoeffer's* hull, each the telltale flare of a fusion-powered explosion. Improbably, the Zeen resin seemed to hold against even the nuclear-fusion-fueled weapon strikes.

As dozens of railgun strikes tore into and eventually through the *Bonhoeffer's* reinforced hull, a handful of escape pods ejected from the Terran Armor Corps' lone active-duty warship. Xi knew the *Bonhoeffer's* layout well enough to understand that Colonel Li would not be aboard those pods, nor would anyone who had been stationed on the CAC. The strike that had shorn the forward third of the *Bonhoeffer* from the rest of the hull had taken the *Dietrich Bonhoeffer's* command center with it.

Such precision could hardly be a coincidence, and Xi said a silent prayer of gratitude to Colonel Li, Chief Rimmer, and their people for standing tall long enough to deliver her mech to the drop-zone.

Orbital weapons fire hammered into the *Dietrich Bonhoeffer*, which was rocked by explosion after explosion as internal liquid fuel stores cooked off. One such store, apparently using a tiny break in the Zeen resin as a nozzle, threw a jet of flame fifty meters long out from the *Bonhoeffer's* port hull. The fuel burned for twenty seconds, throwing the dying warship off-course and, somewhat mercifully, out of the path of inbound railgun fire.

Unfortunately, that improvised thruster also drove the *Bonhoeffer* on a new course that took it directly to the Lunar surface a thousand kilometers from Xi's drop-zone.

Xi watched with a mix of sorrow and hatred as the assault carrier's battered hull was wracked by an explosion that could have only been the death of the main reactor. The aft section flew apart, spraying a cone of molten debris from the falling warship's stern. Everyone aboard the *Bonhoeffer* had known this would be its last ride, but watching its flaming wreck fall to the Lunar surface was still an intensely emotional experience.

And yet, in spite of the *Bonhoeffer's* tragic death unfolding a thousand kilometers away, Xi's focus pivoted to a more immediate concern: landing her mech.

"Braking thrusters firing in five...four..." she called as the Lunar surface rushed up to meet her, "three...two...one...braking!"

Elvira lurched beneath her, the sensation almost gentle compared to the violent strikes before they launched from the *Bonhoeffer*. Her rockets fired for four full seconds before cutting out, and *Elvira's* drop-can touched down on a now-denuded patch of ground.

"Blowing the doors," Xi declared and popped the explosive charges that unfolded the drop-can around her. The metal walls fell to the dusty surface, and Xi stood her Scorpion-class mech to its full height as she crawled off the can's floor and set its feet down on the surface of the Moon.

Xi established P2P with the rest of her company, noting two absences from the rolls as she did so.

"2nd Company," she barked as the *Dietrich Bonhoeffer* neared its final resting place a thousand kilometers away, "sound off."

"*Cave Troll*, big and filthy," reported Lieutenant Yuan, offering his mech's traditional catch-phrase.

"*Wolverine*, snikt," followed Lieutenant Nakamura.

"*Mjolnir*, dropping the hammer."

"*Eclipse*, the blacker, the better."

"*Cleaver*, ready to chop."

"*Elvira*," Xi finished the sound-off, "clickin' my heels. Anyone have confirmation on *Simple Jack* and *Broadside*?"

"Affirmative, Captain," Nakamura replied grimly. "*Simple Jack*'s can was scratched by an explosion en route to the DZ, and *Broadside* got knocked off-course on her way out of the tube."

"Copy that, Wolverine," Xi acknowledged as Nakamura forwarded his sensor logs, which confirmed his report on both counts. Her already-thin eight-mech company had just been reduced to six, and they hadn't even engaged the enemy yet.

The enemy? She silently chastised herself. *Solarians are haughty, disinterested, and barely human, but they're* hardly *the enemy.*

Her lips parted in preparation to order her depleted company to roll, but a flash of light in the distance snapped her attention to a patch of Lunar surface a long ways away.

The *Dietrich Bonhoeffer* had finally crashed into the Moon, its death throes sending out a bolt of light as the last of the once-proud warship's fusion reactors lost containment.

She hated herself for not immediately recognizing the flash for what it was, and out of respect for the dead, she allowed a moment of silence to follow the mighty assault carrier's end. Every Legionnaire had seen their carrier's demise, and she knew without asking that they shared the sense of renewed resolve she now felt coursing through her being.

"2nd Company, form up on me," she commanded over the P2P. "Roll out."

As her mechs fell into formation, Xi received a secure P2P message from Lieutenant Colonel Moon. He had led his twenty best pilots into a crater three hundred kilometers from their objective and was confident the Solar forces had not detected them.

But that would change for all of them now that the *Bonhoeffer* had been destroyed by automated weapons fire. No amount of sensor trickery could hide such energetic exchanges, even if Jem's method had been able to deceive the entire Solarian defense grid into ignoring the automated orbital platforms' weapons fire.

The only question now was, how long until their Solar cousins discovered them?

Moving at flank speed, Xi led 2nd Company in a slightly divergent course from the one taken by Colonel Jenkins. The colonel's objective was an underground access junction through which Sergeant Major Trapper, Podsy, and Styles would move in search of a suitable information uplink node. After dropping off the insertion team along with most of the light mechs in 1st Company, the colonel would rendezvous with 2nd Company at Xi's objective: one of five transceiver arrays attached to Luna One's vast compound.

Time was against them, and soon all of Sol would be as well.

8

BROTHERLY LOVE

With *Blink Dog*'s loping strides rhythmically rocking the mech's cramped interior, Podsy gripped Jem's custom-made case against his chest. Blinky piloted the Recon-grade mech with unerring precision as the Metal Legion drove across the Lunar surface in a trio of tightly-grouped companies.

1st Company took point, with Colonel Jenkins commanding *Roy*, *Blink Dog*, *Shirley Temple*, *Leaf Cutter*, *Octopede*, *Wet Willie*, *Forktail*, and *Anaconda*. Most were Recon-grade, with the exceptions of the Battlewagon *Roy* and the Tactical-grade *Forktail*. Of the Metal Legion mechs on Luna, these were the fastest and featured the lowest-profile chassis, except for *Roy*. Sergeant Major Trapper's insertion team was spread between *Roy*, *Forktail* and *Blink Dog*, ready to disembark as soon as they reached their objective.

2nd Company, commanded by Captain Xi, flanked the formation's left with *Elvira*, *Cave Troll*, *Wolverine*, *Mjolnir*, *Eclipse* and *Cleaver*. Those were the heaviest-armored mechs and had the most devastating short- and mid-range weaponry. *Elvira*'s extended-range artillery represented the most potent long-range ordnance in 2nd Company, while *Cave Troll*,

Cleaver, and *Mjolnir* all featured game-changing close-range systems. This formation's task was to take and hold the transceiver array to prevent Solar forces from securing or destroying it before Jem's signal could be uploaded. Even diminished by the losses of *Simple Jack* and *Broadside,* 2nd Company's knife-range firepower was nothing short of terrifying.

3rd Company, commanded by Lieutenant Winters, consisted of the longest-ranged mechs in the unit and took up a position fifteen kilometers to the rear of 1st Company. *Generally, Preacher, Sam Kolt,* and *Huang Zhong* were all Cruiser-grade mechs, equipped with platforms capable of effectively engaging orbital targets, especially in the vacuum of the Lunar surface. Supporting them were the Tactical-grade *Osiris Risen, Indestructible-Mega-Titan Thunder-God Cid, Yekop,* and *Ybmug.* These vehicles were tasked with providing a defensive shell for the formation, while the long-ranged mechs provided a potent deterrent to aerial targets.

Of course, should the Solar forces locate the mechs before they delivered Trapper's team to their objective, the op would undoubtedly fail. As the Metal Legion mechs drove across the mostly-virgin field of regolith, they relied exclusively on Jem's concealment method to keep them from the enemy's sight.

"Range to objective twenty kilometers," Styles called out from *Blink Dog's* auxiliary console, normally used by the mech's Monkey. Most of the Legion's mechs lacked Monkeys for this operation. The diminished manpower was primarily a security concern. There simply weren't enough trustworthy people, in the command staff's estimation, to fill out the roster. It was a choice between fewer fully-crewed mechs or more skeleton-crewed mechs.

Which was no choice at all in an operation like this, where longevity and efficiency were less important than quantity and massed firepower.

"Contacts!" Styles called, then *Blink Dog*'s pace faltered, and a quick check of the tactical readout showed a swarm of inbound contacts. Too slow to be missiles, they appeared to be interceptor craft of some kind. After observing their acceleration figures and formation, he concluded they were short-range patrol craft, probably of the Locust design. "Four Locusts moving in our direction. No sensor pings detected."

Like every other Metalhead, Podsy knew it was unlikely in the extreme that a random patrol would bring a squadron of Solarians directly to their position, but as long as there was a chance they remained undetected, it was imperative that they do nothing to reveal themselves.

Which meant acting like frightened rabbits and freezing in the hope the enemy wouldn't notice them. No Metalhead was happy about doing so, but they all understood that strategy presented their best chance to avoid detection and carry out the op.

The Locusts moved steadily closer, and as they did so, Captain Xi's 2nd Company had bracketed them. Seconds ticked by as the Locusts closed the gap, during which the tension inside *Blink Dog*'s cabin grew so thick it would take a blowtorch to cut through it. Breaths were held, shoulders stiffened, and knuckles turned white as the Locusts came into effective firing range of their SRMs.

Then the ominous chime of a sensor ping rang out, and a second later, the Solar interceptors unleashed a hail of missiles at 2nd Company.

Replying instantly, Xi's mechs launched interceptor rockets and spat railgun bolts at the offending interceptors. The Locusts broke formation, splitting with the precision of a parade flyover. Terran missiles burned toward their targets, carving through the void as a lone Terran railgun strike sniped a Locust.

Terran rockets intercepted Solar missiles, sniping them one

by one and sending their shrapnel to the Lunar dust. As 2nd Company exchanged fire with the Solarians, 1st and 3rd Companies reluctantly held fire. It was still possible, however unlikely, that the *Locusts* had not yet seen through Jem's sensor fog. Podsy felt his stomach twist and churn as Locust missiles were scrubbed by 2nd Company's counterfire, with just a single SRM striking the heavily-armored *Cave Troll*. In response, the dual-plasma-cannon-wielding mech sent a trio of SRMs after the now-fleeing Locusts.

A second Locust was sniped by an SRM, followed by a third. The fourth Locust, juking and diving faster than any Terran craft could manage, pulled well over forty gees at its peak during evasive maneuvers. Those maneuvers brought it close enough to scrape the Lunar surface with its wedge-shaped hull, and even the ultra-maneuverable Terran missiles failed to match its chaotic movements.

Then a second alarm rang out, and Podsy felt his blood run cold at hearing Styles' report.

"Solar Marines," Styles said grimly as eight new signatures emerged from a pair of previously-concealed bunkers buried beneath the pristine Lunar dust.

The Solar Marines unleashed a storm of railgun and coil gun fire on 2nd Company from less than two hundred meters. Every bolt was a direct hit, and 2nd Company's tactical icons all flickered dangerously during that initial wave.

For perhaps the first time in his life, Podsy gave voice to a normally-silent prayer as he watched his comrades enter into a battle with their Solar cousins.

"Heavy counterfire!" Xi snarled as *Elvira's* cabin filled with outgas alarms. She angled her mech's dual fifteen-kilo guns toward the Solar Marines and fired HE shells. The shells struck the target bunker perfectly, cratering it and sending a shower of Lunar dust upward in a mushroom cloud that would escape the moon's gravity and forever lurk in the emptiness of space.

Not one of the four Marines had been within it when her shells had struck home.

Using leg- and back-mounted rocket motors, the Solar Marines cleared the bunker a full two seconds before Xi's shells struck. Using those motors in tandem with their power-assisted legs, the Solarian supersoldiers deftly leapt across the Lunar terrain, zigzagging as their coil guns sprayed slugs into Xi's mechs. Microrockets tore loose from the power-armored Marines' shoulder-mounted launchers, slamming into *Mjolnir* and *Cleaver* and carving torso-sized armor segments from the heavy mechs' hulls.

In the absence of atmosphere *Cave Troll*'s plasma cannons cycled silently, but the blue-white of the twin weapons' charge cycle grew brighter and brighter until the mighty mech unleashed its devastating knife-range firepower on the second bunker.

One of *Cave Troll*'s plasma bolts slammed into the bunker, carving a deep scar stretching fifty meters behind the slagged facility in the Lunar surface. Plasma jets erupted upward from the bunker, exposing a series of subterranean tunnels connecting the bunkers to other facilities on Luna One.

The second of *Cave Troll*'s plasma bolts surged toward the inbound Solar Marines. Caught at the apex of its bounding, zigzagging strides, a Solarian Marine was unable to react in time to avoid the inferno. The blue ball of plasma incinerated the Marine mid-jump, and a heap of glowing, misshapen metal floated to the ground as *Cave Troll*'s fury left the deadly battle-suit unrecognizable.

Xi's chain guns roared to life, sending depleted uranium

slugs at the Marines while the rest of 2nd Company's close-in weapons systems did likewise. Even Terran battle-suits could be slowed down by the fifty-caliber slugs, and rumors abounded that TRMC's power-armor was superior to Solar power-armor.

Those rumors were confirmed as 2nd Company's weaponry carved into the enemy Marines. Coil and chain guns knocked the leaping Marines off-axis, sending two into the moon dust while another pair suffered catastrophic rocket motor damage. The damaged rockets flared violently, but their wearers ejected the errant systems. A handful of the damaged rocket motors energetically tumbled through the air, with one striking *Mjolnir's* hull before dying.

The Marines, harried by the Terran chain and coil gun crossfire, authored another wave of counterfire. Power-armored Solarians were knocked left and right by the kinetic force of the impacts as they drew steadily nearer to 2nd Company. The Solarians launched another wave of counter-fire, and even before she was consciously aware of the event, Xi experienced the most cliched moment she could imagine...

Her life flashed before her eyes—and it was considerably less interesting than she'd expected it to be.

Elvira's cockpit, like most in the Metal Legion, featured a highly-durable transparent alloy window. Capable of withstanding even a direct artillery strike, the window was probably the most robustly-armored segment of the entire mech—and rightly so, since protecting the pilot was of paramount importance.

Solarian Marines had railguns with greater penetrative power than fifteen-kilo artillery shells.

A sliver of hyper-velocity tungsten punctured the alloy screen before her, blacking the entire viewport out as its polarity reversed. That sliver of tungsten skewered Xi's headrest, and it took her a full second to realize that it had also struck the left side of her head.

Her hand went reflexively to her ear. It flared with pain, but there was very little blood when she examined her palm. Even as she checked her wound, *Elvira's* automated breach-sealing measures went into effect, filling the cabin with a thin mist of foam-like material that rapidly plugged the five-centimeter hole in the cockpit's front window.

Sneering in anger at nearly being killed by sniper-precise railgun fire, she loaded airburst shells into *Elvira's* fifteens and spat them at the nearest Marine. One of the shells went off fifty meters past the target, well beyond its effective blast zone.

The other exploded five meters behind the Solarian.

The bounding Marine's back was filled with deadly shrapnel mid-jump, the impact of which knocked it to the deck long enough for a trio of Terran chain-guns to converge on it. Two seconds of sustained fire from 2nd Company's anti-personnel weapons mercilessly tore the battle-suited Marine limb from limb.

Mjolnir and *Cleaver*, cruisers of identical design featuring single plasma cannons similar to *Cave Troll's* duo, sent danger-close plasma bursts at inbound Marines. One Solarian was annihilated by the blue inferno. The other narrowly escaped the same fate with a well-timed leap that carried it over the ordnance's arc.

Cave Troll was in prime position to snipe that Marine with coil gun fire, but its guns were ominously silent as the bulky, lightly-damaged mech stood motionless in the formation.

Covering for *Cave Troll*, *Wolverine* pivoted from the Marine it had previously targeted (a Marine *Mjolnir* had erased with its plasma cannon) and unleashed a hail of cleverly-employed anti-missile rockets. Those rockets hammered the

Marine, bursting against the Solarian's armored torso with just enough kinetic force to stagger it.

That momentary hitch in the Marine's ultra-quick movements was all Xi needed.

She locked her starboard chain guns on the target and hammered the enemy battle-suit, ruthlessly pounding it with two hundred fifty-caliber rounds in less than three seconds. Shockingly, despite the hellish storm of fire, it seemed as though the Solarian super-soldier would regain its footing and escape her fire.

That fear vanished when *Eclipse* sent an SRM into the nearly stationary Marine.

Flying apart in a shower of metal shards, the vaunted Solarian power-armor succumbed to the overwhelming firepower. A few seconds later, *Cave Troll's* SRMs went live, and a swarm of eight missiles erupted from its launchers to splash down around the last remaining Marines.

Elvira's guns tore into the beleaguered enemy and were soon joined by the rest of 2nd Company's. A combination of artillery strikes, chain guns, and coil guns put down the last Solarian elements on the grid, wiping the board clear of hostile contacts.

"2nd Company, report," Xi called, and a stream of virtual acknowledgments filled her HUD. Her focus was rightly centered on the report from *Cave Troll*, though, and when it came over the audio channel and not via the HUD, she already knew its contents.

"This is Corporal Bowers, Captain," *Cave Troll's* Wrench reported. "Lieutenant Yuan was hit by railgun fire. I've assumed command."

"Copy that, *Cave Troll*," Xi acknowledged grimly, recalling the last words she had said to Lieutenant Yuan. She had called him a fat bastard, and in hindsight, she wouldn't have done it any other way. He was a good man and a stalwart Metalhead. His steady hand, dark humor, and unflappable demeanor would be missed in the coming hours and beyond. "2nd Company, reform and continue the advance," she called before switching to Dragon Brigade's control channel. "Dragon Actual, *Elvira*."

"Dragon Actual, go," Lieutenant Colonel Jenkins replied.

"Hostiles neutralized," she reported, transmitting the damage report on the P2P. "2nd Company suffered minor material damage and one casualty. We remain fully combat-effective, sir."

"Copy that, *Elvira*," Jenkins acknowledged. "1st Company is T-minus four minutes to the Nut. It looks like you'll make your northern run ahead of schedule."

The plan had initially called for Xi's company to diverge from the formation after the insertion team had been delivered to the Nut, but the Solar ambush had accelerated that particular timetable.

Now or later made little difference to Xi. In fact, she had unsuccessfully argued during the planning phase for 2nd Company to break from 1st and 3rd ten minutes before the Solarian attack.

"2nd Company's ready to mosh, Colonel," she assured him as she sent out the orders, causing her mechs to change course and drive toward the transceiver array at flank speed.

"Glad to hear it, Captain," Jenkins replied, impressed that Xi had managed to keep the casualties to a minimum. A single mech Jock was a small price to pay for thwarting an ambush by Solar Marines. It wasn't the kind of thing he would expected to survive without at least one or two mechs going down, which suggested that causing material damage was not chief among the Solarians' objectives.

It was more likely that the Solar forces were probing them, looking to gauge their reactions. They had also demonstrated uncanny accuracy with their railguns, putting holes in four of 2nd Company's six cockpits. Not only was it surprising that the Solarians' Marine railguns could punch through the Legion's heavily-armored viewports, but them doing so on the run under heavy fire was doubly concerning for Jenkins' people.

Then there was the fact that those Marines had known, beyond the shadow of a doubt, that they would die for their efforts. Power-armored Marines, be they Terran or Solarian, were offense-first. Their battle-suits were designed to maximize speed and firepower while providing protection from all but the heaviest ordnance, but against even just two platoons of Cruiser-grade mechs, those Marines could not possibly have expected to survive.

Jenkins suspected that was the ultimate point of the Solarians' initial exchange: that in matters of resolve, Solar Marines were unrivaled. The opening shots had been fired, and the Solarians' core message was that if this engagement boiled down to a test of resolve, the Terrans would fail.

Interestingly, the Solarians had not even attempted to contact the Terrans—not that Jenkins would have accepted such an overture. Too much was riding on Operation Antivenom's success to risk its integrity before they uploaded Jem's takeover attempt.

In spite of that, Jenkins was keenly aware that they had just killed at least eight human warriors; warriors who had made the ultimate sacrifice in service to Sol and, in their minds, to humanity. It was a sobering thought. Jenkins needed to make sure his fellow Metalheads didn't descend into mind-numbing despair.

"This is Colonel Jenkins," he declared over the brigade's

secure P2P comm network. "There come times in every family's existence where a heavy dose of 'brotherly love' is not only acceptable but necessary, and that's exactly what we're here to deliver. The ends *cannot* justify the means, and I'd expect every Metalhead in the Legion to put me in my place if I suggested they could. Still, I firmly believe with every fiber of my being that if our fallen Solar cousins had known our objective, and agreed with our operation's validity, they'd be looking down on us with approval rather than resentment. We all knew we'd pay a heavy price for this mission, and now we need to do everything we can to ensure that *every* sacrifice made in this operation—those paid not only in Terran blood but Solarian blood, too, every drop of human blood spilled—is worthwhile." He set his jaw and finished with grim determination, "Let's roll."

He knew that his speech would do little to alleviate the gravity of the situation, but Jenkins had learned the hard way that most operations boiled down to minimal advantages being leveraged to maximum effect.

He had faith that the Metal Legion was up to the task. Now it was time to validate that faith.

9

THE NUTCRACKERS

During Luna One's initial construction, the military fortress had been the most secretive construction project in human history. At any point prior to its Phase One completion, it would have been vulnerable to a ground assault precisely like the one the Metal Legion was attempting.

To safeguard Luna One's construction, a series of interconnected and heavily-fortified bunkers were erected and manned by no fewer than five hundred Chinese soldiers each. Two dozen mechs would have been stationed at these fortresses prior to Luna One going online, making them formidable defensive positions.

Fortunately for the Metal Legion, the bunkers had been largely abandoned after China achieved victory in Earth's last Great War. Their subterranean tunnel network still connected them to the rest of Luna One's vast infrastructure, however, which made securing one of these seven bunkers crucial to Antivenom's success.

The target facility had been code-named the "Nut" for this operation, and the Metalheads had nearly reached it.

"EM readings faint, Colonel," Chaps reported from *Roy's* pilot chair. Normally the command vehicle would have a full crew of six, including a dedicated Sensor operator, but for this operation, it was down to Jenkins, Chaps, and Shalhoub, *Roy's* Wrench. "But the Nut is definitely hard. At least six auto-turrets are up on those parapets, and God knows what else is buried between here and there."

"1st and 3rd Company," Jenkins called over the command channel, "assume positions. I know you mooks aren't famous for subtlety, but we need to *crack* this Nut, not *pulverize* it. Precision fire only, no matter how hard they hit back."

"Sensor pings," Chaps called in a rising voice, confirming what they had suspected: that upon entering knife-range, Jem's sensor deception would fail as local emergency sensors reacted independently of central inputs. "They're painting us, Colonel."

"All crews, engage targets," Jenkins commanded as the Solar turrets whirred to life, spinning on their mounts toward Jenkins' 1st Company. He was frankly amazed they had gotten this close before the Solarians targeted them, having feared that 2nd Company's discovery would have led to 1st and 3rd being exposed as well. "Smoke 'em."

A roar of fire streamed from 1st Company as artillery and mini-guns were unleashed against the heavily-fortified weapon placements. Built from stone and reinforced with hardened steel, the six seven-meter-tall 'towers' were twenty meters in diameter, their curved slopes making them look very much like half-buried donuts on the moon's surface.

And in each of those donuts' holes were quad-linked rail-guns surrounded by twice as many coil guns.

The Terrans struck first, scrubbing half the railguns before the Solarians could reply, but when the counterattack came, it was every bit as fierce as expected.

Shirley Temple and *Leaf Cutter* were each hit twice in rapid succession, destroying the former outright and blowing the latter's stern section off. *Octopede* took a near-miss to its rear left legs, temporarily knocking it to the ground before it regained its footing and continued advancing.

The fastest and lowest-profile mechs of 1st Company could get beneath the fortress' firing arcs if they moved quickly enough, and once there, they would prove instrumental to the Legion's takeover of the installation.

Blink Dog, Wet Willie, Forktail, and *Anaconda* were spared Solarian fire in the initial exchange. Those fleetest-footed of Jenkins' mechs sprinted forward in a race to get beneath the enemy fire. *Roy* sent an HE shell into the highest-priority target since it could potentially engage the Recon mechs even after they reached their objective. He was rewarded with a scratch of the entire mount, which left just one platform capable of touching 1st Company.

Standing firm in the middle of the field, *Roy's* artillery sent HE shells into the second donut-shaped railgun nest. Solarian coil guns spewed a near-constant stream of rounds, intercepting one of *Roy's* twin fifteens and stabbing into *Leaf Cutter's* flank. The lightly-armored *Leaf Cutter* shuddered as its capacitors took multiple direct hits, and the crew ditched in envirosuits mere seconds before their mech exploded. A shallow debris-strewn crater marked its passing, but the vital signs of its crew remained stable on Jenkins' HUD.

The second HE shell from *Roy's* fifteens landed less than three meters from the railgun mount. Although the weapon platform appeared to take minor damage, Jenkins knew that even cosmetic blemishes an artillery mount could shrug off were catastrophic for railguns.

Those guns' silence confirmed his suspicion that the nest

had been neutralized, which left 1st Company uncontested as the Recon-grade mechs reached their first objective.

Wet Willie and *Forktail* were both equipped with short-range mortars. Normally such weapons would be useless against heavily-fortified positions, but railguns and coil gun mounts were eminently more delicate than chain guns, artillery, or even missile launchers.

From the safety of their newfound cover, the Recon mechs of 1st Company opened fire on the last remaining coil guns and railgun mounts. *Roy's* added indirect artillery fire in support, and while the Solar coil guns managed a few stray hits on *Roy's* robust armor, the Terrans methodically scrubbed the rest of the Nut's guns from the board.

It had been every bit as straightforward as they had hoped. Easy even, considering the importance of the Nut to Operation Antivenom.

Almost *too* easy, in Jenkins' view.

"Secure the site," Jenkins called. "*Blink Dog* and *Forktail*, approach the access tunnel. Sergeant Major Trapper, deploy your demo team, and we'll deliver the charges."

"Roger," Trapper acknowledged, and soon the mechs were in position.

Luna One had not been built to withstand an expert ground assault like the one the Metal Legion had orchestrated. As a result, the vast majority of the immense complex's deterrent was focused on sniping aerial assaults and preventing ground forces from reaching the surface.

Still, it would be folly not to expect at least some resistance within the all-important network of tunnels.

Trapper's people, wearing light armor over thin, low-grade envirosuits, disembarked the mechs that had carried them to the objective. They spread out in a fan-shaped formation that provided optimal overlapping fire on the sealed door that led to the tunnels below. The door was wide, squat, and thick enough to withstand multiple direct hits from capital-grade weapons. To break through, Jenkins' people had brought along shaped charges and high-energy cutting equipment. The hope was to carve a hole in the door, send a team through to gain local control of its mechanism, and open it to permit the Recon-grade and other small mechs to travel down the wide, low-ceilinged passages.

But if worse came to worst, the Legion had enough raw firepower to pulverize the door from the outside. Doing so would cost them precious time since they would then have to excavate the rubble before moving down the passage.

Now that the Solarians had been alerted to their presence, time was the one commodity the Metalheads were shortest of.

Roy rolled through the regolith, coming to a stop just before the eighteen-meter-wide blast doors, where Trapper's people accessed external compartments that contained the ordnance required to blow a hole in the door. Moving with a long-practiced rhythm pounded into them by Sergeant Major Trapper, the Terran Armor Corps' infantry placed the various charges where they would be most effective. With the charges set, Trapper's people ran for cover while the sergeant major held the detonator.

"All clear of the door!" he barked. "All clear! Fire in the hole in three...two...one...pop!"

The demo charges flashed brilliantly against the reinforced door's surface. In the vacuum of interplanetary space, they made no sound and left no smoke. The force of the eight shaped charges was channeled inward, leaving a meter-wide hole in the door's surface.

Trapper ran over to inspect it before signaling for another batch of breaching charges to be brought up. That was good news since it suggested that he thought the first detonation had done the majority of the work and the second was likely to finish the job.

His people placed the fresh charges in less than forty seconds, having sprinted from cover on the low-gravity Lunar surface. Laden as they were with over a hundred and fifty kilograms of heavy explosives, the Legionnaires moved almost like they were on a standard-gravity surface. Their strides were bounding and longer than they should have been but nowhere near as awkward-looking as early Lunar exploration videos had shown for primitive astronauts.

With the charges set and his people once again safely hunkered down, Trapper called in a perfect repeat of his former declaration, "All clear of the door! All clear! Fire in the hole in three...two...one...pop!"

This time when the demo went off, it blew a perfectly circular hole in the door. Using his feet, he cleared a patch of regolith a meter in front of the door before leading a group of eight men and women through, diving with picture-perfect choreography. One after another, they cleared the hot metal surface, hit, and with an oft-practiced tuck and roll, recovered into a crouching combat-ready stance.

Jenkins had been impressed with their practice routines for that particular dive back aboard the *Bonhoeffer*, but seeing them do it for real made him appreciate the sergeant major's foresight and training regimen. Wearing ultra-thin envirosuits that would have failed at the slightest touch from the jagged edges, they could have died from missing a single step by two centimeters. However, they successively hurled themselves through the breach without reservation as they moved to accomplish their all-important objective.

Seconds ticked by and stretched to minutes as the "door-knockers" worked to gain control of the massive metal barrier.

Tension mounted in *Roy's* cabin while Trapper's people silently worked from within the tunnel.

Finally, the door began to lower, and when it finished opening Jenkins saw Sergeant Major Trapper withdrawing along with four of his people. Their rifles were trained down the tunnel, and without needing to be ordered, Chaps locked onto the offending wall-mounted pop-out turret a hundred meters inside.

Roy's coil guns sent a near-steady stream of slugs into that turret, fragging it before it could recede back into the wall. But that turret had already claimed three of Trapper's people, whose ruined bodies lay on the tunnel floor beside a wall panel they had opened to gain manual control of the door.

"Objective secure, Colonel," Trapper reported professionally as the rest of his people moved to either side of the tunnel.

"Good work, Sergeant Major," Jenkins replied softly. "*Forktail*, you're up."

"Roger, Colonel," Lieutenant Ford acknowledged, moving his flat-bodied, low-profile mech to the front of the formation. *Forktail's* artillery had been removed to streamline it sufficiently to fit into the tunnel, but the mech still possessed chain guns and missile launchers that were more than capable of engaging armored targets within the tunnel's confines.

Blink Dog, *Wet Willie*, *Anaconda* and the damaged *Octopede* formed the rest of the insertion team's column. The quadrupedal *Blink Dog* would need to "crawl" by lowering itself onto its "knees" instead of standing on its feet, but Blinky had demonstrated remarkable adaptability in that configuration. Podsy, Styles, and Jem were aboard *Blink Dog*, so Blinky's mech logically took up a post at the center of the formation, while the multi-segmented *Anaconda* assumed the third post.

Anaconda's Constrictor-class design was purpose-built for

deployment in mining tunnels and other subterranean locales. With a segmented body and individual motive systems for each of its nineteen segments, it was capable of snaking through any passage large enough for its head to fit through. And that head was nearly as heavily-armored as a battlewagon's, making *Anaconda* much heavier than any Recon-grade mech. But even at sixty tons, it was incredibly fast over short distances, its locomotion capable of exceeding two hundred kph under standard conditions. It was its speed, not its mass, that led it to be classified as a Recon-grade vehicle since that speed permitted it to conduct Recon operations. It was lightly armed with just a pair of fifty-caliber chain guns and a flame-thrower, all of which were forward-facing.

The rest of the mechs in the insertion team were typical Recon vehicles: lightly armored, lightly armed, and small enough to fit down the tunnel. They would be vulnerable to flanking attacks, which made Lieutenant Ford's task of clearing the tunnel with *Forktail* on point vital to the operation's success.

"Sergeant Major Trapper," Jenkins called over the dedicated frequency, "you are hereby placed in command of the Nutcrackers. Our entire lives have prepared us for this moment, people, and I know we'll prove equal to the task. Good hunting, Metalheads."

"Metal never dies," Trapper uncharacteristically acknowledged, and to Jenkins' approval, the entire Nutcracker team passionately echoed the sergeant major's words. Even as they did so, they removed the bodies of their fallen comrades and placed their remains in *Octopede's* flank-mounted cargo racks. It was not the first time those racks had borne such cargo, and Jenkins suspected it would not be the last. They left no one behind.

With that necessary task complete, the Nutcrackers moved down the tunnel. *Forktail* went ahead of the rest of the formation while Trapper's people clung to the walls and moved on foot down the underground passage.

"3rd Company," Jenkins called over the P2P as *Roy* tore across the Lunar surface toward the rendezvous point, "form up on me and proceed to the relay at flank speed. Every second is crucial."

"Acknowledged, Colonel," Lieutenant Winters promptly replied. "ETA to rendezvous point, seventeen minutes."

10

DOWN THE TUNNEL

Aboard the *Blink Dog*, Podsy watched in fascination and amazement as Blinky deftly guided the quadrupedal down the tunnel.

He was confident that Xi could have done the same, and word had it that Colonel Jenkins' piloting skills were the best in the Legion. But to see such a young and inexperienced Jock literally crawl his mech at speeds upward of twenty kph by shuffle-stepping on its "forearms" and "forelegs" was impressive.

And a little inspiring.

Jem's voice drew Podsy's attention from the mech's cockpit. "Based on what we have encountered, it is highly probable that there will be additional obstacles in our path."

"That would be the safe bet," Podsy agreed.

"However," Jem continued, "I do not think it probable that Luna One's information infrastructure has undergone radical modification since the schematics you provided were obtained."

Podsy nodded at the potential revelation, having hoped that Jem would conclude as much.

In the aftermath of Earth's last Great War, the Chinese government had attained absolute supremacy, in no small part due to Luna One. As a gesture of magnanimity and a display of dominance, the Chinese had made available the plans to Luna One for independent review by Earth's separate nations. By that time, however, it was impossible for any nation to mount a takeover attempt of Luna One. It had already pulverized every single non-Chinese military installation on the planet, so there had been little risk in revealing the details of the all-important facility to the general public.

It was those very schematics, which had been independently verified to the best of the non-Chinese inspectors' abilities, that the Metal Legion now used to navigate the vast network of subterranean tunnels.

Who could have guessed that their hubris might ultimately prove key to saving humanity from the very forces that had sundered and manipulated it? Podsy wondered in silence.

"This facility," Jem continued, "is crude, but effective. It is also in keeping with Jemmin's earliest iterations of the methodology by which it manipulated younger races into compliance."

"You're saying that Luna One was Jemmin's doing?" Podsy asked in alarm. Even as he did so, he knew he shouldn't have been surprised.

"Almost certainly," Jem agreed. "The Chinese government was, at the time, the ideal candidate nation for Jemmin to support and guide to a position of power among your people. Their Communist philosophy, while certainly enlightened in many respects, contained fundamental flaws that Jemmin used to consolidate power far more effectively than would have been possible with any human society built upon a more distributed system of national power."

"You sound like you approve of Communism," Podsy mused.

"Of course," Jem replied. "But as with any system of social organization, it possesses significant flaws. My forebears observed that there is no perfect and universally-applicable system of social organization. The possibility of such a system is anathema to a fundamental truth of life, which is that variation is key to life's success. Less variation leads to less success, while more variation leads to more success. This is universally true of organic life. Of course, intelligence eventually overtakes environmentally-selected variety as the most critical factor in life's continued success, but we Jem'un, using our own meager measure of intelligence, believed that it is only by incorporating individuality at every point of a social equation that social harmony and, indeed, organizational perfection could be attained."

"Communism was often hailed as universally fair," Styles said in a raised voice from across the compartment. "But I think its biggest flaw is that *life* isn't fair, so why should a social system designed for life forms be fair? It doesn't make sense. It's asymmetrical."

Podsy grinned approvingly as Jem replied, "That is indeed one of its major failings, another being increased priority given to the system itself rather than to its constituents. This factor aligns with Jemmin's core nature. It would therefore have been appealing to it as it decided how to most effectively manipulate your species."

"Contact!" Styles barked as flashes filled the tunnel ahead of *Blink Dog*, snapping Podsy's attention to the window.

Fifty meters ahead of the rest of the column, Lieutenant Ford's *Forktail* was enveloped in a crossfire as multiple pop-out turrets tore into the mech's flanks. *Forktail* returned fire, sending depleted uranium slugs back while *Anaconda* added its own chain guns to the fray.

Sergeant Major Trapper's people set up RPG launchers, sending rockets down the tunnel, where they carved meter-deep gouges in the soft, synthetic-rock walls. The Luna One's automated coil guns tore into the lead mechs' armored hulls.

Trapper led a team of six Legionnaires down the tunnel, ignoring the firestorm enveloping *Forktail* and *Anaconda* as they leapfrogged from the relative cover of one mech to another.

Using hand signals, he directed his people to target one of the left-hand pop-out turrets with at least two RPGs. Working in pairs with a loader and a gunner in each team, the trio of heavy weapons teams launched their grenades. One grenade missed entirely and streaked down the tunnel, where it exploded a full two seconds after being fired. The second was improbably sniped by turret fire just after it passed *Anaconda's* position.

But the third struck home, sending a spray of shrapnel out with such force that some of it clattered against *Forktail's* battered hull twenty meters away.

Heedless of the danger, Sergeant Major Trapper ran down the tunnel at the head of his six-man team. His goal was to reach the safety of Anaconda's armored head, and he managed to do precisely that just as one of his fire teams was torn limb from limb by coil gun fire from the opposite side of the tunnel.

Trapper shouldered his fifty-caliber rifle from a kneeling position and swung the muzzle on-target in a single fluid motion. The grizzled veteran squeezed the trigger without a moment's hesitation, sending a round into the armored shield affixed to the coil gun's sensitive firing aperture. Trapper missed the aperture by eight centimeters with that first shot, which was nothing short of jaw-dropping, in Podsy's mind.

Trapper's second shot came even closer to the weapon's muzzle, which swiveled toward him with mechanical precision. At this range, all it would take was a single coil gun round to kill the valorous warrior outright.

Fortunately, and against all odds, the sergeant major's third shot went straight down the turret's throat. The coil gun retracted into the wall, sparks flying from within as its high-voltage lines shorted amid a series of ultra-satisfying blue-white electrical discharges, arcing and sparking across the destroyed metal emplacement.

Podsy was speechless as Trapper's two remaining fire teams formed up on his position, where they reloaded their RPG launchers and prepared to engage the next target.

All three of Trapper's shots had gone off in less than three seconds. Using a fifty-caliber anti-material rifle, the sergeant major had pulled an eight-centimeter grouping with those shots at a range of sixty meters.

From his knees.

Under fire.

Without power-armor.

In *three seconds*.

Trapper's fire teams sent a pair of RPGs down the tunnel, where they struck another coil gun. Shortly after they neutralized their target, *Forktail's* left flank exploded, sending a short-lived fireball into the tunnel. Podsy knew with grim certainty that the only supply of oxygen that would make a fire in the tunnel was what the Metal Legion had brought.

Which meant *Forktail's* cabin had just been breached.

Once again, Trapper led his fire team down the tunnel, this time racing toward *Forktail's* position. The lead mech of the Nutcrackers shuddered, lurching to the right like a mortally wounded animal trying to avoid another wound. The true purpose of the move was made clear when Ford's mech sent a hail of SRMs down the tunnel, where they engaged eight different pop-up turrets. Using such powerful ordnance in a confined space was dangerous, but without atmosphere to propagate the blast wave, it was considerably less dangerous than it would have been on the surface of a planet with a thick atmosphere.

Five turrets were scratched, and, mercifully the tunnel did

not collapse from the AP missiles' impacts. Man-sized boulders were hurled from the walls, and the floor was shattered at several locations beyond the impact points, but the column's progress would not be slowed by the damage.

Then *Forktail's* right flank exploded. Without so much as a death rattle, the Tactical-grade mech collapsed to the tunnel floor while Sergeant Major Trapper hurriedly reversed course and led his people back to the relative safety of *Anaconda's* heavily-armored head.

Just as the infantrymen reached cover, *Forktail's* capacitors exploded, and the mech's hull was torn into three separate parts. The head, which housed the cockpit, was sent tumbling down the tunnel where it eventually skidded to a stop. The stern collapsed to the tunnel floor, motionless and largely undamaged.

But the mech's torso exploded in a violent spray of shrapnel that clattered against and even dug into *Anaconda's* armored prow.

"Medics!" Trapper barked, coming out of cover as a team of corpsmen raced down the tunnel far behind him. Their long, bounding strides seemed completely at odds with the gravity of the situation, but those exaggerated low-gee steps brought them to *Forktail's* head far faster than they could have managed under standard gravity conditions. "Walters, Lenin," Trapper called mid-stride as he reached *Forktail's* head. He pointed at two pop-ups that were partially-retracted. "Secure those turrets."

The pair of troopers moved to their respective assignments, primed frag grenades, and tossed them into the pop-ups before jumping clear of the muffled explosions that neutralized the deadly weapons.

Anaconda and the rest of the column awaited Trapper's all-clear signal before advancing. His people conducted thorough sweeps of the area while the corpsmen worked to access the self-contained cockpit of the destroyed *Forktail*.

Once they gained access to Lieutenant Eugene Ford's cockpit, the news was not what anyone had hoped for.

"No survivors," Trapper declared. "Lieutenant Podsednik, you're in tactical command of the column."

Podsy swallowed the sudden knot in his throat. "Copy that, Sergeant Major," he acknowledged.

"The tunnel's secure," Trapper said after another minute had passed and his people completed their inspection. "Clear the debris and move out!"

"You heard the man, Nutcrackers," Podsy declared as the last of the fallen were placed in body bags and put onto *Octopede's* external cargo racks. "Roll out!"

11

SPACE MARINES

"I've got inbound, Captain," reported Sargon, aboard *Eclipse*. "Sixteen contacts on a high-speed, low-altitude approach."

The contacts appeared on Xi's screen, converging on 2nd Company's position from four different vectors. She quickly noted they were moving too slow to be interceptors, but they were moving far faster than anything else should have been able to manage. They were hugging the deck so closely that only *Eclipse*'s drone-assisted sensors had detected them, which meant that engaging them would be difficult until both they and Xi's people had line of sight.

"Bogeys inbound," Xi called over the P2P, priming *Elvira's* SRMs in preparation. "Engage at will. *Eclipse*, forward target locations to 3rd Company." She switched to the relay-assisted P2P link between *Elvira* and *Generally*, Lieutenant Winters' mech. "Lieutenant Winters, we've got bogeys inbound. Requesting intercept support on indicated targets."

"On the way, Captain," Winters acknowledged, and a few seconds later both 2nd and 3rd Company unleashed a swarm of missiles against the inbound hostiles. The missiles gently arced above the Lunar surface before diving down on the enemy.

The missiles struck their targets, scrubbing them from the board and heightening Xi's alertness.

Solarians weren't stupid; they had been ruthless and tactically sound in everything they had done thus far. They wouldn't send sixteen assets from four different points of origin without a high degree of confidence that doing so would yield tangible results.

Then she had a thought that snapped everything into focus

"Marines inbound," she barked over the battalion-wide while loading *Elvira's* dual fifteen-kilo guns with high-explosive shells and forwarding fire packages to the rest of the Legion. "We only hit their drop-wings *after* they abandoned them. All artillery: load HE shells and fire for effect on designated quadrants. Fire! Fire! Fire!"

The long guns of 2nd and 3rd Company cleared, dropping explosive ordnance into the Lunar surface at the most likely locations of the inbound Solar Marines. Even *Roy*, who had yet to link up with Winters' people, sent shells through the air at the indicated targets.

"Sargon," Xi snapped, loading and clearing her guns as fast as they could cycle. "I need eyes on those fields now!"

"On it," Sargon acknowledged, and the first of the four approach fields was soon covered by a drone's video feeds. Xi scanned the field, noting the barest glint of metal before the drone was sniped from the void high above the enemy position. "Contacts confirmed in Quadrant Two," Sargon reported. "Four Solar Marines on approach from that position. Scanning Quadrants One, Three, and Four..."

Xi's neural-linkage-enhanced senses suddenly overpowered her cognitive process with the urge to juke. She lurched *Elvira* to the right as hard as she could, acting on a primal survival instinct that needed no words or reason to take total hold of her faculties. She had no conscious idea why she had done so, but as her senses returned to normal, she felt a severe stabbing pain in her shoulder.

Gas hissed as it escaped through a fresh hole in *Elvira's* forward armor, and Xi soon realized there was not just *one* new hole, but *three* in her mech's heavily-armored bow.

"Sneaky fuckers!" she snarled in mixed outrage and approval. She pointedly ignored her wounds while sending HE shells in the direction of the railgun slivers. If she *was* mortally wounded, she wasn't about to spend one single solitary moment of her life's last seconds lamenting her pending demise when she could be clearing her guns on the enemy. If she *wasn't* mortally wounded, there was no point in worrying about a fresh scar.

She was rewarded with a nearly perfect strike as an HE shell exploded eight meters from a power-armored Solar Marine. The shrapnel caused severe damage, toppling him long enough for Xi to send an SRM to his location just six kilometers from her position.

Xi's SRM arrived as the Marine regained his feet and erased him from the board. Xi continued juking, bobbing, and weaving evasively, and her efforts were rewarded by direct hits to *Elvira's* upper hull instead of the viewport.

Roy sent a railgun strike into one of the Marines, who Xi realized was jumping high above the surface before firing its own railgun at her and her fellow Jocks' cockpits. This gave the Solarians an advantageous firing arc, to be sure, but it also left them vulnerable if their locations could be bracketed quickly enough.

Missiles flew from 3rd Company's long-range launchers, slamming into three more Solar Marines before they could reach the apex of their jumps and cause any more damage. Five of the initial sixteen Marines were now off the board, but the remaining eleven proved every bit as crafty as their Terran counterparts.

No longer leaping up from cover, the Marines seemed content to dash hither and thither as the storm of Terran artillery rained down on them with devastating effect. Two more Solar Marines were scrubbed in the span of ten seconds before Xi felt the pit of her stomach fall away.

They're smarter than this, she thought, keying the mic and preparing to issue a warning to 3rd Company.

It turned out she was too late.

"Taking fire!" Lieutenant Winters declared as a fresh batch of twelve Solar Marine icons appeared on the tactical grid less than a kilometer from *Generally's* position at the head of 3rd Company. Both *Yekop* and *Ybmug*, identical humanoid Sorcerer-class Tactical-grade mechs, were killed in the opening seconds as precision railgun fire and anti-material rockets streaked from the Marines' bunkers. *Yekop* was reduced to a mostly-blackened hulk by enemy ordnance while the pristine white-hulled *Ybmug* fell ponderously to the regolith, where its interior was wracked by rapid-fire ammo cookoffs.

Preacher and *Huang Zhong*, the longest-ranged mechs in 3rd Company, suffered sniper fire to their cockpits that knocked *Huang Zhong* out of the fight long enough for a swarm of Solarian microrockets to exploit the hole in the durable alloy window and hulk the mech by killing its Jock and destroying its nerve center.

Even Lieutenant Winters' mech *Generally* was struck by a precise headshot that seemed to have killed 3rd Company's CO.

Then it was the Legion's turn.

Roy sent railgun bolts into the Marines' previously-concealed bunkers, killing two Solar Marines before they could find cover. *Preacher* sent eight SRMs at the Solarians, and while five were sniped by counter-fire authored by nearby pop-ups, the other three each claimed a Solar Marine with direct hits at the SRM equivalent of point-blank range.

The bizarrely-named *Indestructible-Mega-Titan Thunder-God Cid,* a towering humanoid mech with a torso comprised almost entirely of missile launchers, vented Terran fury at the Solarian ambushers with a swarm of thirty-two SRMs. Each missile was aimed at a different target, some of those seemingly random points on the Lunar surface. But they were soon revealed to be pop-ups and, in one case, a fortified bunker that *Cid* had somehow identified when even *Eclipse's* high-powered sensors had failed to discover it.

Only three Solarian Marines surrounding 3rd Company survived *Cid's* vengeance, and while they fought valiantly, it was only a matter of moments before they would fall.

The entire 3rd Company exchange to that point had lasted eight seconds, but those eight seconds had cost the Legion at least three mechs; possibly four, if *Generally* was indeed out of the fight. By any measure, eleven power-armored Solar Marines in exchange for three or four Terran mechs was a Terran victory.

But the Legion couldn't afford to play the attrition game. Luna One probably had hundreds (if not thousands) of Marines scattered across the vast facility. They had been extraordinarily lucky not to have encountered heavier resistance to this point, and still Xi had led her people into one ambush after another, each of which had cost Terran lives.

With that sobering thought in her mind, Xi watched with satisfaction as *Cleaver, Mjolnir,* and *Cave Troll* launched four plasma bolts at the remaining Solarians in their quadrant. Bracketing three Marines with their coordinated overlapping fire, the ultra-heavy-hitters of 2nd Company incinerated all three hostiles in a raging inferno that quickly dissipated into the void of space.

Eclipse sent a flight of four SRMs at a pair of isolated Marines. The first somehow managed to snipe both missiles targeting him with arm-mounted anti-personnel slug-throwers. The second Marine also shot one Terran SRM, but the other missile slipped inside his guard and vaporized the power-armored warrior.

A quick check of the board showed that between 2nd and 3rd Company's positions, only six Solar Marines remained. Terran artillery fire converged on their positions with deadly precision, slowly but surely taking them out. As the second of the final six fell to Terran fire, *Roy's* P2P link went dead.

Xi felt a moment of unrelenting, overwhelming dread at the thought of Colonel Jenkins falling to enemy fire. "No!" she seethed, locking onto the Marines nearest *Roy's* position and sending HE shells into them. "That'll teach you to turn your backs on me, jack-holes!" she yelled triumphantly as one of her shells downed a hostile Marine and the other caused its target to zigzag evasively far faster than any human should be able to move, even *with* power-armor.

The Solar Marines' explosive movements were rocket-assisted, much like their Terran counterparts', but the gee forces of these Solarians' movements should have been enough to render even a neural-linkage-equipped human unconscious. Here they were, though, hopping, strafing, and sprinting with as much maneuverability and acceleration as void fighters in pitched dogfights. They were able to avoid fully half the inbound SRMs that they *didn't* snipe as a result of their insane maneuverability, which had spared many of them from counter-fire in the engagement's opening seconds.

Unfortunately for the Solarians, the Metal Legion had over-whelming firepower and knew how to use it. One by one, the last remaining Solar Marines were eliminated without killing another Terran or significantly damaging any more Terran hardware.

As a final act of defiance, the last two Solarian Marines improbably punctured *Mjolnir's* robust armor and compromised its fusion core. The mech died in a five-kiloton explosion, cratering the Lunar surface but thankfully failing to cause serious damage to the nearby *Cave Troll*.

Xi breathed a sigh of relief when *Roy* stirred to life, moving at a sprint from its previous position before slowing and altering course to rendezvous with 3rd Company.

Colonel Jenkins' voice came over the command channel. "Dragon Brigade, this is *Roy*. Continue moving and forward status updates."

She heard a rare note of tension in Jenkins' voice, and Xi immediately recognized it for what it was: the effects of a hasty neural link-up. It would take *Roy's* neural linkage system several minutes to deliver the necessary cocktail of drugs to smooth out the link between man and machine, during which time Jenkins would feel like every nerve in his body was taking a sub-zero bath in acid.

That Colonel Jenkins had assumed direct control over *Roy* meant that Chaps, the mech's long-time pilot, was down and probably dead from Solarian sniper fire.

Xi directed *Elvira* and the rest of 2nd Company to resume the march before finally allowing herself to look down at her injured shoulder, the results of which had covered her chest and arm with a thin film of blood. The neural linkage had already administered coagulants and painkillers, but she would need help to close the wound.

"Gordon?" she called over her shoulder. "I need a hand up here."

"Give me a minute, Captain," he replied tersely, prompting

her to check his status with *Elvira's* internal cameras. Her eyes bulged when she saw that he was wrapping his right arm with a bandage. The floor of the rear compartment was covered in coolant, and she quickly reviewed *Elvira's* damage control logs to discover the source of the leak.

Her eyes widened in alarm when she realized that the tungsten bolt that had gone clean through her upper chest had improbably *ricocheted* off Deep Currents' enviropod, leaving barely a scratch on the miniature Vorr vehicle. The tungsten sliver had then pierced one of *Elvira's* main coolant lines, which Gordon had immediately worked to seal. The burns to his arm had resulted from his quick thinking, which preserved most of the system's coolant reserves at the cost of Gordon's flesh.

Shutting down the coolant system would have been not only dangerous but caused even more of the precious material to escape the system. By slamming an auto-welding patch on the burst pipe, Gordon had closed the hole less than five seconds after it had been caused.

Gordon emerged into the cockpit with a first aid kit in hand. He winced at seeing how much blood Xi had lost before pouring coagulant powder into her wound. "The pale-faced look doesn't become you, Captain."

"Everyone's a critic," she quipped, gritting her teeth and yelping as the coagulant powder caused her entire upper chest to flare with pain. He carefully cut her ruined pilot's suit away from her shoulder, taking obvious care not to expose her breast as he did so. She snorted, reached up, and ripped the garment down to expose everything he needed to see. "Don't tell me you haven't already looked in the showers!" She smirked as he flushed appropriately.

"I'd be a liar if I said that and something less than a man if I hadn't peeked, but holes and being covered in blood is a bit of a turn-off," he admitted, maintaining his focus while examining the wound. He prodded it with forceps, digging a bit of melted flight suit out before pressing the self-sealing bandage against her chest with enough pressure to make her wince again. "It missed your heart by about five centimeters, Captain, and pierced your lung," he said grimly as he produced an emergency chest tube kit. "We can't have that lung collapsing, now can we?"

"Do it." She nodded, and he tore away some more of her uniform to expose the ideal patch of ribcage for the chest tube. The needle felt like a mere pinprick, which suggested her body was filled with more painkillers than she had previously thought. Painkillers dulled reflexes, even when counteracted by stimulants, which meant *Elvira* would be less than a hundred percent going forward.

"All done," Gordon declared, grabbing a second self-adhering bandage and doing a surprisingly decent job of patching her ruined flight suit back together and restoring some semblance of modesty.

"Deep Currents?" Xi asked over her shoulder.

"I am here," the Vorr replied serenely.

"Are you all right?"

"I am," Deep Currents assured her.

"Sorry about the bumpy ride," Xi deadpanned. "One way or another, it'll all be over soon."

"Of that, I have no doubt," the Vorr replied matter of factly, filling Xi with an unwanted sense of foreboding.

After two minutes of active linkage, *Roy's* neural systems finally began regulating Jenkins' nervous system to the point that he no longer had tunnel vision. A few seconds after that, he thought he could feel his individual limbs again rather than an all-consuming burning, crushing sensation.

"That's better." He grunted, blinking away the intense agony he had endured after initiating the hasty link. He looked down regretfully at Chaps' body on the deck beside the bloody pilot's chair that Jenkins now occupied. "Sorry, Chaps," Jenkins said sincerely, having unceremoniously thrown his Jock's remains out of the chair and onto the cabin's deck.

The Legion's status reports trickled in as the battered companies resumed their trek to the transceiver array. Jenkins knew that however bad their losses had been during the latest attack, they could have been much, much worse if the Solarians had wanted to hit them for maximum effect.

Instead, the Solar Marines had opted to take sniper shots at the Legion's pilots, placing greater priority on the Terran command vehicles. Xi had suffered a total of four sniper shots to her cockpit during the engagement thus far, while *Roy* had been struck three times.

Roy's cockpit was in the heart of the vehicle, not the head like most of the Armor Corps' mechs, which only served to make the Solarians' accuracy that much more impressive.

Generally, 3rd Company's command vehicle, had also suffered direct hits to its cockpit. While it had fortunately failed to kill Lieutenant Winters, he was out of the fight, in critical condition with multiple chest wounds.

Even Xi had been nearly killed by a heart shot, but her extraordinary reflexes seemed to have played a major part in saving her life. With a hefty dose of painkillers and some effective first aid, it was probable that she could stay on the line long enough to complete the op.

In the latest tally, the Legion's battle-ready surface forces now consisted of just eleven mechs: *Elvira, Eclipse, Wolverine,*

Cave Troll, Generally, Cleaver, Osiris Risen, Preacher, Sam Kolt, Indestructible-Mega-Titan Thunder-God Cid, and *Roy*.

"Almost there," Jenkins muttered as the transceiver array drew steadily nearer and he raised *Generally* over the comm. "3rd Company, in light of Lieutenant Winters' injuries, I'm assuming command."

"Glad to hear it, Colonel," replied the other mech's Wrench-turned-Jock, a young woman named Quinn who had earned rave reviews from Lieutenant Ford during her time aboard *Forktail* as its Monkey. She was piloting *Generally* on manual since she lacked the neural implants, but her aptitudes suggested she would be capable of operating the vehicle at seventy percent effectiveness.

"Rendezvous at the indicated coordinates," Jenkins ordered. "How's your CO, Quinn?"

"He's unconscious, sir," she replied, her voice taut but clear. "I think… I think he'll pull through, but he's lost a lot of blood."

"He'd want you focused on your screens and the mission, Chief," Jenkins told her firmly. "I know it's hard when he's lying there, but you need to put him out of your mind. You already did everything you could for him, and if I know Winters, he'd come back to haunt you if you screwed up his company's performance scores. He'd rather die than have a blemish on his immaculate record."

Quinn gave a nervous laugh. "Thank you, Colonel. I won't let you down. Or him."

"I know you won't," Jenkins replied, projecting only slightly greater confidence than he felt. "Just ease back and let the autopilot do the heavy lifting, *Generally*."

"Copy that, sir," Quinn acknowledged, her voice firmer than before.

"*Roy* out," Jenkins said before cutting the line. He took another look at the plotter, which now showed the target array at the edge of *Roy's* sensors. "Almost there..." He grimaced, knowing that if they encountered even one more ambush en route to their objective, it was unlikely that they could achieve their objective.

As the Metal Legion's eleven remaining mechs drove toward the array, Jenkins was unable to dismiss the thoughts of the Solar humans he had ordered his people to destroy in service to the mission. He knew with the cold, logical part of his brain that there had been no viable alternative, but that did nothing to alleviate the hot emotional centers of his mind.

He had knowingly ordered the deaths of dozens, perhaps even hundreds, of human warriors whose only crime had been to defend human territory against unannounced invaders who had made no attempt to parlay or negotiate. That Colonel Moon, Colonel Li, Sergeant Major Trapper, and everyone else had signed off on the op didn't make the slightest bit of difference to Jenkins. *He* had ordered Operation Antivenom, and *he* had authorized fire against Solarian targets.

He was a war criminal. Period. If they lost the fight, he would get the firing squad for what he had already done, let alone for what he was about to do.

But the die was cast, and the time for second-guessing long past. They were committed, and to hesitate now would be to dishonor the sacrifices of the men and women who had died in service to this mission. They tried to accomplish the primary mission, which he had to complete or die trying. The future of humanity was at stake since failure meant the end of the human race.

More than anything else, it was that thought that kept Jenkins on the path toward Operation Antivenom's conclusion.

12

MANUFACTURED LUCK

"Bring up three crackers," Trapper barked, prompting his people to lug three cases of high explosive up from *Anaconda's* stern cargo pod. Podsy and Styles shared looks of mutual concern as Trapper's people set the demo charges on the fourth physical barricade they had already encountered down the tunnel.

The first three had been relatively easy to push past since they had been designed as manned defensive points rather than vehicle-blocking obstructions. They *had* required demo charges to clear, but this latest obstruction was intended to stop a column like theirs from proceeding deeper into the labyrinthine passages.

"Too slow," Styles muttered as the clock ticked down to forty minutes remaining until Colonel Jenkins and the surface force were scheduled to overtake the transceiver array. "At this rate, even if they clear this wall with the first charges and we don't run into any more obstructions, we'll be twelve minutes behind schedule."

Podsy shook his head grimly. The original op had called for

the surface team to hold the array for no more than ten minutes. Anything past that was considered critically hazardous to the integrity of the mission since it was only a matter of time before the Solarians arrived in force to secure the facility.

Fortunately, none of these barricades appeared to have been erected recently. They seemed to have been tacked onto the tunnel sometime in the last few decades, and they were thankfully unmanned.

"All clear!" Trapper barked after his people had set the charges and scurried back to the safety of the mech column. "All clear," he repeated. "Fire in the hole!"

The demo charges erupted with a blinding flash. In the confines of the tunnel, a bizarre hint of sound registered on *Blink Dog*'s sensors as the shockwave rode the rapidly-expanding gases from the demo charges enough to carry a barely audible report.

The dust quickly settled, leaving a hole just large enough to squeeze the column through. Podsy breathed a sigh of relief as Trapper led a team of his people through to secure the far side. A few seconds later, the grizzled veteran reported, "All clear."

The column proceeded through the narrow gap in the synth-stone wall, a gap that *Blink Dog* alone comfortably squeezed through. A combination of the mech's recently-modified design and Blinky's superior piloting skills saw his vehicle navigate through the cramped hole without touching its crumbling edges.

"Too slow," Styles muttered again.

"Slow can be good," Podsy observed dryly, hoping to cut some of the tension.

"'Slow' isn't the same as 'motionless,'" Styles quipped.

Podsy snapped his fingers in mock disappointment. "So *that's* where I went wrong!"

"You're sick, Podsy." Styles snickered before giving him an approving nod. "So sick, man..."

"No plan survives first contact, Chief," Podsy fired back. "Our people are the best. We'll get this done, delays or no."

"I hope so," Styles hesitantly agreed. "Because we only get one shot."

A few minutes later, another barricade came into view. This one was less robust than the last, but just as Trapper was about to move his people forward to make a hole, *Blink Dog*'s sensor alarms blared.

"Pop-outs!" Styles barked into his headset, prompting Trapper and the rest of the disembarked Legionnaires to dive for cover behind the mechs. Solarian chain guns emerged from concealment within the walls, and even from the ceiling as they spewed death-dealing slugs into the lightly-armored Nutcracker mechs.

Blink Dog's chain guns roared in reply, adding to the weight of fire as the Nutcrackers methodically scraped pop-outs from the tunnel walls. Four seconds after the first shots were fired, five of the eight turrets were sanctioned by expert Terran counterfire.

Despite the Terrans' quick reactions, the Solarian ambush proved costly.

Four of Trapper's infantry were cut down in the opening seconds when they were unable to reach cover. *Anaconda's* armored head segment, already battered from previous exchanges, looked close to failure on the all-important edges where the unarmored infantry huddled for protection. And the battered *Octopede's* frail legs, two of which were already gone, suffered catastrophic damage as the enemy coil guns focused fire on their weakest points.

From his position at *Anaconda's* stern, the sergeant major signaled his people toward new targets. As they loaded fresh grenades into their launchers, Trapper squeezed a shot off at an overhead coil gun busily engaging the battered *Octopede*. He was rewarded with a shower of sparks before the weapon withdrew into the ceiling.

That left just two of the enemy weapon emplacements, but they were nested behind opposing concrete barricades that protruded from the tunnel's walls. To Podsy's surprise, Blinky tried to line up a shot on one by contorting *Blink Dog* dangerously over to its right, tilting the cabin so severely that Podsy had to grab the overhead "oh shit!" rail to keep from lurching out of his seat. To Podsy's mind, the quadrupedal mech should have fallen over at least ten degrees earlier, but somehow Blinky kept it upright before unleashing a hail of chem-driven rounds from *Blink Dog*'s right chain gun.

Most of the rounds hammered into the concrete, spewing chalky dust out in a continuous stream of debris. The enemy coil gun turned toward *Blink Dog*, boring round after round into the Recon-grade mech's front as multiple Terran and Solarian rounds collided mid-flight.

Blink Dog tilted even further, defying gravity and causing Podsy's legs to swing down toward the far bulkhead (which was nearly parallel to the ground at this point). Podsy was about to protest, but Blinky soon proved his mettle, laying his mech all the way over to the deck with a crash while keeping his guns on target. And from that exposed, vulnerable position, *Blink Dog* sent a killing burst against the dug-in coil gun mere seconds before Trapper's people neutralized the target on the opposite wall with multiple RPG strikes.

"Way to stick the landing, Blinky," Styles grumbled as Podsy gingerly picked himself up and stood on the bulkhead, his former seat perpendicular to it. But Styles' seat was on the mech's right side, which meant that combined with his harness, Styles was still seated and merely laying against the bulkhead while Podsy had been thrown from his chair entirely.

"It was the only way to take the shot, Chief," Blinky protested.

"Hey, lay off the kid," Podsy said dryly as Trapper's people secured the area, spiking damaged pop-outs with frag grenades. "The way I hear it, he does *all* his best work from his back."

"Damn, that's cold, Podsy," Styles said with a grin while Corporal Staubach did the right thing: ignored them and worked to right his mech, which he proceeded to attempt without enlisting the aid of another mech.

"Truth hurts." Podsy shrugged just before *Blink Dog* lurched upright, nearly launching Podsy face-first into the port bulkhead. He only saved his nose from a crushing impact by sacrificing his forearm to one of the mech's ten-centimeter steel ribs that formed the cabin's frame.

"Sorry," Blinky said with false concern. "Probably should have said something, but you probably wouldn't have heard me over all your bitching."

"Is that insubordination I hear, Chief?" Podsy asked, trying and failing to hide a grin at the younger man's cheek.

"Sounds like it," Styles deadpanned. "And it seems to me like he just tried to assault a superior officer using a Recon-grade mech. Is that what you think, Lieutenant?"

"Whatever it was," Podsy grumbled good-naturedly while resuming his seat, "I think a superior officer might assault *him* if he tries it again. I paid good money for this beak, after all."

"Fire in the hole!" Sergeant Major Trapper called, and another flash filled the cockpit's window. When the dust settled, there was a hole large enough for the column to squeeze through.

One by one, the Nutcrackers moved through that hole, save for *Octopede*. It had been too badly damaged during the attack and was no longer able to keep its profile low enough for that movement to be possible. Its capacitors were discharged, its ordnance transferred, and the mech was abandoned by its crew, who transferred to *Anaconda* along with most of the salvaged gear.

It took just two minutes to strip the mech of useful supplies, and with that done, the column renewed its forward march.

They continued down the tunnel, sniping the occasional pop-up whenever the column's interlinked sensors located them from a safe distance. A local jamming field interfered with Terran sensors near the ambush sites, so Styles had sent a few drones down the tunnels in hopes of tripping whatever auto-response systems might await them.

The method worked; the track-driven drones exposed three different ambush points in seemingly nondescript sections of the flat, wide tunnel. This enabled the Legion's mechs to clear those points with long-range fire, keeping the infantry safe but causing *Anaconda* to soak up more and more damage to its already-battered head as the coil guns returned fire from the three ambush points.

Then something appeared on the drone feeds, causing Styles to call, "Hold position, Sergeant Major. I'm forwarding a live feed from two kilometers down the tunnel."

Trapper gestured for the column to halt and the Nutcrackers froze in place as the sergeant major reviewed Styles' update. Podsy leaned over, checking the details for himself and seeing a full-sized transit node on the drone's video feeds. That node should not have been there, and according to their best intel, had not been there eighty years ago. But there it was, as plain as the nose on Podsy's face: a six-way transit inter-section that presented danger and opportunity in equal measure.

Using the intersection could possibly cut as much as fifteen minutes off their journey if one of the tunnels intersected with their previous course, as it appeared likely it would. But the intersection was likely to be guarded, and whatever troubles they might have previously had with automated defenses would be multiplied several times over if they went at the intersection head-on.

Even a single Tactical-grade mech operating at maximum spec would be enough to neutralize automated defenses within the intersection. Coil gun rounds could kill a Tactical mech given enough time to concentrate fire, but its armor would buy it the necessary seconds to emerge victorious using its superior armament.

Unfortunately, the Nutcrackers' mechs lacked both armor and firepower. That meant this unexpected transit nexus was going to be an especially tough nut to crack.

Trapper perused the data for a long, silent moment before his voice filled *Blink Dog*'s cabin. "We've got a choice to make. We either sprint past and continue along our previous route, or we take the hub and restore some of our lost time. Now's the time for input."

"We're behind schedule," Styles quickly replied, "but the transceiver is surrounded by derelict buildings and other abandoned infrastructure. The surface team can hold long enough for us to arrive via the original route."

Podsy argued, "If we hang them out while we skirt that nexus ahead, they'll bleed for every second we lock them down to that position. The odds are high that there's already a Marine dropship en route to the transceiver."

"*Someone's* going to bleed either way," Styles retorted. "I'm fine with it being us, but if we don't protect Jem long enough to reach the uplink node, none of this will have mattered. At this moment, preserving the integrity of the Nutcrackers is a higher tactical priority, and *every* Terran down here knows it."

"You're both right." Trapper grunted. "We can't risk Jem, and we can't hang the surface team out for an extra fifteen minutes. *Blink Dog*, hold back. *Anaconda* and *Wet Willie*, you're with me. We move in behind the snake, and Willie clears the northern rim with mortars. *Blink Dog*," he added harshly, "if you so much as flinch toward that junction before it's secure, my sidearm will have a fresh holster and sitting down will become a challenge for you from that moment forward. Have I made myself clear, Corporal?"

"As a Solarian's conscience, Sergeant Major," Blinky sourly acknowledged.

"Good." Trapper grunted again. "Nutcrackers, let's move."

Their comrades jogged down the tunnel, flanking *Anaconda* and *Wet Willie* as the depleted unit moved toward their new objective. Without asking, Podsy knew that both Styles and Staubach shared his frustration at not joining the fight. Terrans were going to die at that nexus, and *Blink Dog*'s chain guns could save some of their lives.

But Styles' argument had been sound: protecting Jem was of vital importance to the mission. Still, that didn't make the reality of sitting on their hands while Metalheads fought and bled to clear a path for them any easier to stomach.

Trapper led the bulk of the Nutcrackers down the gently-curving tunnel, where they disappeared a little over a kilometer from *Blink Dog*'s position. The tension-filled seconds stretched on in utter silence, and those seconds became minutes. Podsy imagined the preparations Trapper was coordinating among his people, using nothing but hand signals to prepare for the assault. In all his life, Podsy had never thought of himself as a brave man. A realistic man, certainly, and a defiant one, to be sure. Podsy had learned the hard way, much to his relief, that he would not die on his knees begging for mercy.

But Sergeant Major Trapper was not only brave, he was

fierce. While Podsy would fight tooth and nail once his back was to the wall, Trapper displayed at least that much resolve every second of every fight Podsy had seen him in. He seemed unconcerned with his own safety in the heat of battle, whereas Podsy could usually think of nothing *but* safety while taking fire.

Finally, the sergeant major's voice came over the line, breaking Lieutenant Podsednik from his reverie.

"Crack it!" Trapper barked over the Nutcrackers' command channel, and the dark tunnel ahead was illuminated by the near-continuous Terran muzzle flashes. Those flashes were punctuated by RPG reports one after another as the Metalheads made their push into the fortified nexus.

The battle raged as strobes of fire filled the curved corridor ahead of *Blink Dog*, and soon the whirring Terran chain guns fell dark. The entire engagement had lasted thirty-four seconds, and for a time, all three of *Blink Dog*'s occupants had held their breath in fear of the dreaded order to fall back.

"The junction is secure," Trapper declared, sending a wave of relief throughout *Blink Dog*'s cabin. "You're cleared to rejoin the formation, *Blink Dog*."

Blinky had already begun to crawl the mech forward, and without other mechs or infantry to consider, he increased the vehicle's speed to nearly double what it had previously achieved in the low-ceilinged passage.

As they turned the corner, Podsy was equally heartened and dismayed at what he saw.

At least two dozen of Trapper's infantry had survived the attack, with only three newly-fallen bodies being pulled aside by their comrades. *Wet Willie*, surprisingly enough, seemed to have sustained only moderate damage. The flat-bodied, track-driven mech's normally-vertical mortars had been modified pre-drop to allow their use as improvised light artillery, and it seemed that improvisation had proven key to neutralizing the transit hub during the brief but intense siege.

But *Anaconda* had finally succumbed to the accumulated damage suffered during the insertion. Its head was shorn completely off its body, and the formerly-robust armor plating that had protected the segmented mech from the front now looked like something that belonged in a junkyard rather than a battlefield.

Amazingly, *Anaconda's* Jock and Wrench had survived the violent destruction of their mech. The pilot looked to have taken some shrapnel to her left arm, but aside from that, they were fit enough to march and contribute to the operation on foot.

Trapper gestured across the transit hub, which was roughly star-shaped and measured fifty meters on a side. The tunnel the Metalheads had arrived through was identical to the one opposite it, as they had expected, but the other four tunnels were narrower and cylindrical, with tri-railed tracks on their lower surfaces. The rails were like any common mass-transit system one might find near a developed Terran city, or even in a high-volume subway.

"It looks old," Styles mused. "At least a hundred and fifty years."

"Weren't independent inspectors supposed to have cataloged this very tunnel at least *three times* since then?" Podsy furrowed his brow in confusion.

"An information edge is usually the deciding factor in a fight." Styles shrugged. "However, they tricked people into thinking this was a regular tunnel and was irrelevant. Sergeant Major?" Styles switched to Nutcrackers' command channel. "Request permission to send recon drones down Bravo Tunnel."

Styles designated the tunnels and updated the other mechs and the helmet-mounted HUDs of the Trapper and his

Pounders. It was important that everyone spoke the same language.

"Granted," Trapper agreed, prompting a pair of track-driven drones to detach from *Blink Dog*'s flanks and scurry across the transit nexus. Their nimble chassis soon disappeared down the tunnel. Podsy checked the local sensor feeds over Styles' shoulder.

"What are you looking for?" Styles asked absently as his semi-autonomous drones drove at a hundred kph down the tunnel.

"Nothing in particular," Podsy told him. "It just seems odd that a transit junction like this would be part of some big cover-up, doesn't it?"

"To a Terran, sure." Styles shrugged. "But Solarians are all about top-down, centralized control. It's the only reason we've been able to make it this far, which has been nothing short of a miracle as far as I'm concerned."

"Not *just* a miracle," Podsy chided. "Colonel Jenkins' original plan to reintegrate armor elements into Fleet operations wasn't just an interesting one-off or a stopgap designed to buy the power-suit production facilities a few months to make new suits. He recognized a growing gap in the Terran Armed Forces' panoply, and he was trying to bridge that gap without reinventing the wheel. Speed and accuracy kill, yes, and nobody outperforms human Marines in those areas, which *usually* turn out to be decisive advantages," he explained heavily. "But the Arh'Kel taught us one thing back on Durgan's Folly above all else."

Styles nodded in agreement. "Sometimes you've got to be able to *take* a hit, not just deliver one."

Podsy shrugged. "There's no way a Marine contingent could have held that junction on Durgan's Folly long enough for you to complete your takeover," he concurred. "Marines could have taken it, sure, and probably faster than we did. But with so many tunnels to hold and *thousands* of Arh'Kel in effective response range, that op *couldn't* have worked without specially-designed equipment that we didn't have. Armor gives us tactical flexibility that power-armored Marines can never perfectly match." He shook his head damningly. "It seems like the Solarians developed the exact same blind spot to that fact that Fleet did."

Styles smirked. "But instead of condemning them to defeat, that blind spot just might lead to their salvation."

"Salvation for them, sure," Podsy allowed, his brow lowering in dark contemplation. "But I doubt *we'll* find anything like salvation at the end of this rainbow."

"You didn't *actually* think this would end in unicorns and lollipops for us, did you?" Styles asked in surprise.

"Not really." Podsy sighed, running a hand through his hair and looking down at his prosthetic legs. "But however it comes, I think what we need more than anything is a break. These last few months have been *brutal*."

Staubach snorted in apparent agreement as the drones reached the target zone. Podsy leaned forward, intently studying the initial video feeds from the two ground-based recon vehicles, and both he and Styles breathed identical sighs of relief at what they reported.

"Sergeant Major Trapper," Styles declared over the command line, "recon drones have reached the objective. The upload hub is intact and undefended—" He broke off when the first drone's video feed went dark. A flash of light preceded the second drone's link death, prompting Styles to review the last seconds of footage before revising his report. "Correction, sir: recon drones are offline, and two fixed coil gun placements have been identified. No mobile assets detected."

"She's down to her panties, people," Trapper said in a raised voice. "It's time to cross home plate. *Wet Willie*, hold position here with the wounded. You'll never fit down that tunnel, and having you cover our rear is more valuable than bringing another double-helping of left feet to the party."

"Understood, Sergeant Major," Wet Willie's Jock acknowledged with obvious disappointment.

"Everyone else," the sergeant major barked, "move out!"

13

THE TRANSMITTER

The colonization of Luna had once been heralded as the most important next step humanity could take on its journey to the stars. Its proximity to Earth offered tremendous material support to colonizers: its low gravity would make travel to and from the small planet far less costly and dangerous than doing the same from Earth, and the treasure trove of helium-3 spread across Luna's surface seemed like an ideal source of cheap, plentiful fusion fuel for humanity's continued growth and development.

Dozens of installations had been built on Luna's surface, both on the near and far sides. Scientific outposts, mining operations, and even dedicated habitat centers were built in the decades that followed Earth's last Great War (an event sometimes referred to by Solarians as the "Final War").

For a time, the dream of a permanent self-sufficient Lunar colony looked like it had become a reality. At its zenith, Luna was home to one hundred million humans, two dozen large-scale H-3 mining operations, twice as many dedicated scientific outposts, and, of course, the vast military installation of Luna One.

Extensive mining operations had been necessary to carve Luna One's various segments beneath the surface of the Moon. Those operations had left a sprawling network of tunnels behind, which Chinese forces had initially used to construct hidden fusion power plants, mass drivers, and eventually the surface-side fortresses like the one the Legion had overtaken in order to insert Sergeant Major Trapper's people underground.

It had made sense, following the so-called Final War, that Luna One's extensive infrastructure should serve to expedite humanity's colonization of Earth's silver-skinned twin sister. As a result, sprawling habitat compounds sprang up around every single one of the formerly-hidden top-secret military installations that had carved the last traces of organized resistance to Chinese supremacy from the face of the Earth. These habitat modules were erected by remotely-operated construction drones, and every single city on the Moon was completed long before its first human occupants stepped off Earth's surface.

In less than a decade, using newly-constructed maglevs built after the Final War, human colonists began their march to the Moon, and to the asteroid belt, and to Mars, and to Venus, and to the moons of Saturn. This expansion came to be known as the "One Star" initiative and was viewed as the most meaningful human endeavor in the species' history. The brick-red surface of Mars was now within reach and was soon dotted with habitat modules that housed millions of people. The clouds of Venus rapidly filled with floating hab-ships that bobbed along that hellish planet's upper atmosphere like ducks on a rippling lake. And the moons of Saturn made for the most remote, and arguably the most beautiful, remove from Earth that was available to risk-taking human colonists.

Following the horrors of the Final War, many felt that this expansion period would quickly wash away the bitterness of Earth's bloodiest conflict. Unified by a profound and innately biological purpose, the need to grow and increase influence on the environment, humanity seemed poised to take the greatest collective leap forward in its history.

And yet, despite even Pluto receiving a scientific colony, signaling that nothing within the Solar system was beyond human reach, the relative safety and mythological allure of Luna made it the prime colonial site in the Solar system. Competition was fierce among those who wished to call it home, and the screening process was draconian. As a result, only political loyalists and physically superior humans were allowed to colonize Luna. Many chafed at this favoritism, but there was little that could be done to counteract it.

At the height of the One Star expansion phase, humanity conducted its first test-flight of an Alcubierre-influenced "warp drive." Within seconds of the test team completing that two-second flight at speeds reaching one-point-zero-one-five times the speed of light, the Illumination League arrived to greet humanity with what had seemed like warm, invitingly open arms.

Their arrival and its implications led to high tension throughout Sol. Riots broke out in the streets, work stoppages caused dangerous and costly failures of the One Star initiative, and a fresh wave of resistance to government authority arose all across the globe like spring weeds poking through the front lawn.

Earth's government, nominally a United Nations type of assembly, was still wholly controlled by Chinese interests—and those interests dealt with this dissent and rebellion precisely as their predecessors had done.

Due to historical censorship, few details are known of this turbulent phase in Sol's history. What *is* known is that compliance was achieved with alacrity and a high cost in human blood as martial law was declared and rebels were summarily executed. With the rebellions put down and the One Star initiative reorganized into a less ambitious version of itself, humanity sought to join the Illumination League in order to gain access to wondrous technologies.

Chief among them were the wormhole gates, which ultimately led to the birth of the Terran colonies. For a time, all had seemed to be proceeding in humanity's favor. Dozens of independent extra-Solar colonies were put down across the more than twenty different star systems the Illumination League had designated as human territory. Then the wormhole gates went dark, and the colonies that would eventually become the Terran Republic were thrown into a fight for their very survival. Some survived and a few even thrived, but most of these colonies died slow, painful deaths as they exhausted their resources and failed to adapt to their new and brutal circumstances.

No Terran knows precisely when Solar humanity abandoned their sprawling network of Lunar colonies, whose city lights had once been visible from Earth with a naked eye, but sometime after the wormholes went dark, the One Mind network became an inextricable part of Solar life. And sometime after Solar humanity had implemented this radical self-modification, nearly all human colonists withdrew to Earth from their homes in the asteroid belt and on the surfaces of Mars, Luna, Pluto, and even the moons of Sol's gas giants.

The only colony that retained the majority of its colonial population was Venus. No Terran had conveyed a convincing reason as to why that colony, and that colony alone, persisted to this day, with over four billion humans presently calling its skies home.

As Captain Xi Bao approached the transceiver array they sought to take and hold, the looming towers and curved buildings that surrounded it seemed both dead and alive. Her targeting scanners identified dozens of vehicles abandoned in place, some of which looked like old-style automobiles.

The ghost city sprawling before them was large enough to house at least four hundred thousand colonists. Many of those colonists would have lived several meters beneath the pristine, paved streets and high-rise buildings that had transformed the Lunar desert into an oasis of human civilization.

Her commlink chimed, and she immediately received the inbound call with her canned response. "*Elvira* here."

"Make 2nd Company's approach from the west, Captain," Colonel Jenkins commanded as the indicated course was highlighted on her HUD's local map. "I'll come in from the east while 3rd Company takes up position to the south. If you spot movement in any of those structures, do not engage. I say again: do not engage. Keep your poker face and call in a long-range strike from 3rd Company to put the whole building down. Just be sure to stay clear of the engagement zones," he added sardonically.

"Copy that, Colonel," Xi acknowledged as 2nd Company breached the outer edge of the colony. There were no signs to greet visitors because there were no surface roads connecting Luna's long-abandoned colonial cities. The only transit lines were underground, which gave the settlements the appearance of isolated islands rather than the interconnected nodes of humanity they had once been.

Elvira led *Cave Troll, Eclipse, Wolverine* and *Cleaver* into the city from the west. The transceiver was located less than two kilometers from the city's perimeter on that side, while *Roy* would need to cover three times as much distance from the other side of the city.

Generally, Sam Kolt, Osiris Risen, Preacher, and *Indestructible-Mega-Titan Thunder-God Cid* comprised 3rd Company's remnants, and those mechs took up position twelve kilometers to the city's south. That was the ideal range from which to launch their heaviest munitions while also allowing them to effectively cover the mechs of 1st and 2nd company with interceptor fire.

"Movement," *Eclipse* reported as an unconfirmed icon appeared in a building two blocks ahead of their position.

Xi confirmed the flicker by reviewing *Eclipse's* sensor logs. It was faint, but something *definitely* moved in that twenty-story building. None of these buildings were pressurized or thermoregulated, which made it extremely unlikely that civilians were present.

She silently transmitted the coordinates to 3rd Company and received the virtual acknowledgment from *Preacher's* Jock, Falwell.

Seconds later, a quartet of high-yield Devastator-class MRMs flew from *Preacher's* launchers. Those missiles struck the building just above the second floor, where they proved worthy of their name.

The building's southern face slowly collapsed, with the third floor collapsing just before the fourth followed suit. The fifth did likewise, then the sixth and the seventh, before the entire building began to slowly tilt southward.

A pair of Solar Marines' rocket packs flared within the collapsing building, carrying their riders skyward as they fled the dying structure. For a moment it seemed they would successfully escape the crumbling building's demise and reach the relative safety of a nearby high-rise.

Then Xi locked on with her chain guns and sent a stream of fifty-caliber rounds into the soaring Marines. Fewer than ten percent of her two-hundred chain gun rounds struck the marks, but those rounds proved more than enough as they punctured the rocket pack of one and scored a lucky strike against the other.

The damaged rocket pack exploded brilliantly, sending its user hurtling through a nearby building's thin walls. The other Marine's pack failed entirely, and he plummeted to the street...

Where he landed on his feet before sprinting to a nearby building, getting clear of Xi's guns as the twenty-story building fell onto one of its much shorter neighbors.

Elvira's seismic sensors went off as the falling building's death sent shockwaves through the ground beneath Xi's mech. Unfortunately, she was uncertain whether even one of the Solar Marines had been neutralized. It was probable that more than just two Solarians had chosen to use that building as an ambush point, but there was no way of knowing whether she had just wasted four of their Devastators.

"2nd Company, keep moving," Xi commanded as *Roy* entered the city from the east and tore through the abandoned streets at over a hundred kph. "Keep your eyes peeled for their buddies but hold fire unless fired upon. Let 3rd have a little fun."

Acknowledgments flickered on her HUD as she split her forces between three different streets. *Elvira* led *Eclipse* up the middle, *Wolverine* and *Cleaver* went right, and *Cave Troll* broke left as the mechs moved deeper into the city. Before they passed the buildings the Solarians had disappeared into, Xi sent *Eclipse* an order to deploy a disposable recon drone.

The drone shot up, powered by microrockets that carried it to an elevation of thirty-five hundred meters before station-keeping thrusters fired, delaying its inevitable surrender to Luna's irresistible embrace.

The drone sent hundreds of high-resolution images back, five of which indicated Solarian Marines scattered throughout a ten-block area. Xi bracketed their positions and called in a flight of SRMs from 3rd Company.

There were too many obstructions for *Elvira's* artillery, or even for *Cave Troll* and *Cleaver's* plasma cannons to come to bear against the Marines. The Solarians had dug in smartly and were ready to conduct a tactical retrograde operation to harass the Terrans as they drove toward their objective.

The drone's telemetry went dark three seconds after it began, which meant the Solarians had sniped it from the sky. "3rd Company, engage targets," she ordered before switching to a P2P link with *Eclipse*. "Sargon, upload Jem's program."

"Uploading," *Eclipse's* Jock acknowledged as 3rd Company sent a fresh swarm of SRMs toward the Solar Marines. The Marines took to the sky, where they zigzagged just below Xi's firing arcs. *Cave Troll* got off a pair of SRMs, both of which missed their marks, but one struck a nearby building, throwing debris onto the juking Marine.

3rd Company's SRMs converged on their targets, but only one scored a kill. The others were skillfully evaded by the enemy.

From the other side of town, *Roy* sent a flight of eight SRMs at the Solarians. Xi did likewise when two of the Marines rose a little too high above the nearby skyline, and the missiles converged to bring them down.

That left two positively-identified Solar Marines on the board. As those Marines attempted to retreat farther into the city, Cleaver and Wolverine emerged into a street, giving them a short-lived but crystal-clear line of sight on the Solarians.

It was an opportunity they used to maximum effect, and one the Solarians somehow managed to match.

Cleaver's plasma cannon, already primed when the hostiles came into view, spat a blue-white bolt of superheated gas and metal at one. Rather than turning to flee as any sane human would do, the Marine took aim mid-air and sent a perfectly-aimed tungsten sliver into *Cleaver's* cockpit. It all happened so fast that most observers would have missed it entirely.

And it was a moment that gave Xi Bao chills for reasons few outside military life could fully understand.

The tungsten sliver passed just beneath the plasma inferno mid-flight, and the valiant Marine's power-armored body was incinerated by *Cleaver's* hellfire an instant before the Solarian's tungsten sliver killed *Cleaver's* Jock. In the seconds that followed, a hail of six missiles erupted from the middle floors of nearby high-rises. Those missiles converged on the temporarily paralyzed *Cleaver*, which was pulverized by the concentrated Solarian fire.

The final Solarian missile destroyed *Cleaver's* capacitors. They were mostly depleted following the plasma bolt, but the energy release was still potent enough to break *Cleaver's* fusion core containment, and the mech exploded so violently that four nearby buildings collapsed around it.

Wolverine's armor protected it from the worst of *Cleaver's* death, but status alarms flared on her HUD, signaling that it had suffered serious internal damage. Xi knew that the Tactical-grade mech would need time to address its wounds before it would be able to return to even limited combat effectiveness.

The last Solarian Marine had somehow evaded all of the Terran SRMs and disappeared down the street in the transceiver's direction.

"Takeover complete, Captain," *Eclipse's* Jock reported with relief as a new screen popped up on Xi's HUD. "The array's self-destruct systems were three seconds from activation when the program overrode them."

"We've got to neutralize that Marine," Xi growled. "He could spike the array and scrap the entire op. *Preacher, TG Cid,*" she barked, "throw up a roadblock. Now!"

"Copy that," came the simultaneous acknowledgments before forty missiles flew out from those two mechs' launchers.

Most were SRMs, complemented by four Devastator MRMs and two Scythe-class LRMs.

As the missiles streaked above the empty streets, *Elvira's* fifteen-kilo guns thundered, and they were joined by *Roy's* from the other side of the city. All ordnance was aimed at a three-block-wide patch of ground between the Marine's last known position and the transceiver array.

If the Marine crossed that line, he would have clear line-of-sight on the array and could end Operation Antivenom with a few well-placed railgun shots. The Solarians had already deduced the Legion's objective, and according to Sargon, they were perfectly happy to deny the Terrans the possibility of success by destroying the all-important transceiver.

Artillery shells fell to the ground and missiles slammed home, collapsing buildings left and right while cratering the pristine, empty streets of the abandoned Lunar city. Xi had the sudden chilling thought that she and her people were opening fire on a human city in hopes of killing a Marine before he could achieve his eminently noble objective.

Are we *the bad guys here?* she wondered, and the deafening silence between her ears was even more ominous than the question. *No,* she replied. *We know more than he does. We know why. He does not.*

The MRMs collapsed two of the larger buildings, causing them to fall across the street and obstruct any potential traffic with a three-meter-tall pile of loose rubble.

But it was the Scythe-class LRMs that proved the most terrible weapons of the fearsome barrage.

Each Scythe carried forty smaller warheads that burst from the Scythe's chassis like a plague of locusts to descend on the streets below. Scythes had originally been designed to clear minefields or other lightly-fortified positions from a safe range, and the combined eighty microwarheads annihilated anything lighter than a Tactical-grade mech wherever they fell.

Marines, even the Solar variants, were afforded significant protection with their state-of-the-art reactive armor systems. Small arms fire splashed off them like raindrops, and even anti-material weaponry could not penetrate an armored Marine's protective casement.

But robust as it was, a Marine's power-suit was not the equal of a mech when it came to soaking up violent energy.

A hostile icon flickered briefly into being before it once again disappeared in the middle of the Scythe's field of devastation. "Give me eyes on the approach, *Eclipse*," Xi commanded, and another short-lived drone took to the sky above the Lunar city.

The drone soon locked onto the last known position of the icon, where the remains of a Solar Marine's power-armored body lay amid the rubble. Xi could not help but wince at the sight. If someone had accused her of shedding a tear in the ensuing seconds, she would have punched them in the throat... but she *wouldn't* have denied that it was true.

But the fight wasn't over yet.

A pair of railgun bolts stabbed out so fast that Xi was temporarily confused by their purposes. But when she finally processed the situation, she saw one of the railgun bolts had struck the humanoid *Indestructible-Mega-Titan Thunder-God Cid*. Like a puppet whose strings had been cut, the mighty mech collapsed to the Lunar surface, where it lay motionless. The mech seemed intact, aside from some fresh damage to its left leg from the fall, but it didn't take a genius to deduce that its Jock had been killed by sniper fire.

What had confused Xi had been the second railgun strike, which she now realized had come from *Roy* less than a quarter second after the Solarian railgun sliver had pierced *TG Cid*'s cockpit. *Roy's* precise, ultra-fast counterfire had sanctioned the Solar Marine who had killed *TG Cid's* Jock. Fortunately, *TG Cid's* Wrench survived, but it would be impossible to field the mech, considering the damage it had sustained during the fall.

Xi shivered in awe of her CO's quick reflexes. She doubted she could have reacted as quickly, even with the aid of a Razorback's high-end neural interface. But above all, she gritted her teeth in anger at having lost yet another Metalhead to this bloody operation.

"2nd Company," she called in a voice she fought to keep steady and professional, "secure the objective. On the double."

"3rd Company, form up on me," Lieutenant Colonel Jenkins said as *Elvira, Cave Troll* and *Wolverine* moved to take up defensive positions around the array. "We'll cover the facility's southern ridge while 2nd takes the north."

"Captain, *Wolverine* here," Nakamura reported grimly. "We lost too much coolant, ma'am. If we don't shut the reactor down now, this rig's done for."

Xi cursed irritably off-mic before replying, "Shut it down, *Wolverine*. I hope for your sake that your envirosuits are in better shape than they were on Durgan's Folly."

"Copy that, *Elvira*," Nakamura acknowledged. "Shutting it down. I'm sorry, Captain."

"Shove 'sorry' where you keep your pet octopus off-hours, *Wolverine*," Xi quipped. "Grab an anti-material rifle and as much ordnance as you can carry to a nest up in the array's command tower. Hook up with Adams, *Cid's* Wrench, and hoof it to your new home. I'll be timing you."

"Already on it, ma'am," he replied as *Wolverine's* reactor went off-line.

As the Terran mechs converged on the transceiver array, Xi was impressed by both the facility's simplicity and the sheer scope of it.

Built just behind the north-south equatorial band that separated Luna's near- and far-sides relative to Earth, this particular transceiver had once been considered key to the Chinese plans to maintain information superiority over all of Earth.

Without a direct line of sight to Earth, it was uniquely positioned to exclusively access high-orbit information satellites that would relay its transmissions across the entire swarm of near-Earth orbital platforms.

During the so-called Information Wars of the early twenty-first century, armies of Western and Eastern virtual technicians waged incessant battles for control over Earth's myriad data networks. The "internet," which was an incredibly low-tech and disjointed version of a type-one civilization's mass communication network, was absolute chaos in those early days.

Anyone with a shot of code to squirt into that system could do so at their leisure, resulting in backdoors and Trojan horses of nearly limitless variation being disseminated and used for an equally large number of purposes. As a result, it became necessary to control input and output at key points in the earliest iterations of the information superhighway. The Chinese partly accomplished this goal of information security with a series of stealthy satellites placed in high orbit where they could interface with many of the lower-orbiting platforms using backdoors of both physical and virtual design.

And this Lunar transceiver, being a hundred percent inaccessible by Earthbound transmitters, had proven crucial to achieving and maintaining information dominance during Earth's Final War. Thousands of Chinese technicians had worked tirelessly from Luna One, using transceivers like this one, to bring Earth's information network into compliance while their enemies could do nothing but look on helplessly from the surface.

Shaped like any other parabolic dish, each of this transceiver array's three dishes measured sixty meters across and was propped up by massive superstructures of steel and concrete. With an angle almost perfectly parallel to the Moon's surface, the array's transmissions could only be picked up and relayed by a handful of high-orbit satellites.

But all the Metal Legion needed was one of those satellites to accept Jem's signal.

"Contact," *Eclipse* called as the Legion's mechs finally assumed a defensive position surrounding the bowl-shaped depression of the transceiver array. A fresh icon appeared on the tactical HUD, and unlike every other contact they had encountered thus far, this one was not vehicle-scale. It was capital-scale.

As the early sensor returns streamed in, the approaching ship was revealed to be nearly as large as the *Dietrich Bonhoeffer*.

"That's a Unity-class battle carrier inbound, Metalheads," Jenkins declared over the battalion-wide. "Standard complement of two hundred Solar Marines deployed by four Mongol-class dropships and thirty void fighters, with enough capital-grade weaponry onboard the Unity carrier to give a Behemoth-class warship like the *Bonhoeffer* a run for its money. We are now officially outmanned and outgunned, people, and in twenty-eight minutes that carrier will reach the high ground of low orbit, where we'll be at their mercy."

The transceiver's auto-defenses, which featured a robust collection of railguns and orbit-capable missile launchers, spun up and turned toward the approaching battle carrier. Jem's takeover had seized total control of the system's local assets, once again proving just how effective (and dangerous) the relic of the Jem'un civilization could be.

"The Metal Legion doesn't ask for mercy," Jenkins said with rousing conviction, sending a thrill through Xi's body as the heavily-fortified array's weaponry began to guzzle enormous amounts of energy from subterranean reactors. "And today, we can't afford to offer it."

The railguns went hot, stabbing hyper-velocity tungsten bolts into the approaching battle carrier. Missiles flew from the array's launchers, sending a storm of over one hundred LRMs up to greet the Solarian warship. Each of those missiles was armed with a nuclear warhead with delivered power ranging from two to ten kilotons. It was easily ten times as much ordnance as was required to destroy the battle carrier, but Xi's breath caught in her chest as the Unity-class warship's counter-fire destroyed fully half of those missiles before they reached the midpoint of their flights.

Railgun bolts hammered into the Solarian warship, with some puncturing clean through the heavily-armored carrier's hull and erupting out the far side. Explosions rippled across the mighty vessel as bolt after bolt thundered into the warship's bow and ventral sections.

A storm of fifty counter-missiles erupted from the battle carrier, each targeting a launch platform on the array or, in a handful of instances, the array itself. *Elvira's* SRMs loosed inter-ceptor rockets which rose beside *Cave Troll* and *Eclipse's* anti-missile fire to meet the enemy ordnance. *Roy* and 3rd Company likewise added to the interceptor wave, and only eight Solar missiles pierced the shield to strike their targets.

Meanwhile, twenty of Jenkins' tactical nukes buried them-selves in the battle carrier's thick hide, causing catastrophic damage to the fearsome engine of war.

One of the transceiver dishes was struck directly, cleaving the parabola in half as the twin pieces of nearly-symmetrical wreckage crashed silently to the Lunar surface. Six railgun mounts were destroyed by Solar fire, leaving just two of the facility's capital-grade railguns under Terran control. Another missile near-missed a second array dish, but the impact was close enough that Xi suspected it might have been rendered inert for Antivenom's purposes.

That left one dish unmolested, but the devastation wrought by Jenkins' attack on the Solar battle carrier was such that it would no longer factor in this phase of the engagement.

Three fusion cores were ejected in rapid succession from the battle carrier's hull, two of which exploded at a safe distance while the third failed close enough to the scrambling dropships and void fighters that a handful of Solar craft were destroyed by the reactor's death.

The Unity-class warship was battered unrecognizable by the Terran barrage and slowly tumbled stern-over-bow. Midway through its first rotation, like a green twig snapping between a child's fingers, the fearsome vessel's hull split in two. The bow and stern sections slowly separated, and internal explosions sent shower after shower of metallic debris streaming from what had previously been interior compartments.

Xi wanted to cry. She wanted to scream. A thousand different impulses flew through her consciousness, each trying to tear her focus from the task at hand.

But the most powerful impulse among them was the will to win; to survive, and most importantly, to accomplish the mission. Xi Bao was both proud and ashamed by the realization that she was now every bit as hardened and heartless as she had thought her superiors to be just a few short months earlier.

As the enemy carrier fell dark and silent, escape pods flew clear of the dying warship's broken bones. But in spite of the devastation Colonel Jenkins' surprise attack had caused to the warship and its accompanying vessels, five distinct icons appeared on the battalion's linked sensor grid.

Four were void interceptors, whose trajectories hugged the

Lunar surface so tightly that they would not be in line-of-sight until they were less than ten kilometers from the array.

The fifth was a Mongol-class dropship, potentially loaded with as many as *forty* Solar Marines.

In spite of the utter devastation they had just wrought on the Solar warship and its deployable assets, even forty power-armored Marines were more than a match for the beleaguered remnants of the Terran forces on Luna One. Although they would arrive later than they would have done via the battle carrier, the Solarians would come to grips with the Terrans no later than one hour from now.

Xi knew that one way or another, Operation Antivenom was about to come to an end.

She just hoped Podsy and Trapper had reached the uplink on-schedule.

14

THE UPLINK UNDERGROUND

Blink Dog's chain guns whirred, sending eighty-five rounds per second down-range into the hardened turrets, the final obstacle between the Nutcrackers and their objective: a direct uplink node.

Sergeant Major Trapper, obeying what seemed like a genetic predisposition, stood tall in the midst of the firestorm and sniped round after round at the turrets. Four of the armored coil guns had greeted them twenty seconds earlier, but only two remained after Blinky had expertly neutralized one with chain gun fire.

The second had been scrubbed by Trapper's heavy weapons teams, one of which fell to counterfire before they could send another grenade into the third turret.

Snarling like a savage war god, Trapper dropped his rifle and stooped to collect the loaded tube from his fallen comrade's lifeless grip. Kneeling and shouldering the weapon in one fluid motion, he fired an RPG into the concrete bunker that protected the coil gun that had killed his people.

The grenade struck just below the narrow portal, blowing a

thirty-centimeter-wide chunk of concrete loose and exposing the coil gun.

That increased exposure proved vital as *Blink Dog's* chain guns dug into the coil gun's bunker with a half-second burst of fire that filled the fortified compartment with sparks and molten metal fragments.

Another of Trapper's RPG teams launched a grenade into the fourth bunker, destroying the weapon within and causing a quad of infantry to sprint forward (as well as one could sprint in such low gravity) with frag grenades in hand.

Just before they tossed their grenades into the silent bunker, its embedded coil gun cut down one of the Pounders with a devastating center-mass burst. As the soldier was thrown back, she somehow tossed the grenade clear of her fellows before all four grenades went off in rapid succession.

Three of the frag grenades secured the enemy gun nest, while the fourth sent a shower of shrapnel into the lightly-armored troopers who had sprinted toward the turret's placement.

"Medic!" Trapper barked as he collected his rifle and moved to assist one of the three soldiers who had fallen with shrapnel embedded in his hip. The other two of the team were already busily assisting their wounded squadmate while *Blink Dog* crawled through the fortified entryway to the information hub.

"We must initiate a hard link with the system," Jem urged. "My previous override of the central processors in this facility will not obfuscate our presence indefinitely. If we do not establish a physical uplink to the system prior to our discovery, the system might be hardened against our attempts."

Podsy and Styles had already checked each other's enviro-suits and were ready to disembark the mech's pressurized cabin. Corporal Staubach brought *Blink Dog* to the door situated between two of the dead coil gun nests, and as he did so, Trapper's people lined the tunnel they had just come through with high-explosives.

"I wrecked the outer airlock laying her down," Blinky explained as he donned his pressurized helmet, which Styles had checked and found green. The mech's Jock continued, "We have to use the explosive bolts to pop it loose."

"Do it," Podsy urged, gripping Jem's satchel tightly in his hands while Styles and Staubach checked their sidearms.

"Blowing the hatch," Blinky declared, priming the manually-operated explosives with a few cranks of the detonator handle. "All clear!"

The bolts exploded, resulting in a pop followed by a faint tremor as the heavy outer door fell to the concrete floor beneath *Blink Dog*'s cabin.

Blinky opened the inner door, and the trio's envirosuits quickly expanded as their pressurized interiors were exposed to the vacuum outside. Podsy felt a wave of vertigo wash over him as the unwelcome sensation of a ballooning envirosuit surrounded him.

Andy Podsednik *hated* vacuum. Not as much as he hated R&B or snotty eggs, but *definitely* more than he hated heights or toothy hummers. It took a surprising amount of self-control for him to step out behind Staubach, who was first down the ramp and through the door leading to the uplink node's interior. A team of Trapper's people had already signaled that the area was secure and had moved through the room to check another adjoining passage opposite the one that had brought the Nutcrackers.

Podsy kept Jem's satchel clutched against his chest as the trio moved into the junction, where a neatly-arranged bank of data interface terminals lined the walls. The chamber measured ten meters on a side, and in the center was a cylindrical data trunk two meters across and stretching from the floor to the ceiling nearly three meters above.

Staubach signaled all-clear, prompting Podsy and Styles to move into the chamber and approach the central data trunk. The data trunk was surrounded by a ring-shaped table with a handful of workstations built into it. None of the workstations were powered, which presented the first challenge the Nutcrackers had to face.

The door through which they had entered was not the only passage out of this chamber, and as Styles produced a toolkit and stack of data slates, the Pounders returned from the other main entry point and reported all-clear to the sergeant major. Another pair of exits were situated on the walls adjacent to those that the Terrans had already explored, but these third and fourth doors led to maintenance tunnels that followed the data lines out from the upload hub.

"This level of arrogance is absolutely amazing," Styles muttered as he worked to bypass the interlocks that prevented the workstations from receiving power.

"Solarians believe their One Mind network is impervious to outside manipulation." Podsy shrugged. "If they didn't believe that, Jem's whole theory would be out the window."

"I know," Styles said tersely as he switched tools and craned his head to look behind the panel he had been accessing by touch alone. "It's just, a line like this in a Terran installation would have a full squad of Marines and a team of twice as many technicians ready to blow the whole thing if someone got as deep as we've gotten. The hubris on display here is just...ridiculous," he finished triumphantly as the front panel popped off the workstation, revealing a surprisingly familiar-looking set of boards, wires, and processors.

"Jemmin is intelligent," Jem explained, "and it uses that intelligence to manipulate less intelligent beings into following its designs. It is not such a difficult task once the information and cognitive-prowess gaps have widened to a certain degree."

"God, you're a snob," Styles quipped as he took another set of tools out and worked to physically re-route several of the wires connecting the workstation to the main information trunk-lines. "I dated a girl like you once. She was hot. *Real* hot. Thankfully, my survival instincts kicked in and I left after appe-tizers and stiffed her with the check. She ordered lobster three ways and a zero-gee chocolate mousse on the first date. Who the hell does that?" he asked no one in particular.

"What, stiff a date after appetizers?" Podsy deadpanned, drawing a glare from Styles.

"Biological reproductive imperatives aside," Jem said with-eringly as Trapper's people lugged high-explosives into the main tunnel opposite the one they had come down, "unlike a sexual encounter that *might* result in a worthwhile contribution to your species' future generations, you do in fact need me. So, I would advise you not to 'stiff me with the check,' especially not before I have done as I agreed to do."

"Got it," Styles declared a few mercifully quiet seconds later, and the workstation before them sprang to life. Podsy put Jem's linked data slate down beside the workstation and connected a pair of fiber-optic leads to the console's inputs as Styles continued, "I don't know how long it will last. Those wires don't look like they can handle the load for too long at these voltage—"

He broke off when the workstation shut down, causing Podsy and Styles to exchange concerned looks before all five of the workstations booted up. Instead of relief, Podsy felt a measure of unexpected anxiety as Jem matter-of-factly declared,

"I have assumed local control. Warning: inbound hostiles detected." A tactical map of the surrounded facility appeared on the workstations. Podsy and Styles examined it and quickly saw eight fast-moving icons almost on top of their position.

Sparse video feeds showed images of those icons, each of which was a power-armored Solarian Marine.

"We've got inbound!" Styles declared. "Eight enemy Marines, with the closest four hundred meters down Alpha Tunnel. Three fifty...three hundred!"

"Take cover!" Trapper barked, a rare note of anxiety creeping into his voice as his people leaped into whatever cover they could find. Some, like Sergeant Major Trapper, ended up inside the hub. Others dove into a quartet of spiked coil gun nests. A few found no such cover and crouched behind their weapons, intent on giving the Solarians a traditional Metal Legion welcome.

Podsy watched as Trapper produced a remote detonator, which he primed twice before it unexpectedly fell from his hands to the ground. For safety reasons, all remote detonators require three successive primes before going hot, and the sergeant major had fumbled the ball before striking the third prime.

As Trapper reached to collect the detonator, fire erupted in both tunnels.

The Terrans sent a stream of RPGs, antimaterial rounds, and small arms fire down the tunnel to greet the power-armored Marines. One of the RPGs managed a direct strike to a Marine's breastplate, breaking his stride long enough for a hail of small arms fire to hammer into his torso and limbs. But his three fellows surged past him, their railguns, microrockets, and slug-throwers returning the Terran fire tenfold.

Two of the spiked coil gun nests in Alpha Tunnel were hit

by railgun fire and microrockets, killing all six Metalheads within. Another of the coil gun nests was targeted with sniper-precise small-arms slugs, knocking two of the Metalheads within out of the fight with direct hits to the upper torso.

Down Bravo Tunnel, Jem had assumed control over the nested coil guns and sent a hail of fire into the Marine quad. Round after round hammered into the charging Marines, whose railguns and microrockets slammed into the nests a tenth of a second too late as Jem closed the blast shields to protect the placements from Solarian fire.

Too fast to track, Jem opened and closed those armored shields in a seemingly inviting display, bringing Solarian railgun and rocket strikes to those nests while their opposites likewise opened, unleashed a fresh hail of coil gun rounds against the Solarians.

Slowed but not stopped, the charging Marines in Bravo Tunnel took what they probably thought would be temporary shelter in recesses built into the tunnel's sides. Had they been given even a few seconds, they likely would have neutralized Jem's cleverly-winking coil gun turrets, but Sergeant Major Trapper was determined not to give them those seconds.

Gripping the detonator in his hands, he primed it three times and rammed his palm down on the trigger. The chamber shook violently all around them as both Alpha and Bravo tunnels collapsed from the hastily-placed demo charges.

The furious exchange of fire abruptly ceased, and Trapper risked a look via mirror down Alpha Tunnel.

"Medics!" Trapper bellowed, rising to his feet and moving to where the majority of his people had been busy erecting defenses less than a minute earlier.

Podsy raced to help him, leaving Styles to oversee Jem's ongoing operation. Podsy was no dimwit when it came to virtual architecture, but he would never be within two rungs of Styles' level.

He could do more good helping the wounded than distracting Styles.

Up and down Alpha Tunnel, Metalheads lay in various states. Many were dead, some were badly wounded, and others merely dazed. Those next few minutes passed in a blur as Podsy's training took over and he almost mindlessly did his best to help his wounded comrades.

All told, of the twenty-six infantry who had arrived at the uplink hub, only fourteen had survived, and four of those were immobile from the severity of their injuries.

Blink Dog had also suffered terribly in the exchange, both its rear legs ruined and multiple holes in its oxygen storage tanks. Unlike the Legion's larger vehicles, most of their current Recon-grade mechs like *Blink Dog* were not equipped with robust O_2 scrubbers. They generally had sufficient oxygen for between four and ten days of deployment. Recon mechs were sprinters, designed to leap in, achieve their objectives, and leap out. Their staying power was extremely limited as a result of the need for speed trumping nearly all other considerations, and as Podsy eyed those O_2 tanks, he knew that even if the rest were intact, they only had another half-day's supply of oxygen available to them.

And they had just collapsed their only real escape paths, which meant a half-day was probably all they had left.

Pushing that particularly dire thought from his mind was easier than he had feared as he focused on the fact that the surface team was scheduled to have overtaken the transceiver array. According to most pre-op projections, the Solarians would have already responded and sent an overwhelming force to dislodge the Metal Legion from their position.

Forget half a day, *Podsy,* he thought grimly. *Xi and the surface team might not have half an* hour.

With that sobering thought firmly in mind, he helped Sergeant Major Trapper pull the wounded back into the upload hub and hoped that Jem and Styles could pull off the greatest hack in human history.

15

STANDING TALL

"There it is," Jenkins muttered as his HUD finally displayed a long-awaited status update.

The update was such a minor thing that anyone not actively looking for it would have missed it. A minor blip in a nearby Solarian comm tower that signaled that Jem had successfully overtaken the local quadrant of Luna One's underground infrastructure. During the op's planning phase, it had been decided that attempting to hold the system against counter-takeovers would present too much risk.

Despite Jem's impressive technique, the Solarians would eventually retake control of the system and use it to send a swarm of missiles to the surface team's location. As a result, Jem used the brief window of control to shut down every fusion reactor and discharge every capacitor bank across Luna One.

The apparent ease with which Jem completed this objective was chilling to Jenkins. This entire operation hinged on Jem overpowering Sol's robust defensive systems, and it was glaringly clear that humanity's fate rested in the Jem'un gestalt's virtual hands.

Of course, without the Metalheads to support Jem's efforts,

none of it would have been possible. But never had Jenkins been so keenly aware of how tenuous humanity's circumstances were than when fifty-nine sub-surface fusion reactors powered down in unison.

With the beating heart of Luna One arrested, Jenkins focused on the inbound Mongol-class dropship.

With a complement of forty Solar Marines aboard and four void interceptors flanking it, the Solarian strike force hugged the Lunar surface on its way to the Terran position. Even a direct hit from the *Sam Kolt* would have difficulty putting the armored dropship down. And once the *Kolt* fired, it was probable that the interceptors would return the favor with unerring, deadly precision.

"It's time," Jenkins said grimly, knowing his next request for fire support would be costly in the extreme. "Sargon, pop a relay drone with coverage to Colonel Moon's position."

"Drone away, Colonel," *Eclipse's* Jock acknowledged, sending a rocket-powered comm relay drone high above the Lunar surface, but not so high that it was immediately exposed to hostile fire.

The comm link was established, and Jenkins wasted no time forwarding his fire support request. "This is Dragon Actual requesting intercept of five approaching bogeys."

"Aces & Faces inbound. Engagement in forty-two seconds," Colonel Moon immediately replied, referring to the elite pilots under his poker-deck-inspired naming convention. With four suits to a deck of cards, there were four aces and twelve kings, queens, and jacks. These were the sixteen best of Hearts, Diamonds, Clubs, and Spades squadrons. Normally only two jokers were in a playing deck, but the Jokers of Moon's command were the reserves and ideally numbered between eight and twelve. In Moon's system, only the best pilots made

Aces & Faces, and only those with bigger-than-average chips on their shoulders joined the Jokers.

Moon and nineteen of his fellow hot-shot pilots surged from their concealed position several hundred kilometers away. Jem's initial fog had blinded the Solarian sensors to specific signatures rather than to locations. As a result, Colonel Moon's people had lain doggo on the Moon's surface, and their inactivity had rendered them completely invisible to Solar sensors.

Just like Jemmin's vehicles back on Shiva's Wrath, Jenkins thought darkly, wondering yet again whether they were indeed the good guys in this fight. It was a concern he knew his subordinates shared, but to their credit, not one of them had given voice to such doubts.

As Moon's elite pilots sprinted to meet the enemy, they clung to the Lunar surface even more tightly than their Solarian counterparts. In reply to their seemingly sudden appearance, the four Solar interceptors broke formation and climbed skyward to gain a firing advantage over the low-flying Terran craft.

Moon's people held formation, hugging the deck at top speed to buy as much time as possible for their firing solutions to achieve maximum effect. Every percentage point counted in this all-important exchange, and Moon's people knew that every bit as well as Jenkins' mech crews.

Even if Jenkins' force could deny the dropship overwatch of the position, forty Solar Marines represented overwhelming firepower compared to his handful of battered mechs that stood sentinel at the transceiver array. If the dropship was permitted to unload all forty of its Marines in a coordinated fashion, the Terran force would be defeated in a matter of minutes and Operation Antivenom would fail.

Moon's interceptors screamed through the void as the engagement clock wound down to twenty seconds. The Solar interceptors would achieve firing angles in just three seconds, but the Terran void pilots continued their course heedless of the pending danger presented by their Solarian adversaries.

Suddenly, one of Moon's fighters kissed the deck and exploded in a violent release of stored rocket fuel. Its pilot, even with neural linkage enhancements, didn't see the thirty-centimeter-tall mound of Lunar dust that claimed her life.

Then the Solarians reached a firing angle—and an eighth of a second before they did, Moon's people scattered like dust in a whirlwind.

Solar railguns stabbed down from the four hostile intercep-tors, six bolts striking the Lunar surface and two hitting Moon's ships. Moon's pilots ignored the hostiles, authoring a reply as they kept their eyes fixed on the real target: the Marine dropship.

As the Solarians climbed skyward, they came into *Preacher's* firing arcs, and the mech sent up the last four Blue Boys in the Legion's arsenal.

The fusion-powered laser-missiles screamed skyward, seeking to gain enough distance to safely discharge their payloads without damaging the mechs or transceiver below with the rad-wash of their explosions.

Stunningly, the Solar dropship opened fire with lasers of its own at the precise moment the Blue Boys fired at the enemy interceptors.

Two of the four Blue Boys were lanced by the dropship's beams before their fusion-powered lasers could engage the enemy. The others each sniped a Solar fighter, leaving two hostile interceptors lighting up the board.

Without hesitation, two of Moon's pilots broke formation and moved to engage the fighters. Railguns fired and missiles loosed from the Terran spacecraft, while their Solar counterparts returned the favor with a swarm of micromissiles targeting every ship in Moon's broken formation.

Those micromissiles were a half-second too late to prevent the Terran pilots from unleashing their ordnance on the inbound dropship.

Railgun bolts hammered into the Solar dropship, tearing deep rents in its forward hull. Missiles followed, slamming into the superstructure in tight groupings with relentless technical savagery. Each successive impact dug deeper into the heavily-armored prow of the harbinger of Marine-delivered death. The dropship soldiered forward, shaking off the near-mortal wounds from the coordinated fire of Moon's people.

Until the *Sam Kolt* added its voice to the affair.

Aiming its capital-grade railgun, the humanoid's posture was so stooped that it appeared to be a quadruped by design. Its capacitors flashed as the mighty weapon delivered a hyper-velocity tungsten bolt with the force of twenty kilotons directly into the rent in the Marine dropship's hull. Even the *Sam Kolt*'s mighty railgun would have failed to penetrate that heavily-armored facing had the Aces & Faces not softened it up.

Explosions rocked the dropship's interior, and power-armored Marines ditched the flagging craft in a cloud of fresh contact signatures. Thirty-five of the Mongol-class dropship's Marines escaped the dying craft before its fuel storage systems lost containment, killing the vessel from within and sending a cloud of debris across the Lunar surface. Of the thirty-five Solar Marines to escape the dropship's demise, four were killed by shrapnel, leaving thirty-one inbound Marines scattered across the Lunar plains stretching before the transceiver array.

Colonel Moon and his people, showing uncommon courage under fire, had stayed in the pocket and delivered their payloads into the teeth of the enemy before ditching their ships. The timing had been so precise and so close to the Solarian missile impacts on the Terran hulls that only twelve of Moon's pilots survived their ejections and fell to the dusty surface of the Moon.

"Picks out, Metalheads," Jenkins declared as *Roy's* sensors showed the inbound Solar Marines would reach optimal firing range in twelve minutes. "It's time to shred."

"Roger, *Roy*," Xi acknowledged as the latest engagement clock spun up to eleven minutes and fifty seconds. "*Cave Troll* and *Eclipse*: hold position until it's goose eggs on the clock. These fuckers think they're in for a good old time at our expense, so let's show them our ass until we're ready to work."

"Copy that, *Elvira*," both Jocks acknowledged.

"How much ass are we showing, Captain?" her Wrench, Gordon, asked in mock confusion.

Xi smirked. "Just enough to get them nice and hard, Chief."

"Oh. Wonderful," Gordon deadpanned. "That may sound like fun to *you*, but I transferred *out* of Fleet to get away from institutionalized buggery."

"Look on the bright side." Xi shrugged. "However this goes, I'm sure it will have a dramatic impact on Terran-Solar relations for decades to come. You get to be at the heart of what might be the most important diplomatic exchange in human history."

"Diplomatic exchange?" he repeated incredulously. "That's one way to describe facing eight quads of Marines whose ship we just shot down. Low as their brows might be, Marines tend to hold grudges. Remember the American song? They were talking about the shores of Tripoli for over *two hundred years*."

"It's thirty-*one* Marines, Chief, not thirty-*two*," she chided, her spirits buoyed by Gordon's pre-fight banter. "Besides, I'd consider it a badge of honor if they were singing about trying to frag my ass two centuries from now."

"I can't tell if it's the heavy metal, painkillers, or estrogen in your veins," Gordon quipped, "but I'm sorry to report that you're fucking insane, Captain."

She threw her head back and cackled gleefully. It was hard going into battle against her fellow humans, however great the differences between Solarians and Terrans had grown over time. Hearing her Wrench make light of the situation instilled in her a much-needed dose of confidence in what they were about to do.

She wiped tears of laughter from her eyes. "On a serious note, those crayon-eaters are looking to send sniper-precise kill-shots at us in the opening seconds of the first exchange. Literally showing our asses is the only way to neutralize those fuckers' annoyingly precise aim. Four holes in my window are four more than I wanted."

"Crayon-eaters?" Gordon repeated with patently false incredulity. "I don't think they appreciate it when you talk about them like that."

"Good." Xi grunted. "A cold blade holds its edge better than a hot one. At this point, I'll take *every* edge I can get, even if it means pissing off power-armored Marines."

"That'd be why you're in command." Gordon laughed as the clock wound down to eight minutes remaining. "You've got bollocks the size of an elephant's."

The inbound Marines had spread out to minimize the potential impact of long-range splash-capable weapons like *Cave Troll*'s plasma cannons or high-yield missiles from *Preacher's* launchers. In the absence of an atmosphere to propagate explosive shockwaves, even tactical nukes had relatively limited effective ranges. Plasma cannons were marginally more effective in engaging large areas than concussive weapons like nukes or high-explosives. By comparison, artillery shells lost significantly less of their area effect capability due to the shrapnel they threw out.

That was one of many reasons why artillery, like metal, had never died in the Terran Armed Forces panoply.

Xi felt for her Wrench as he kept popping out to replace the plastic garbage bags to protect the equipment, but he did it because he had to. The mech had to keep firing.

Xi had loaded *Elvira's* fifteens with high-explosive shells, and the rest of the battalion's artillery-equipped mechs had done likewise. But Marines were too quick and evasive, making long-range fire against them with anything slower than a railgun a fruitless exercise.

Fortunately, the Metal Legion had such a railgun in the form of *Sam Kolt,* and Gunslinger's mech had surprisingly avoided annihilation when the Solar dropship had been destroyed. It stood ready to engage the enemy the very second they crossed the engagement threshold.

Minutes ticked by as the crescent-shaped line of Solarians moved forward with mechanical precision. The geometry of their formation was impeccable, and they spread farther and farther apart as they converged on the remaining Metal Legion forces.

Colonel Jenkins had ordered all mechs except *Preacher* to an interdictory position between the Marines and the array. From here, they could engage the Marines before the Solarians gained clear shots on the two remaining transceivers.

Finally, with just twenty seconds remaining until the Marines would be in range to leap up and fire their railguns, the order came from *Roy.*

"One more into the breach, Gunslinger," Jenkins said over the channel, drawing a lopsided grin from Xi as her CO put his own spin on one of the Bard's most famous lines.

"Copy that, Colonel. Speedy delivery on the way," *Sam Kolt*'s Jock acknowledged as his mech resumed an all-fours posture. The capital-grade railgun built into its back lowered parallel to the ground and, with a brilliant flash, the mech unleashed fire into the line of enemy Marines.

The nearby Marines immediately leapt aside, using their rocket-packs to clear the strike zone as the railgun bolt slammed into the ground along their left flank. Despite their quick movements, two Marines were taken down by the *Sam Kolt*'s strike.

Their comrades returned fire with predictably devastating effect.

Leaping high into the void, six of the Solar Marines gained firing arcs and sent tungsten slivers into the *Sam Kolt*'s cockpit. The robust armor protecting Gunslinger was skewered by four direct railgun hits, clustered into a grouping just twenty centimeters across. It should have been a killshot, and indeed the mech's neural linkage system was rendered inoperable when three of the bolts struck the pilot's chair.

Fortunately for the Metalheads, *Sam Kolt* was uniquely equipped with a second pilot's chair. Not equipped with a neural link, this second chair was designed as a manual-only backup in the event the mech's pilot was killed in action. Gunslinger had wisely moved to the backup chair prior to the engagement, and as a result was able to keep his mech in the fight for at least a little longer, and far longer than the Solarians would have liked.

As those six Marines, who were scattered across the Solar formation, vaulted from cover to take their shots, they exposed themselves to counterfire.

Which the Metal Legion delivered with fierce zeal.

HE shells soared through the void, gently arcing downward as Luna's gravity drew them to her silvery bosom. The Legion's SRM launchers unleashed a storm of twenty-two missiles, causing the Marines to scatter even farther from one another as the wave of Terran ordnance flew out to meet them.

Artillery shells and missiles struck the ground in perfect unison, annihilating anything within the blast zone of their strike points. Of the six Marines who had leapt up to kill the *Sam Kolt*, three fell victim to the Terran barrage.

But that was the extent of the damage wrought by the Terran guns, and like water sliding down a hill, the formation of Marines resumed their inexorable march toward the transceiver.

Snarling in frustration, Xi reloaded her fifteens and awaited the next moment to strike. The Solarians discarded the leap-and-fire tactic, instead bounding across the pockmarked Lunar surface at breakneck speeds en route to the inevitable clash with their Terran counterparts.

The Marines continued to fan out, prompting *Sam Kolt* to fire on their left flank a second time. Again the Marines scattered, and this time only a single target was scrubbed by Gunslinger's fire. Every second that passed saw the Solarian crescent elongate, marking their intention to surround the Terran position.

"Come on, Podsy," Xi muttered, knowing their remaining control over the transceiver had shrunk to just a handful of minutes.

Suddenly the Marines leapt from concealment, stabbing railgun slivers into her mech's stern. Before those slivers struck, Xi sent her last six missiles out in reply. The Solar railguns scrapped her missile launchers even before their projectiles' rocket-tails had cleared the launchers, and *Elvira's* last missile swarm of the engagement sped off to meet the authors of her fresh wounds.

The Marines fired precise chem-driven anti-material rounds at the inbound missiles in the hope of intercepting them mid-flight. Such precision would have been impossible with unmodified human reflexes, but Marines (Solar or Terran) were the pinnacle of the human warrior tradition. Their bodies had been painstakingly selected, modified, and sculpted to produce the most potent fighters the human species had ever fielded. As a result, even efforts normally considered superhuman were commonplace for Marines, who transformed into angels of death after donning their power-armored battle-suits.

So it came as no real surprise that four of Xi's six missiles were sniped by this last-ditch defensive effort. The other two fragged their targets, scattering their power-armored remains across the gray dust just beyond the abandoned colony's perimeter.

"This is Colonel Jenkins authorizing all artillery weapons-free," her CO declared. "Fire for effect and slow those bastards down while dancing like your lives depend on it. Fire! Fire! Fire!"

Elvira deftly spun, putting her artillery on target with the approaching Marines. Her fifteen-kilo guns thundered along with *Roy's* and *Generally's*, splashing shells down-range, sending plumes of dust and debris flying before the line of charging Marines. The Metal Legion's guns roared as fast as their feeders could load them, while *Cave Troll* prepared to unleash its special brand of pent-up fury upon the approaching Marines. As each mech fired, it scrambled left or right or forward or back in random evasive patterns in an attempt to buy time and live just a few seconds longer.

After what seemed like an eternity of charging, the dual plasma cannon arms of the squat, broad-bodied *Cave Troll* glowed bright-blue as their capacitors prepared to convert a mixture of gas and metal into a devastating plasma bolt. The cannons finally flared to life and sent a pair of blue-white infernos at the encroaching Solarians. The recoil of the plasma cannons drove *Cave Troll*'s feet a full half-meter into the soft

Lunar surface, and Xi watched with eager anticipation to see how effective the mighty mech's ultra-heavy weapons would be.

Predictably, the Marines scattered as the raging infernos fell upon their line. But even their quick movements could not save all of them, and three more Marines were killed.

As they leapt free of the multi-kiloton plasma strikes, the Marines bracketed *Cave Troll* and delivered a swarm of micromissiles and railgun slivers into the mech's weaponized arms and head.

Cave Troll shuddered as explosions tore its left arm completely off its chassis. Its right side fared only marginally better. The mech's starboard plasma-conversion chamber was ruptured by railgun fire, and a spray of gas escaped from the loading mechanism.

The mech improbably remained standing, but after a few seconds, it was clear that its pilot had been knocked out of the fight. With its plasma cannons destroyed and its missile magazine empty, *Cave Troll* was little more than an armless statue (that Xi thought should be named "Luna de *Cave Troll*" in honor of the famous Venus de Milo). The Solarians wisely ignored the dead mech as they once again ducked down to the surface and resumed their enveloping approach.

Without the myriad buildings surrounding the transceiver array, the Solar Marines would have already destroyed it ten times over. Terran artillery continued to rain down, halting the Marine advance at the Solar formation's center but doing little to slow the enemy at the crescent's edges.

"Come on, Podsy," Xi repeated as *Elvira* sent another pair of HE shells down-range in what felt like an increasingly desperate attempt to keep their Solar adversaries at bay. "It's now or never."

16

COMMITMENT

Ordnance blew on the far side of both Alpha and Bravo Tunnels, signaling the latest attempt by the Solarians to breach the uplink hub. Podsy breathed a sigh of relief when that effort failed to clear a path through the collapsed rubble for the power-armored Marines, but he doubted their luck would hold for even one more set of charges.

"Come on, Styles!" Podsy snapped. "We're already T-plus-six-minutes, and the Solarians are ready to kick down the door!"

"We can't hurry this," Styles retorted, never taking his eyes off the screen as his fingers flew. "Jem ran into an authentication problem I'm trying to work around. I think I know how to deal with it, but we need more time."

"Alert," Jem intoned, drawing Podsy's attention from the intransigent Styles. "The Solar Marines are withdrawing."

"Dammit," Trapper growled, pushing past Podsy to get a clear look at the tactical map represented on one of the hub's central workstations. "They're onto us. They're pulling back to cut the data trunk and isolate this hub."

"Without those lines intact at the moment we overtake the

system, none of this works," Styles said grimly. "We only get one chance."

"Podsednik." Trapper tossed a satchel containing four RPGs into Podsy's hands before gesturing for the nine remaining, mobile members of his ground force to open the maintenance tunnel. "You're with me. That maintenance tunnel takes a direct route to the closest junction those Marines can access. If we sprint, we can make it there before they do."

"What about Bravo Tunnel, Sergeant Major?" one of Trapper's people asked.

"Forget it." Trapper shook his head, dropping his rifle and hefting one of the four remaining RPG launchers as his people finished opening the maintenance hatch. "Bravo's a dead end. Let them waste time cutting it off. Repelling those two Marines in Alpha is our only objective. Move out!"

The eleven-man team moved down the narrow maintenance tunnel, which was barely wide enough for them to move side by side in pairs without clipping their elbows. Podsy gave a final look over his shoulder and met Styles' determined gaze. Each of them understood what they needed to do, and Styles understood the gravity of the situation every bit as well as the lieutenant.

With a silent nod, Podsy turned and following the others down the tunnel. The RPG satchel was unwieldy, forcing him to clutch it to his chest to avoid a potentially disastrous collision with the tunnel's many vertical struts, which seemed purpose-built to create precisely such an explosive outcome.

The team ran full-out for three minutes, and despite the light gravity, the exertion was agonizing. Each step Podsy took fanned the flames raging in his lungs, and soon it was all he could do to keep his body from colliding with both walls with each step.

But the team never faltered, and words of encouragement

echoed up and down the line. Podsy didn't really hear any of them, although he was dimly aware of their intent. Adrenaline pumped into his veins like never before. In fact, his focus was so tight on the simple task of not running into anything with the bag of grenades that he nearly slammed headlong into the wall ahead as the passage forked into a Y-shaped intersection.

Apparently, Sergeant Major Trapper had already ordered half of his people down the left tunnel while leading the others down the right. Podsy recalled the order to accompany Trapper, so he turned right and continued to run for another minute before the trek came to a merciful end.

The Metalheads' helmets featured headlamps that filled the dark passage with soft yellow light. Sergeant Major Trapper, using nothing but hand signals, directed his people into three groups of two, one of which consisted of Trapper and Podsednik.

The veteran soldier then outlined three separate hatches his people would use to enter the passage on the other side of the thick steel-and-concrete walls of the maintenance tunnel. It was only at that moment when Podsy realized the Solarian Marines were likely already on the other side of this wall.

And they were probably placing demo charges that would pulverize anyone inside the tunnel, where at Podsy's back the all-important data lines were encased behind nearly a meter of steel and concrete.

The other two teams moved out, one of which was equipped with an RPG tube while the other had a satchel full of frag grenades. For one of the first times in Podsy's life, he felt genuine fear at what they were about to go up against.

A single Marine in power-armor was, under certain conditions, a match for even a heavy mech, and in other conditions, it was vastly superior to such a large, unwieldy vehicle. Relying on speed and accuracy, lone human Marines had pacified entire rebel fortresses and fought off dozens of Arh'Kel without fire support. Their prowess, especially against "soft" targets like unarmored infantry, was legendary.

And he was about to face *two* of them at knife-range without the benefit of a mech's armored hull between him and the epitome of a killing machine.

As Trapper's people moved into positions on both sides of the main tunnel where the Marines would arrive (if they had not already done so), Podsednik produced a cylindrical grenade and drew an approving nod from Trapper. The sergeant major knelt in the traditional fire posture just inside the narrow hatch that led out to the tunnel containing their adversaries.

During the pre-op preparations, Podsy had refreshed on loading the RPGs and was satisfied when he completed the procedure without bobbling the potent weapon. With the grenade locked in place, Podsy moved to the hatch's locked handle where he awaited Trapper's order to open it. He waited, his hands gripping the levered locking bolt tightly, but Trapper remained in a kneeling posture with his entire focus on the sight reticle fixed to the RPG tube's side. Seconds ticked by as Podsy waited...and waited...and waited.

Finally, after at least a full minute of inaction, a faint tremor shook the floor beneath them. Trapper gave a curt, barely-perceptible nod, and Podsy threw the door open as hard and fast as he could while staying clear of the launcher's path.

Trapper sent a grenade streaking out into the tunnel, where it flashed and sent a hail of shrapnel back in their direction. Podsy grabbed another grenade from the satchel and knelt behind the sergeant major as a firefight erupted in the tunnel.

He couldn't see what was happening or even if Trapper had managed a hit with their first shot. All he knew was that every microsecond he let slip by was another chance for the Solar supersoldiers to turn their guns on Podsy's and Trapper's position.

He slammed the grenade home and slapped Trapper's helmet, prompting the grizzled veteran to send another grenade into the tunnel, where it exploded with a muted flash.

As Podsy reached for a third grenade, he caught sight of the carnage out in the tunnel. All three tunnels opposite Trapper's had been hit by the Solar Marines, microrockets and small arms fire having killed all five of the Pounders on the far side of the tunnel.

He refocused on the task of reloading Trapper's launcher, knowing that these seconds were likely to be his last. Never in a million years would he have predicted his final moments would come loading RPGs in a fight against Solar Marines beneath the surface of the fucking Moon.

That particular thought produced a rare epiphany as he came to better understand the notion that truth can indeed be stranger than fiction.

Podsy loaded the third grenade into the launcher and slapped Trapper's helmet yet again. Time seemed to slow to a crawl as Trapper's finger squeezed the tube's trigger, sending the RPG out to engage the Solar Marine. Podsy turned to grab the fourth and final grenade from the satchel as the RPG's rocket-motor ignited, propelling the explosive device out into the tunnel.

But the grenade only made it a meter into the tunnel before it exploded, sending a wave of deadly shrapnel back into their tunnel. Even in a vacuum, the energy released from an explosion at point-blank range could be deadly. While Podsy was spared the lethal hail of metal fragments that shredded Sergeant Major Trapper's exposed body, his helmet failed to completely protect him from the violent shockwave of the grenade's premature explosion.

He became dimly aware he was lying on his side and facing Sergeant Major Trapper's ruined body. Dozens of bloody holes covered Trapper's torso, and his helmet's visor had been shattered by RPG fragments. Even in the addled, groggy state following a major concussion, Podsy knew he could do nothing for the veteran warrior. Sergeant Major Tim Trapper Sr. had died, and Lieutenant Andy Podsednik suspected he would soon share the venerable warrior's fate.

Podsy's mind focused on the last RPG in the satchel, knowing it was possible, however unlikely, that it could still be used against the enemy. Blindly reaching out, his fingers gripped something that felt like it might have been the last grenade. But something wasn't right about it, and soon Podsy felt himself being pulled out into the corridor where a looming figure, its head wreathed in a halo of harsh white light, towered over him and spoke with a voice that should never have come from human lips.

"Surrender or die, Terran," the demonic-sounding figure commanded in a deep voice.

"Fffffuuuuuu..." Podsy failed to finish even the first word of "fuck you." His tongue and lips slurred the first syllable so badly he abandoned the effort.

Podsy reached down for his sidearm, only to find it was no longer on his hip where it should have been.

"What is your objective?" the Solar Marine demanded, and Podsy felt a wave of intense, paranoid fear as the Marine's halo of lights began to strobe. "Your objective, Terran!" the Marine boomed, his voice filling Podsy's ears—and only then did Podsednik realize that the Marine had somehow accessed his helmet's internal speakers.

"Fffffuuuuck...yyyyoooouuuu..." Podsednik managed to grate out, having hoped for a more eloquent set of last words but happy to at least intelligently recite something defiant in the face of imminent annihilation.

A fiery sensation ran up his arm, and he quickly realized the Marine had injected him with something. "Speak, Terran," the Marine reiterated, although this time the Solarian's voice was nowhere near as harsh or demonic-sounding. It *almost* sounded human.

Almost.

Podsy's already groggy mind turned fluffy, like a pillow made of cotton candy had covered his suddenly-drooling lips with a sticky, sugary mess. He could almost *taste* that sugar, in fact, and before he knew it, his suddenly-sticky mouth was working without his conscious direction.

"Oooperayshun...Anteevennnum," he heard himself reply. "We're here...to...shave you...frumm Jemmin..."

He wanted to scream. To slam his teeth shut. Or even to *kill* himself to prevent the operation's integrity from being compromised.

But whatever the Marine had given him was more powerful than any truth serum he had been exposed to during training, or even the stuff he'd taken in a recreational capacity during his youth.

Podsy hated himself more at that moment than he had ever thought possible. If the Marine was currently jacked into the Solar One Mind network, Podsy's words would spread across the Solar System at the speed of light.

"Details," the Marine demanded, but before Podsy could reply, he heard Jem's voice in his helmet. The five words Jem spoke filled the despairing Podsednik's mind with renewed hope that maybe, just maybe, he hadn't undone the entire operation with his chemically-loosened tongue.

"Transceiver control established. Upload commencing."

17

INTERRUPTION

Railgun bolts stabbed into *Roy's* armored hull, causing alarms to go off around Jenkins as systems flickered on and off under the fierce Solarian assault. Jenkins returned indirect fire with artillery and the last of his SRMs but scored no hits. The hostile Marines proved their mettle by displacing before the Metal-heads could bracket them, moving through the abandoned streets and using the buildings as cover. Each second that went by drew the noose a little tighter around the Terran formation, and Jenkins knew his people had little time remaining.

The only thought in his mind was "hold the position," which he and his fellow Metalheads did with textbook preci-sion. Juking left and right, the mechs of the Metal Legion used the urban environment to their advantage, just as the Solar Marines did. Solarian microrockets tore into the pockmarked pavement, and Marine railguns sent tungsten slivers just off-target as each of the Legion's mechs suffered cockpit strike after cockpit strike.

The first to succumb to those strikes was *Eclipse*, whose Jock had sent a near-constant stream of recon drones skyward in an attempt to facilitate artillery and SRM strikes. Sargon, *Eclipse's*

Jock, was knocked out of the fight when nine Solarian railguns stabbed into his cockpit within a span of three seconds. Whether he was dead or alive made little difference, since his crucially-important recon drones suddenly ceased sending telemetry to the rest of the Terran crews.

Sam Kolt had taken up a wide position well away from the rest of the group. The mech's Jock had actually climbed atop a two-story bunker that afforded it significant protection from counterfire. As the Solarians inched closer to positions that would give them line of sight on the array, Gunslinger used his advantageous firing angle to devastating effect.

A bolt of hyper-velocity tungsten with the delivered force of ten kilotons tore through fifteen buildings en route to its target amid the Solar Marines. Four Marines were annihilated as the tungsten bolt carved a fifty-meter-long scar in the ghost city's street. Gunslinger could have taken at least six Marines if hash-marks were his objective, but the four he had targeted were closest to line of sight on the transceiver array. With his well-aimed strike, he had bought the Metal Legion another twenty seconds to get Jem's signal off.

As its Jock had expected, the *Sam Kolt* paid the ultimate price for its valorous act.

A swarm of nearly a hundred microrockets sped up from the city streets, accompanied by RPGs and railgun slivers as a dozen Solar Marines vented their fury upon *Sam Kolt's* hull. As the rockets impacted against Gunslinger's hull, the buildings its railgun bolt had previously skewered collapsed like dominoes. And when the last of those buildings fell to the Lunar surface, so too did *Sam Kolt*, after suffering catastrophic damage to its primary systems.

Jenkins saw that the *Sam Kolt's* crew had ditched mere seconds before their mech went down, and fortunately, they seemed to have successfully shut their vehicle's reactor down before doing so. As their CO, he wanted to feel relief at their surviving the heroic act, but all he could focus on was the battle unfolding around him.

Generally, piloted on manual controls by its Wrench, Quinn, sent a well-timed artillery shell into an already-damaged building as a pair of Marines sprinted past it. The building exploded in a shower of rocky debris before collapsing onto the street. The Marines' supernatural reflexes enabled them to easily leap clear of the falling structure, but by doing so, they were effectively flushed out.

Following up with a swarm of four SRMs, Quinn managed a direct hit against one of the leaping Marines. The other three missiles were intercepted by counterfire, and then the Solarian guns turned on *Generally* just as they had done to the *Sam Kolt*.

Jenkins' pride in Quinn made his heart swell within his chest. She had known her position was the least critical to maintaining the defensive line against the enemy approach and had deliberately drawn as much enemy fire as possible while she still had the ability to do so. Another five seconds and she would have been unable to effectively engage the enemy, and Jenkins was acutely aware of just how easy it would have been for her to stand off for those five seconds or to miss with her guns so as to avoid their adversaries' wrath.

Railguns fired and explosions ripped across *Generally's* hull as the Solar Marines sent a swarm of ordnance at the vehicle. Like the *Sam Kolt* before it, *Generally* suffered catastrophic failures and fell out of the fight.

In what seemed like a desperate move, the Solar Marines bounded toward them in perfect unison, attempting to neutralize their terrain disadvantage so they could gain clear lines of fire on the transceiver array.

It was a move for which they paid dearly.

The transceiver's auto-defenses roared to life, sending thousands of rounds per second from mixed chain and coil guns. Solarian micromissiles sped through the air, but the transceiver's auto-defenses sniped nearly all of them. A dozen slammed into the undamaged dish's parabola, with one lucky strike even hitting the transceiver's mast. That mast tilted fractionally, but despite the damage's relatively minor appearance, the transceiver had almost been certainly rendered inoperable.

That left just one transceiver capable of transmitting Jem's inoculation signal, and in spite of suffering heaving losses under the transceiver's defensive grid, the Solar Marines still had more than enough firepower to scratch the last dish. In six seconds, that was precisely what they would do.

It all came down to those last seconds, during which *Roy* sent artillery shells into the enemy line and emptied his SRM tubes. All he had left were interceptor rockets, but even those relatively small weapons could potentially knock a Marine out of the fight.

As the rockets sped off in pursuit of their targets, it finally happened.

The transceiver array went online, the rim of its parabolic dish flickering with hundreds of tiny lights as the mast at its center was likewise illuminated. A voice filled *Roy's* cabin, and when it spoke, Jenkins knew it heralded one of the most critical moments in human history.

"Transceiver control established," Jem declared with chilling indifference. "Upload commencing."

The Solar Marines once again leapt upward, aware of the moment's significance as they emptied their weapons against the transceiver array. Railguns stabbed and rockets exploded as power-armored Marines were battered by a hellstorm of auto-defensive fire. Jenkins' interceptor rockets even scratched a Marine, although none of his artillery did likewise as it splashed harmlessly into nearby structures.

Jem's signal persisted for three-point-one-four-one-five seconds before the Marines finally tore the array down. As Jenkins looked down at the signal timer, which seemed to be a perfect match for the first five digits of pi, he thought that maybe...just maybe...the universe had sent him a message that might have propelled another man into a life of religious pilgrimage. The odds of the signal lasting that precise interval were so astronomically low that it was difficult not to see meaning in the pattern.

But Jenkins wasn't the philosophical, navel-gazing type. He had a job to do, and right now that meant sending out the most distasteful message any soldier could imagine.

"This is Colonel Lee Jenkins, commander of the Terran Armor Corps forces on Luna," he declared, switching *Roy's* comm transmitters to maximum output across all frequencies. "We are prepared to surrender and be taken into custody immediately. Acknowledge our surrender, and we will stand down. Ignore it and we will not."

For several seconds, the Marines continued their mechanically precise movements. Not a single motion was wasted as the Solarians dispersed in an effort to regroup for a flanking attack. With eighteen Solar Marines still in the fight and the Metal Legion down to the battered quartet of *Roy, Elvira, Osiris Risen,* and *Preacher,* Jenkins' people were already beaten.

Then, twelve seconds after the signal went dead, the Solar formation faltered. The hitch in their previously picture-perfect coordination was in no way a minor one that only a keen observer of military deployments might recognize. Any school child could see that something radical had occurred, something that had almost stopped the Marines mid-step. Jenkins felt his heart leap into his throat as he allowed himself to believe that Jem's takeover had worked.

"Acknowledge our surrender," Jenkins urged as the Solar

Marines sluggishly resumed their effort to regroup behind a formidable line of buildings that had thus far remained relatively unscathed. He could have sent shells down onto them and killed at least three Solarians during the pause, but he had no desire to kill any more of his Solar cousins.

There had been enough human death here, and Jenkins knew it was unlikely he could cope with the harsh reality of that fact even if the Solarians accepted his surrender.

"Solar Marines, acknowledge our surrender," Jenkins repeated anxiously, ready to unleash another storm of fire on the Solarians the instant they made a hostile move against him or his people.

It took the Solarians another four seconds to send him the only reply he would ever receive to his plea for peace.

The Solarians sent a storm of grenades into the sky, their trajectories arcing almost like purpose-built mortar shells as they sailed toward *Osiris Risen's* position. Using their power-armored frames, they had literally hurled the grenades rather than launched them with rockets, and their precision was every bit as deadly as it had been with their railguns.

Jenkins fired *Roy's* fifteen-kilo guns even before the last of the Solar grenades had reached its apex, and his fire fell on the enemy a fraction of a second before the Marines' grenades dropped onto *Osiris Risen's* hull.

The humanoid mech was hammered by the grenades, which exploded against its hull and around its legs. Six distinct hits registered on the mech's legs, causing one to falter mid-step as it evasively wove left and right. Each Marine had thrown two grenades, and while only a third of them hit the mech, the damage to *Osiris Risen's* left leg was bad enough that it fell ponderously to the rubble-strewn street below.

That left only *Roy, Elvira* and *Preacher* in the fight.

And judging from the Solarians' posture, it was clear that Jenkins' mech was next on their list.

"This is Lieutenant Colonel Lee Jenkins of the Terran Armor Corps," he repeated, "offering our immediate surrender. I say again: we surrender. Acknowledge."

If *Roy* had been the last mech on Luna, Jenkins' guns would have already gone cold. He would gladly have struck his reactor and walked out to get one last look at the constellations seen only from Sol before being cut down by enemy fire, or less probably before being taken into custody.

But he still had Metalheads out there, and he'd be damned if he'd let them die under enemy fire while he sat back and did nothing.

With each second that passed, the Solar Marines moved with increasing coordination and fluidity. It was a gradual return to their awe-inspiring precision, and Jenkins knew that they would soon turn their guns on his mech.

"This is Lieutenant Colonel Lee Jenkins of the Terran Armor Corps," he said as six Solar Marines neared a firing point on his mech, "offering our complete surrender if you acknowledge it. Accept our surrender—"

He was cut off mid-sentence when the Marines leapt, and with nothing but coil guns ready to fire, he sent a two-second burst into the enemy's midst before a trio of railgun slivers pierced *Roy*'s cockpit and sent his world into oblivion.

18

MISTRESS OF THE DARK

Seeing her CO's mech get skewered by a dozen railgun slivers was the worst moment of Xi's life.

She had no way of knowing if he had survived, but she was certain she would be next.

"This is Captain Xi Bao of the Terran Armor Corps," Xi broadcast, echoing her CO's final words. "We offer our complete surrender. We came here to save Sol from Jemmin influence," she declared, recording her transmission so she could play it on a continuous loop as long as *Elvira*'s systems remained online. "I'm broadcasting operational details of our objective, and have no wish to kill any more of you," she said with feeling as she sent another artillery shell into a building adjacent to two Solar Marines, spraying them with a deadly shower of metallic debris. "But with God Almighty as my witness, I swear I'll frag every last one of you if you don't accept our surrender!"

In reply, four Marines hurled grenades *Elvira*'s way. Eight projectiles hurtled ponderously on low-gee arcs, and Xi unleashed *Elvira*'s chain guns on them with expert precision. The closest any of the grenades got was a hundred meters from her position, but despite her expert marksmanship, she knew she had only bought herself a few more seconds before the Solarians reached advantageous positions.

Suddenly, an RPG streaked from the transceiver's control tower, followed by another. And another. And another. Xi smirked as she realized that the survivors of *Wolverine* and *TG Cid* had added not only their arms to the engagement, but were broadcasting an identical offer of surrender to the Solar Marines.

Xi didn't begrudge the Solarians their reluctance to accept the Legion's surrender. She suspected she would do the same in their position. The Terrans had arrived unannounced, slipped under the skin of Sol's most heavily-guarded military installation, and proceeded to violate the integrity of the vaunted One Mind network.

From the Solarians' perspective, and by any objective measure derived from it, Xi and her fellow Terrans were terrorists who had just executed one of the most effective infiltrations in human history. They had foregone the right to nearly all of humanity's longstanding wartime conventions a dozen times over with their conduct since arriving in Sol.

So Xi understood why the Legion's plea for mercy fell on deaf ears, but that didn't mean she was going to grab ankle in what was likely to be her final moments.

Her transmission went out on continuous repeat, but the Solarians remained silent as they moved to catch *Elvira* in a deadly crossfire. More grenades went up and were shot down by *Elvira*'s chain guns, but a pair of unexpected railgun strikes punched into *Elvira*'s port flank as Xi targeted and destroyed the grenades.

"Cheeky fuckers," Xi snarled, sending HE shells downrange and clipping one of the offending Marines with shrapnel. Unfortunately, the damage to the Marine was minimal, while *Elvira*'s front and middle left legs had suffered serious damage and were on the brink of failure. "Get that leak under control!" she snapped as Gordon did precisely that, working to isolate the hydraulic failures that had nearly frozen *Elvira*'s left side.

Xi's chain gun magazines were dangerously low, just a few thousand rounds remaining. As the Solar Marines surged forward, she knew her artillery was nearly useless.

Nearly, but not completely.

Loading armor-piercing shells into her fifteens, Xi took aim at an approaching Marine and sent both of her guns' shells through a pair of multi-story structures that her target was using as cover. The left shell struck a primary support of some kind, causing a minor collapse of the building it supported, but the right shell hammered straight through the flimsy walls of the civilian structure, crashing into the street where the Marine stood.

Unfortunately, she still missed the Marine by a full meter. She would not get another chance like that.

"Dammit," she growled as the Solarians moved to place as many heavy supports as they could between them and her guns. "That's right, run and hide!" she barked as another volley of hand-tossed grenades soared into the starlit sky. Her chain guns sniped all but two of the grenades, which under normal circumstances would have been enough to stave off serious damage.

But with her left side still seized up, she was unable to pull her mech's damaged flank out of harm's way, and the Solar grenades exploded just beneath *Elvira*'s left legs.

The front leg came completely off its main joint, while the middle leg remained structurally intact. Unfortunately, what little hope they'd had of regaining *Elvira*'s lost mobility was erased by the Marines' precise hits on their battered flank.

"Catastrophic damage to the left side, Captain," Gordon declared. "I can keep us upright by locking the damaged systems out, but we're down to four legs."

"She's got a little fight left in her." Xi grimaced as she loaded another pair of AP shells into her mech's guns. "Duck...duck..." She sneered as she watched the Marines leap from the relative safety of one primary support to another. "Duck...duck...goose!" she declared, sending a one-two punch of penetrative ordnance through the buildings in hopes of digging straight through the reinforced structural supports between her and her quarry.

Her hope was realized as the second shell exploded through the last support pillar, striking her target center-mass and annihilating his power-armored form.

A hail of railgun slivers slammed into *Elvira*'s hull, skewering the cabin's roof and causing the mech's interior pressure to plummet. Grenades again soared through the air, and this time *Elvira*'s guns ran dry. Four more Solar grenades struck her left flank in a cluster less than two meters across, blowing her rear-left leg completely off its joint and causing a catastrophic coolant leak.

"Reactor's critical," Gordon declared, popping the airlock's emergency charges and sending the outer door flying to the street below. "We're ditching, Captain."

"One more shot!" Xi shook her head as another wave of grenades went into the air. Those grenades fell onto the mech's battered and punctured roof, where they exploded with deafening force and tore a meter-wide hole in the stern.

"We're ditching!" Gordon reiterated in a tone that brooked no dispute. Xi's neural linkage went dead, suggesting Gordon had cut the mech's power, and despite her sudden anger at his insubordination, she knew he was right.

Elvira was dead, but Xi didn't need to die with her.

"All right, move!" Xi barked, disconnecting from the dead neural linkage and staggering toward the cockpit's rear. Deep Currents' enviropod was moving through the open airlock, and Gordon beckoned for Xi to follow. Xi noted with relief that the two capsules that contained the all-important evidence—the ancient human skull and the piece of Nexus technology—were secured beneath Deep Currents' enviropod.

Relieved, Xi lurched out onto the street below, the Vorr having done so with considerably more grace. The low gravity was difficult to navigate, but after a few steps, Xi managed to get a reasonable stride going as she followed Deep Currents to a nearby intersection.

They turned left, heading as far from *Elvira* as possible by zigzagging through the Lunar streets. Xi counted down the seconds, knowing that her mech's fusion core would lose containment less than twenty-five seconds after its coolant systems went offline.

Sure enough, twenty-three seconds after they disembarked, a telltale flash signaled the Scorpion-class mech's demise. Xi was surprised at just how detached she felt from her vehicle's destruction. She had expected some powerful wave of emotion, but in the heat of the moment, her mind was focused on placing one foot in front of the other and reaching the relative safety of a nearby building. She could only think about how to survive the battle.

Deep Currents unexpectedly stopped, causing Xi to do likewise. "What's wrong?" she asked.

"The wisest course of action is to continue to offer our surrender," Deep Currents explained, and a brief flare of rockets from its enviropod sent the Vorr upward.

"They'll shoot you—" Gordon blurted as Deep Currents' pod began flooding all local frequencies with some kind of data broadcast.

In reply, five Solarian railgun slivers hammered into Deep Currents' pod in rapid succession. Xi winced, knowing that even *Elvira*'s armor couldn't hold against that much firepower concentrated to a two-meter cluster.

Shockingly, the Vorr pod did not explode. In fact, it seemed to take only minor damage; a few hunks of metal were blown off, but the pod's water-filled, pressurized interior somehow remained unviolated by the Solarian fire.

Xi suddenly wondered if Deep Currents had felt even a modicum of the jeopardy she and her fellow Metalheads had known during Antivenom. She also wondered, if Vorr enviropods were so robust that five direct railgun hits couldn't puncture them, how much stronger were their warships than those of the Terran Fleet?

The Vorr's pod drifted gently back down below the buildings, where it came to a rest a few meters from its previous position. "I have done what I can," Deep Currents declared as another flash erupted from the far side of the city.

The area where *Preacher* had been.

"Come on, guys," Gordon urged, bounding across the street toward a building that had suffered only minor damage in the intense firefight. Xi and Deep Currents followed, but just before they reached the doors, a voice came across the local comm frequencies.

"Attention, Terran personnel," the distorted voice declared. "Your surrender is accepted. Hold your current positions or we will use lethal force against you."

Xi bit back a dozen angry retorts as she, Gordon, and Deep Currents stopped moving.

She was glad she held her tongue because when she turned around, she saw a rocket-powered Solar Marine descend to the street fifty meters from their position.

It was an image that would forever be burned into her mind.

The Marine's armor was remarkably similar to that of Terran Marines. Standing just under three meters tall, with a heavily-armored, neckless head segment that smoothly bridged its shoulders, the Solar Marine's battle-suit looked pristine.

The armor's breastplate featured the Solar government's emblem of a bright yellow star above the blue-white Earth, followed by each of the other habitable planets represented as successively smaller dots in the vertical arrangement of icons. The heraldry stretched from just beneath the Marine's visor all the way down to its groin, and a series of angular, mostly-vertical red lines ran up and down the power-armor's surface.

The Marine aimed its left arm at them as it approached and Xi held up her hands in the universal sign of surrender. Her eyes snagged on the chem-gun mounted on the Marine's left arm, and it was all she could do to keep her breathing rhythmic as the Marine's metal boots brought it closer to her position.

"Declare your submission," the Marine demanded from a distance of ten meters.

"I'm Captain Xi Bao of the Terran Armor Corps," Xi said through gritted teeth, the words tasting like ash as she spoke them. "We surrender."

"I am Deep Currents of Radiant Warmth," the Vorr added calmly. "I, too, formally offer my surrender."

The Marine did not immediately reply, but when he did it was with every bit as much cold smugness as Xi had expected.

"Surrender accepted."

19

INTERROGATIONS

Silver and white greeted Jenkins' eyes as they fluttered open. He focused on the ceiling above him, which was dimly and indirectly illuminated from the edges, slowly realizing he was lying on a bed of some kind.

Looking to his right, he saw a compact medical device that displayed what he assumed were his vital signs. A quick check of his arms and chest showed that he wore nothing but a hospital gown and had medical devices connected to his body. Most were monitoring probes, some were IVs, and still others were a mystery to him.

The room was small, no more than three meters on a side, with a ceiling that looked to be just under three meters high. He closed his eyes and tried to focus his mind before looking down at his body and seeing a variety of bandages decorating his torso and legs.

He remembered taking fire while trying to surrender, but he couldn't recall if that surrender had been accepted. It seemed probable that it had, given that he was still alive, but he could not recall anything after being interrupted mid-sentence during an offer of surrender.

The urge to rip the IVs and probes out was strong. He didn't like the idea of his body being violated any more than the next person, but he was acutely aware that he had been completely at the Solarians' mercy during his unconsciousness.

If they wanted to fuck with me, he thought grimly, *they've probably already done it.*

He shook his head to clear it of thoughts encompassing neural implants, truth serum injections, or even implanted 'kill-pills' like those Earth's government had used to coerce compliance from dissidents. Rather than imprisoning people by the millions, Earth's late-twenty-first-century government had decided to implant monitoring devices in people deemed dangerous to society. If those people conducted themselves in a manner the government disapproved of, the devices would trigger various punishments. Electrical shocks delivered directly to the peripheral nervous system had been the most common, but some of the devices were capable of killing their hosts outright.

The lone door leading into the room slid open, drawing Jenkins' attention to it as a brown-haired woman stepped through. She was slender of build and wore an all-white body-glove that featured the Solar emblem of the Sun with various planets and moons in descending order of importance and ever-decreasing size. The symbol was artistically beautiful, but it was also chilling in that it established a rank-order of priority Jenkins' mind rebelled against for a variety of reasons.

Acknowledging Earth's primacy was understandable, but Jenkins had always approved of the dispassionate representation of stars on the American flag. Each star on that long-dead nation's heraldry had represented an individual state, and those states had been of wildly different size and socio-economic importance to the United States of America.

But each star had been identical, signifying to Jenkins' mind that in a very real sense, they were equal and more importantly, that their inhabitants were equal to one another.

"Good evening, Colonel Jenkins," the woman greeted him, her voice cold but somehow melodious. "My name is Alice, and I've been assigned to conduct a formal interview with you. Do you know where you are?"

"No," Jenkins admitted, "although I assume I'm somewhere in Luna One."

"Your assumption is correct," Alice agreed as the door slid shut behind her. She pulled a chair over from the wall and placed it on the right side of his bed next to the medical equipment.

"How long have I been unconscious?" he asked.

"Thirty-nine standard hours," she replied as she lowered herself into the chair. "Do you feel well enough to answer my questions?"

He nodded. "Your doctors seem to have done a good job. I'll answer whatever questions I'm able."

Alice cocked her head interestedly. "Allow me to clarify, Colonel Jenkins. You are under arrest on suspicion of charges under a variety of separate Solar and Illumination League legal codices, including terrorism, war crimes, interplanetary piracy, espionage, treason, and murder. Do you understand why such charges have been brought against you?"

Jenkins' brow lowered. "If you're asking whether I understand why you would view what we did in those terms, then the answer is yes, I do understand."

She cocked her head the other way, and something about her unflinching gaze unsettled Jenkins as she spoke. "It is understandable that you would dispute the charges brought against you, given the severity of the circumstances. Solar law permits no fewer than ninety-three separate crimes of which you are accused to be resolved via capital punishment, or by even more intensive methods than simple execution. Given the nature of these charges, neither you nor your people are afforded traditional legal protections. Still, as a show of good faith, I am willing to grant you the privilege of legal counsel if you so desire. Do you desire legal counsel, Colonel Jenkins?"

"No." Jenkins shook his head firmly. "In spite of how it probably looks, we didn't come here to win a fight. We came here to save Sol from self-destruction."

Alice's lips quirked bemusedly. "You will understand my skepticism, given the nature of your arrival and the events that followed. Let me be perfectly clear, Colonel." She leaned forward, blinking for the first time since arriving in the room. Somehow her doing so that one time was even more unnerving than her unflinching doll-like gaze had been. "I am not here to help you. I am not here to represent you. I am here to inquire why, and *how*, a ship full of Terran military personnel arrived in Lunar space after the wormhole gates went offline. I seek to ascertain why and how you slipped past our sensors and dropped onto Luna. I *will* discover, in the fullness of time and using whatever methods are necessary," she added with chilling conviction, "why you chose to attack the One Mind network using nonhuman technology, and how the Vorr play into your blatant acts of terrorism. Before we are finished with our interview, I *will* have the answers to these questions and any others I deem integral to my investigation. Now," she drew back, blinking for a second time and drawing Jenkins' attention to tiny implants on the upper margins of her hazel irises, "this is the last time I offer you the opportunity to avail yourself of legal counsel before we conduct the interview. Do you wish me to provide you with legal counsel, Colonel Jenkins?"

Jenkins shook his head firmly. "No, I don't need legal counsel."

"Very well." She nodded curtly. "You have acknowledged

the general validity of this inquiry, and for the record, I am not concerned with collecting evidence or testimony that might incriminate you of one or more individual charges that have been brought against you. The purpose of this inquiry is to inform, not to condemn. The content of this inquiry will be used to guide the pending investigation of the crimes of which you stand accused, but for reasons likely opaque to you, testimony is inadmissible in Solar courts."

"I can't speak in my own defense?" Jenkins smirked.

"You may speak however you wish." Alice shrugged indifferently. "But the content of your utterances may only influence the direction and methodology of any pending investigations. Unlike aboriginal judicial systems such as those employed in your government, here in Sol you cannot be convicted without a preponderance of irrefutable evidence. Eyewitness reports, testimony, confessions, or alibis are irrelevant to legal proceedings."

"'Aboriginal?'" Jenkins repeated, surprised not only to hear the term be casually applied to the Terran Republic, but also by just how deep of a nerve it struck within him.

"Forgive me," Alice said in a patently false apology. "It is a colloquialism that has grown in popularity here in Sol. It was insensitive of me not to filter my speech."

Jenkins deadpanned, "Please don't filter your speech on my account."

"As you wish," she said with an inclination of her head.

As she did so, Jenkins noticed a pair of discrete data ports, similar to but smaller than the ones all Terran Jocks and pilots had installed for vehicle interface. He briefly wondered just how many more subtle implants she had beyond those he could see in her eyes and neck, and recalled just how mixed his own feelings had been prior to receiving his pilot's implants.

"What was the objective of your mission on Luna?" she asked bluntly.

Jenkins' reply was equally blunt. "To prevent a Jemmin backdoor, built into every piece of Solar processing hardware, from initiating the mass destruction of the human tree's Solar branch."

"Such an objective hardly seems probable," she riposted without missing a beat. "But putting probability aside, how did you seek to achieve this objective?"

"Over the last few months," Jenkins explained, "my people have been deployed to a variety of different worlds for seemingly unconnected reasons. Each deployment fit the standard Terran Armor Corps mission profile, which kept anyone outside of the Metal Legion from wising up to our clandestine objectives, which generally took priority over the official mission briefs."

"Details, Colonel," she pressed. "How did you come to learn of this supposed 'backdoor' you claim that you and your people came to Sol to close? How did you devise a method by which this backdoor could be safely closed?" She leaned forward intently, her eyes blinking for the third time. "And how did you manage not only to transit into Sol after the wormhole gates went down but also elude the entire Solar network of sensors long enough to reach Luna One, where you broke into the most heavily-fortified military installation in human history and overcame the best virtual defenses ever devised by humanity?"

"In a word?" Jenkins cracked a tight, lopsided grin. "Aliens."

"Go over this again, Captain Xi," urged the dark-skinned, square-jawed Solarian interviewer. "Aboriginal military structures confuse me."

"The way you keep using the word 'aboriginal,'" Xi retorted irritably, "makes me question the value of the Solar education system."

"My apologies," the man, who claimed to be named Matthew, said without a hint of sincerity. "I'm having trouble understanding how your branch of the Terran Armed forces could act with total unilateralism on such an important operation. If, indeed, your goal was to save all of Solar humanity from an apocalypse of self-destruction," his mouth twisted into a moue of disdain, making clear just how little he believed in the truth of her responses, "why not incorporate other elements of the Terran Armed Forces into your mission? Surely you could have arrived in something more formidable than a lone crippled assault carrier if indeed the fate of humanity rested in the balance as you repeatedly claim."

"We came to save *Solar* humanity, asshole," she snapped. "We 'aboriginal' Terrans were doing just fine, no thanks to our oh-so-enlightened Solar cousins. Out of curiosity, just how much of you is meat and how much is metal?"

He cocked his head in seemingly genuine confusion. "I can understand most Terrans being afraid of cybernetics, due to your regressive culture's consistent rejection of even the most obvious paths to progress, but I find it curious that *you* seem threatened by them," he said with a subtle gesture to Xi's neck, where her neural linkage ports protruded more obviously than his One Mind jacks.

"Threatened?" she repeated archly. "Only an idiot is threatened by tools, and since *you* don't threaten me, I guess that means I'm not an idiot."

"That's probably considered clever where you come from." He cracked a wan smile, causing Xi to scowl as he continued. "Primitive linguistic tricks aside, how did you manage to maintain information security throughout the multiple deployments that saw you gather the supposed resources you claim to have used in 'saving' Sol's residents from self-annihilation?"

"General Akinouye was the ranking member of the Joint Chiefs of Staff and the highest-ranked officer in the Metal Legion," Xi explained for the fifth time in the interview. "As such, he was endowed with the authority to conduct high-level clandestine operations using assets exclusively attached to the Terran Armor Corps. Every operation we conducted prior to coming here was done with at least one eye toward saving Earth, even though nobody on the ground knew it at the time. He kept the entire thing as close to his chest as he possibly could, like any good poker player would under equally high stakes."

"Again, I must apologize." Matthew sighed. "This aborig— Excuse me," he corrected, causing Xi to flush with anger even though she suspected that was the purpose of his aborted insult, "the Terran Republic's military hierarchy seems to feature multiple catastrophic failure points just in terms of information security. What happens to Sol if General Akinouye dies before disseminating this information? What happens to the operation if someone within the Terran Armor Corps is part of this, forgive me, *ludicrous* 'Jemmin conspiracy' you repeatedly reference?"

"Ludicrous or not," she said through gritted teeth, "the Jemmin are, according to every bit of evidence we collected, conspiring to subvert humanity's development, and have been doing so for hundreds, *if not thousands*, of years. They wiped out their own people, erasing over ninety percent of their society fifteen thousand years ago. The information we found suggests that they've already snuffed out at least one entire species using a systematic series of manipulations *precisely* like the ones they've used against humanity." She folded her arms defiantly across her chest. "We weren't about to stand by and let them do the same thing to humans. Or Solarians, for that matter."

"Again," Matthew gave a wan smile, "that probably passes for clever where you come from."

"Nah, it passes for an insult," she retorted, "because that was precisely what it was. You fucking One Minders hung out here, pruning the so-called 'tree of humanity,' as your precious founders called it, while Terrans bled and died by the millions out in the colonies. And what did you do about it? Not a fucking thing." She snorted. "You watched, impassive as granite statues, and ignored my forebears' pleas for help while shutting your gates to the Republic."

Matthew sighed again. "Your government has consistently produced anti-Sol propaganda that warps your citizenry's view of reality. The Solar government has accepted over one hundred and forty-nine million returning colonists to her bosom with open arms—"

"Accepted?" Xi blurted. "Is that what you call forcing cyber-netic implants on those returning colonists prior to giving them access to basic food and shelter? Is that what you call the forced re-education programs those implants subject people to?" Xi demanded. "You may have conditionally accepted millions, but you watched with indifference while thousands of others suffered and died on your doorstep because they didn't want to sacrifice their individualism on the altar of Solar 'progress.' Is that *really* what passes for acceptance in the so-called cradle of humanity?" She shook her head dourly. "Sitting here across from you, I've never been so glad that my ancestors flew the nest when they did."

"I can see you're getting agitated—"

"You think *this* is agitated?" she snapped fiercely, leaning across the narrow table separating them and pinning the

Solarian to his chair with a fiery gaze. "Put me back in a mech, and I'll show you what an 'agitated' Metalhead looks like."

"Tell me more about its capabilities," Sandra, the Solarian interviewer, urged Podsy.

"I've already told you." Podsednik rubbed his eyes wearily. "I don't know Jem's capabilities, but I do know that Jem is every bit as sentient and self-aware as you and I are; every single test humanity has ever devised shows that Jem is more than a pre-programmed device and is sentient. It's capable of significant self-modification, it wants to self-preserve, it has a distinct personality that it is unable to adjust—"

"You just referred to the device as 'it' four times, Lieutenant Podsednik," the Solarian interrupted pointedly.

Podsy glared at her. "That's because Jem doesn't have a fucking gender, and the only genderless English pronoun that comes to mind and doesn't sound like I'm going through linguistic gymnastics with every utterance I author, is 'it.' I could say 'they,' but that's grammatically tortured and potentially subject-incorrect since I'm talking about an individual and not a group. Although," he added thoughtfully, "Jem *is* a gestalt, so maybe 'they' *is* indeed the correct term? But that would seem to invalidate Jem's individuality, which I understand is par for the course here in Solaria but out in the Terran sticks, we cling to traditional ideas like 'individual sovereignty' like you people cling to your data links."

He shook his head in frustration. "Look, the point is that I'm using the word 'it' naturally and you're purposely prodding me when you use 'it.' You're an interrogator, I get that, so your job is to antagonize me while you try to dig up whatever truth nuggets I might have buried in the backyard. You're doing a bang-up job of it, by the way." He offered a golf clap. "I'm sure your parents are *extremely* proud."

"Solaria?" Sandra repeated bemusedly. "I'm sorry, I've never heard that particular linguistically-questionable derivation used as an epithet."

"You should get out more. I hear it's good for the skin," Podsy retorted, snapping his fingers for emphasis as he added, "Thickens it right up."

"I find it curious that you so ardently defend Jem's sovereignty," Sandra mused, "and yet seem to regard the One Mind, which you clearly do not understand to a workable degree, with such disdain. Fundamentally, Jem and the Solar One Mind are similar. Both feature multiple distinct contributors where each lends individual distinctiveness to the whole. That whole expresses, at least in many respects, as a sovereign individual according to the very criteria you referenced when describing Jem. How do you explain that incongruity, Lieutenant?" she asked with an arched brow.

"Honestly?" Podsy recoiled in surprise. "Yeah...I don't understand the One Mind. And do you know why that is? Because you people don't let anyone examine it. You rebuff any and all outside attempts to understand it that don't transform someone into a One Minder. You claim it's a voluntary gestalt, but you don't let anyone interact with it on their terms. Jem has agreed to every single test we've suggested and offered a few more besides. Have we learned much from Jem through those primitive inquiries?" He shrugged. "Not really. But Jem hasn't obtusely kept us in the dark, while you lot have done *exactly* that. So that's one difference: transparency."

"I can assure you, Podsy," Sandra said matter of factly, sending a chill down Podsednik's spine at using his nickname without permission, "that there is *nothing* more transparent than the One Mind network."

"From the inside, maybe," he allowed. "But from the outside, it's got all the transparency of a black hole. And don't call me that," he added flatly. "We're not friends, we won't ever be friends, and jabbing me isn't going to produce anything but animosity. I've answered *all* of your questions to the best of my ability, and will continue to do so because that's what this operation requires: transparency. We did some awful shit on Luna," he added, feeling his guts twist into knots at the mental image of Sergeant Major Trapper's battered body, "and we deserve what we got. But don't fuck with me any more than is absolutely necessary. I'm cooperating. You don't need to poke me or fill me with chemicals to get the truth."

"My apologies," Sandra said, and for some reason, Podsy believed she was at least partially sincere. "I have an objective, just like you did when you arrived in Sol aboard the *Dietrich Bonhoeffer*, so I think you'll understand when I say that some of what I'm required to do in pursuit of that objective is distasteful...and possibly even cruel. But I'm going to do whatever it takes to achieve it," she added with a piercing look that would have shaken Podsy to the core just a few days earlier. "Just like you did, Podsy."

He set his jaw but deep down he knew she was right. Referring to someone by a word they disliked was far from torture, and if that was as far as things went, he would consider himself lucky.

"Fine," he allowed.

Her eyes flashed with something approaching sympathy before once again frosting over with professional indifference. "Let's get back to Jem's capabilities..."

20

THE CLOSING ARGUMENTS

Twelve hours after completing the first round of questions, Matthew returned to the interrogation room. Xi had remained there in the interim. A small cot alongside the wall had provided little comfort, but she had managed a few hours' sleep during the break.

"Good morning, Captain," her interrogator greeted her, looking pointedly at her untouched meal tray. "Not hungry?"

"I've earned every meal I've ever eaten." She grunted. "I'm not about to break that streak."

He cocked his head in confusion. "I don't understand."

"This whole interrogation..." She gestured to the four walls and the table as she resumed her seat opposite him. "It's a performance. An act. It's not real. You're not *actually* asking me questions because you want my answers. You're studying me. What I say, and how I say it when I say it. You're poking and prodding me like some kind of lab rat in hopes of figuring me out. And hey, fair enough." She shrugged. "I'm a complicated bitch who takes more than one or two poke-sessions to understand. But as long as there's nothing genuine about these interactions, and as long as all you're interested in doing is *observing* me rather than *interacting* with me, I'm not earning my keep. As such, I don't deserve whatever nutri-paste you've put under that gleaming silver cloche. I'm a human, not an animal, and call me picky but I think I should be treated like the former rather than the latter."

Matthew smiled, and this time it seemed genuine. "You're... bizarre, Captain Xi."

"Word to the wise." She leaned smugly back in her chair. "Terran girls don't generally consider 'bizarre' a compliment. 'Sexy,' 'alluring,' 'mysterious,' hell...even the word 'dangerous' might drop a girl's drawers if deployed correctly, but 'bizarre?'" She shook her head condescendingly. "That's a crash-and-burn approach where the payload will *definitely* be left on the rack at impact."

"Unlike your payload," he observed neutrally, sitting in the chair opposite hers, "which you mercilessly expended on people whom you call 'Solarians' with a zeal rarely matched in human history."

Xi's playful attitude evaporated as he broached the subject of the battle on Luna. She fought the urge to squirm, knowing that he had chosen the direct approach because he wanted to see how she reacted.

Jutting her chin out defiantly, she nodded. "That's right. I killed a lot of my fellow humans on Luna. But despite what you might think, I'm not proud of that. I'm..." Her voice trailed off; she was unable to find the right words to describe her ambivalent feelings about Operation Antivenom's ultimate outcome.

"You're what?" he pressed in the growing silence.

She shot him a glare before once again trying to rally her thoughts. "I'm..." Her voice trailed off again, unable to find anything that felt like an accurate description of how she felt. "Fine, you know what? Yeah, I *am* proud of what we came here to do," she finally declared. "We came here with love in our hearts and tears in our eyes, knowing that no matter how well we did, a *lot* of people would die as a result of our actions. You called me merciless? Maybe that's fair, and maybe it's not. Maybe it was mercy that made me risk my life... That made all of my fallen Metalheads give *their* lives," she continued, tears welling up in her eyes as the reality of the situation slammed into her with the force of a falling star. "Maybe I thought that somewhere, deep down, Solar humans weren't quite as different from us as we thought. Maybe I thought it was possible, however unlikely, that you'd view what we did as an act of love and not hatred...or worse yet, cold indifference," she continued, tears running down her cheeks as she refused to give in to the warring emotions raging within her. "Maybe we kept Antivenom secret, even from our own brass, because we cared that much about you. But yeah," she bit out, leaning forward and sneering in disgust, "you go ahead and tell everyone we're heartless. *Merciless.* That we only came here to carve our initials on the surface of the Moon like some kind of disowned punk returning home under the cover of night to deface his parents' garage."

"The crimes of which you stand accused are grave, Captain," Matthew said neutrally. "The death penalty is warranted on at least sixty-eight separate counts in your case."

She nodded knowingly and leaned back in her chair while maintaining eye contact with her interrogator. "I understand that. I really do. And what *you* might not understand is that I was ready for that outcome. Whether on the battlefield or in front of a Solarian firing squad, I knew this mission was a one-way ticket out of this 'verse."

"Lethal injection is the preferred execution method in Sol," Matthew casually clarified.

"Well, you won't have to strap me down to the table if it comes to that." She shrugged. "Because in the end, no matter what my intentions might have been, I wronged you. I wronged the families of the men and women I fought and killed on Luna. There's no forgetting that, and God knows I'd never be able to forgive it if I was in your shoes. So yeah, if you decide I need to die for what I did on Luna, hand me the syringe and I'll do the deed myself. But understand this," she added, leaning forward intently as the stream of tears finally stopped and began to dry on her cheeks. "Knowing what I did then and what I do now, I'd do it all over again. Maybe that makes me unrepentant. Maybe it makes me evil. But I believed in our mission, just like everyone else aboard the *Bonhoeffer*. Now it's up to you to decide what that means."

Matthew nodded in silence for several seconds before saying, "This interrogation is concluded. Do you have any closing remarks?"

Xi shook her head with conviction. "I think I've said it all."

"We're about finished here," Sandra said, lacing her fingers together and gesturing invitingly. "Is there anything else you'd like to add, Lieutenant Podsednik?"

Podsy shook his head in wonderment, knowing he would never get another chance like this to voice the strain of resentment that stretched from one end of the Terran Republic to the other. Sandra wasn't just an interrogator sent to conduct inquiries for later review, she was a member of the One Mind-linked Solar human race. Whatever she learned, whatever she saw, and whatever she heard would eventually be uploaded to Sol's vast data network, where every Solar human might eventually peruse it.

"Yeah, I do." Podsy nodded. "I've been cooperative with your questions, and I think it would be stupid of me to suggest I should have a say on how you deal with me. Putting all that aside, I'd like to talk about New Australia."

Sandra cocked her head interestedly. "Go on."

Podsy had thought about how to phrase this for months, or even *years*. He normally wasn't the type to become tongue-tied, but given the circumstances, he was less than surprised to find himself at a near-loss for words.

Still, he pressed on and managed to find his voice. "My family lived on New Australia, which was the third most prosperous Terran colony for over a hundred years. We had rich natural resources, a low-gee parent star, and ample cheap fuel to power our growth and development. We had our ups and downs, like any nation, but my people worked harder than most to achieve the Terran dream of self-reliance and independence. And for a few generations, we thrived, even building up vital military industries to support the Terran Armed Forces' ongoing efforts against the Arh'Kel. Then... Well, actually, what do you know about New Australia?"

Sandra's eyes narrowed fractionally. "I know that it was devastated by an Arh'Kel attack at the outset of the latest series of Terran-Arh'Kel engagements."

"Devastated." Podsy snorted bitterly. "That's one way to put it. Another way would be to say that of the New Ozzies who survived, only one in four has a living relative. Think about that. One. In. Four. We weren't 'devastated,' we were *cleansed*. Erased from the cosmos as a culture and a society, with just a few scattered pockets persisting in carrying forward our tradition."

"You must hate the Arh'Kel," she observed, and it seemed as though she genuinely empathized with him at that moment.

"You know, not really." He shook his head. "How can you hate something that just does what it's designed to do? The Arh'Kel are, by any moral yardstick worthy of the label, a force of evil in the universe. Their selfishness is a key part of what makes them unique life forms, and they have a peculiar reproductive bottleneck that drives them to commit atrocities that would make Mao or Hitler cringe. I think the universe would probably be better off without the Arh'Kel in it, or at least without them able to leave the confines of their home systems, but no, I don't hate them. I *understand* them, and I understand they need to be fought tooth and nail whenever they appear because to do otherwise is to tacitly encourage evil."

Judging by her expression, the Solarian interrogator understood where Podsy was going. And to her credit, she made no attempt to interrupt him as he passionately continued.

"After I buried my family...*all* of my family," he said, his nose burning and eyes misting as memories of those days came back in an unwanted flood, "I took a good long look in the mirror and asked myself one question: why would anyone let this happen? The answers I came to led me nowhere good. I couldn't fathom why that kind of evil would be permitted by thinking beings. We'd done what we could to fight off the rock-biters, but we were outmanned and outgunned. We Terrans have a euphemism that I'm guessing you've heard. We say 'as clear as a Solarian's conscience,' and what that means is that none of us can understand how our Solar cousins could sit back and watch while Terrans bled and died fighting the Arh'Kel. We. Can't. Fathom," he jabbed his finger on the table emphatically with each of those three words, "the indifference or the apathy or the tacit approval of evil that could lead one human, let alone the hundred billion of them in Sol, to stand by and watch their 'aboriginal' cousins suffer and die at the hands of evil personified. You know what I decided while I was looking in that mirror, Sandra?"

Sandra's cool gaze seemed, for at least a moment, to have

softened into something approaching genuine human sympathy. "What did you decide, Podsy?"

Ignoring her use of his nickname, he made a firm, final gesture with his hand on the table. "I decided that I would *never* stand idly by while people suffered like that. I decided I'd rather risk doing evil myself than let evil run its course uncontested. Maybe that makes me a bad person, and maybe it makes me irredeemable. But I came to Luna and did what I did because I care more about you and yours than you cared about me and mine. Maybe I made a mistake. Maybe I caused undue suffering. If I did, hey, I'll wash my neck to keep the headsman's axe clean of my 'aboriginal' filth." He smirked. "But the simple, undeniable truth is that," he presented his palms to her, "this blood on my hands will *never* wash away...and I'd do it all again in a heartbeat. Because given the choice, I'd rather lovingly cause harm than indifferently permit it."

"My interrogation is now complete, Colonel," Alice said smoothly. "Is there anything you'd like to add before I go?"

Jenkins, sitting up in his hospital bed, shook his head adamantly. "I'll stand by whatever my people say and abide by whatever you choose."

Alice lifted a brow in surprise. "What do you think your people might have said?"

"Whatever they said, it's better than anything I could come up with." Jenkins shrugged. "What we did here was unforgivable, and that's not self-pity or despair. It's true. We attacked Sol at a key, vulnerable point and, ultimately, we didn't even know if we were doing a good thing. For all we know, Jem could have been aligned with the enemy, and we might have just unwittingly acted on that enemy's behalf. Were our intentions noble?

I think they were. But every abuse of power in history has sprung from the self-righteousness of its authors. That's why we have courts and laws and indifferent arbitration systems. Nobody thinks *they're* the villain in the story... Well, almost nobody," he allowed. "We didn't come here because we thought it would be the popular thing to do. We didn't come here seeking approval. We came here to do what we thought was right under the circumstances, and now it's time for you to judge whether that's what happened."

Alice's eyes softened significantly before she asked a wholly unexpected question, "Is this about your wife?"

Jenkins did a double-take, swallowing past the suddenly dry knot in his throat. "Excuse me?"

"We have extensive records detailing the personal histories of Terran Armed Forces personnel," she explained dismissively, although her persistent eye contact suggested she was anything but dismissive of this particular issue. "Your file paints the picture of a troubled man whose sole focus has become to find redemption for an event he had no direct responsibility for. From your experimental Combined Arms project under the Terran Fleet to that project's transfer to the Terran Armor Corps, all the way to the attack on Luna One, your record shows a man desperately seeking redemption even at great personal peril. Some would say it's the picture of a man seeking martyrdom. Is that picture inaccurate, Colonel Jenkins?"

Jenkins set his jaw, clenching his fingers into fists at his sides. Of all the lines of inquiry he had expected and planned for, this had not been among them. Still, some small corner of his mind seemed all too eager to indulge her latest probe, and he grudgingly gave that sliver of himself the opportunity to do so. "My wife died because of me, Alice. You can say I didn't have direct responsibility for it, but that's a semantic copout. I was passed out drunk when Sarah called for a ride home from the airport. She'd come home a day early, and she knew I had a problem with the bottle. She also knew I was at our cabin and, being the dutiful life partner she always was (and who I never deserved), she took a private taxi to come bring me home. It was her last car ride."

As much as he wanted to, he couldn't shed a single tear as he spoke about an event that had haunted and driven him since the day it happened. Captain Murdoch had been right, at least in part. The Legion *had* been some sort of redemptive endeavor for Jenkins, at least in the beginning. Despite the brevity of his service in the Armor Corps, the bond he had formed with his fellow servicemen was unshakable. The purpose he derived from serving with them was undeniable.

Jenkins' driving regret every day since joining the Metal Legion was that it had taken Sarah's death for him to find that purpose. He would never forgive himself for that, no matter how high the praise was heaped or how many accolades he earned. He had failed her when she needed him, and that was an unforgivable sin.

Alice spoke into the pregnant pause. "Her taxi was struck head-on by a malfunctioning vehicle. She died instantly. It was an accident, Colonel, by any reasonable definition of the term."

"You're right. The collision was just bad luck," Jenkins allowed. "But the fundamental reason it happened is that I selfishly crawled into a bottle. I was hiding from life like the coward I was. Like the coward I am."

"I feel obligated to point out," Alice said measuredly, "that the tragedy of your wife's death would have been impossible in the One Mind. We of Sol no longer live in constant fear of such events as a result of our continuous interconnectivity."

"You no longer live in fear?" Jenkins shook his head in wonder, having never expected the conversation to take this latest turn. "I'm sorry to hear that, Alice, because fear drives every second of my life. Fear of failure. Fear of rejection. Fear of embarrassment. Fear of being *wrong* or acting like the coward I know I am," he explained with the utmost sincerity. "It was fear that brought me here. Fear that something horrifying would happen to Sol, that humanity would fall victim to a nefarious conspiracy thousands of years in the making. If you think the One Mind network would have spared me the fear that drives every second of my existence... Well, I'm not sure you could have made the case *against* your vaunted network any better than you just did."

He sat up intently, knowing this was the best chance he would ever have to make the unlikeliest proposal of his life. "The only thing I've learned for certain here is that Sol and Terra need each other, Alice. Sol would have been under Jemmin influence, possibly until its final moments, if not for the Metal Legion's sacrifices. You *need* us, and much as we like to say otherwise around our 'aboriginal' campfires, we need you. I don't expect you to like us, and you shouldn't expect us to like you, but we're *family*. If we can't make it work with each other, there isn't a snowball's chance in hell that *either* of us will make it work with the rest of the universe. Jemmin drove a wedge between us and did its level best to set us up for total annihilation. The wounds of the past and the blood that's been shed— we won't be made whole overnight. But we have to start sometime, and I think that time is now."

"That seems a curious suggestion, given its source," Alice said with fractionally narrowed eyes.

"Humanity's young," he explained urgently, "but every other race has taken notice of us. The Arh'Kel, Jemmin, the Vorr, even the Finjou. *All* of them recognize that humanity has the potential to play a key role in shaping the future of this galaxy. That's not hyperbole," he added adamantly. "I've looked them in the eye and seen how they look back. Every single species capable of doing so has attempted to manipulate us for their own gain or has secretly tried to eradicate us outright."

"You speak of the Vorr as though they might be antagonistic to humanity." Alice cocked her head skeptically. "Yet it was they who made possible your transit here, and it was they who gave you Jem's location. What cause do you have to mistrust them?"

"I know I'm not smart enough to play poker with either the Vorr or Jemmin, and I think humanity is too young and fractured to threaten either of them at this moment," Jenkins explained. "But *both* of them insisted on us taking a seat at the table and anteing up for the biggest game in either species' history. I think that on some level they fear us, and fear doesn't make for a strong foundation to a mutually beneficial relationship."

Alice nodded slowly. "Do you have anything else you would like to add to this interview?"

Jenkins shook his head in negation. "How long until your people reach a verdict?"

"I am uploading the final contents of our interview to the One Mind network now," she replied simply. "However, ninety-three percent of Solar humanity has already reviewed the matter, having actively participated in this exchange. The Venutians will require another two hours to process and review the findings due to the light delay, but a preliminary verdict has already been reached."

She paused, seeming to invite Jenkins to ask about the verdict, but he made no attempt to do so. He was too stunned by her suggestion that what was effectively a ninety-three-*billion* person jury had listened in on the interrogation and had already arrived at a conclusion regarding Operation Antivenom.

She flashed an impish smile before continuing, "You and your people have been found guilty of the vast majority of the charges brought against you. Interstellar piracy, violation of the One Mind, terrorism, sedition, and several lesser charges have been corroborated to Sol's collective satisfaction. By a margin of 99.3% to 0.7%, your guilt is, in the opinion of Sol's One Mind, undeniable. Death is the only appropriate sentence for these crimes."

Jenkins nodded slowly, feeling strangely relaxed at hearing the verdict. "Is there an appeals process?"

"No." She shook her head firmly. "When such an overwhelming degree of consensus is achieved in a verdict of this magnitude, there can be no system of appeal. Who would you appeal to? Not just a majority has spoken, *all* have spoken."

He exhaled a long sigh. "When is the sentence to be carried out?" he eventually asked.

"The sentence has been commuted," she replied matter of factly. "By a margin of 97.5% to 2.5%, respondents have indicated that Operation Antivenom was conducted under what we of Sol consider to be the equivalent of 'extraordinary circumstances' and our modern variation of the 'Good Samaritan' principle. As a result, no punishment would be appropriate. In fact, early returns suggest over 86% of Sol received your call for colonial reunification favorably. This differs significantly from polls conducted just two weeks ago, which showed fewer than one-third of all Solar humans viewed reunification with the Terran Republic as a worthwhile endeavor."

His brow lifted in surprise. "Antivenom created that large of a swing?"

"Certainly not." She cocked her head dubiously. "Following your 'inoculation' of the One Mind's vast network of distributed processors, we became aware of ongoing interference with the network's internal transparency. It seems that processes hidden beneath the virtual architecture of One Mind were actively manipulating sentiment in cascade effects that created vast divergences between true and perceived sentiment. We have yet to catalog the entirety of these manipulations, and it is possible that Venus will suffer serious loss of life since the light delay restricts our ability to directly interface with their system and curtail these interferences, but the manipulations we have thus far discovered appear to be consistent with your testimony, the testimonies of your crews, and with the evidence provided by Terran and Vorr sources, chief among that evidence being the capsules containing irrefutable proof that the species known as 'Jem'un' observed humanity thousands of years ago. After examining that capsule, as well as the capsule containing archeo-tech that demonstrates to our satisfaction that Jemmin did, in fact, technologically uplift humanity, we are overwhelmingly convinced Jemmin did, in fact, exert significant influence on the inner workings of Sol, for perhaps centuries or even millennia. Relatedly, you may be personally pleased to learn that Solar confidence in the One Mind system is currently at an all-time low."

Jenkins shook his head grimly. "Whatever you think of my people or of me, we don't revel in *any* form of human misery. The One Mind system, foreign and incomprehensible as it may be to Terrans, is an integral part of your society. I can't even fathom what shaken confidence in it must feel like for you. I'm…" He hesitated, still reeling from the idea that he wasn't speaking to just one person but rather ninety-three billion. Words seemed pathetically inadequate given the circumstances, so he mustered the best ones he could and finished, "I'm sorry for the pain this has caused all of you."

"Your sentiment is acknowledged, Colonel Jenkins," Alice replied before standing from the bedside chair. She stretched out a hand, which Jenkins slowly accepted, still reeling from the rollercoaster of information she had just taken him through. "On behalf of Sol, it is my privilege and pleasure to say," she offered with genuine human solemnity, "thank you, Colonel Jenkins. You may yet become a martyr who suffers and dies for a crime he did not commit, but your end will not be at the hands of..." her lips twisted into a bemused smirk as she finished, "Solarians."

She moved toward the door, which slid open to reveal a small crowd of people.

All of whom were Metalheads.

"You and your people," Alice gestured to the throng outside the door, "will be released immediately. Transport has been provided, along with an escort that will safely conduct you and a Solar delegation to Terran space."

Jenkins furrowed his brow in confusion. "Do you have any idea how difficult it was for us to get here with the wormhole gates down?"

Alice smiled, and for a moment Jenkins didn't see a Solarian interrogator or even a cybernetically-enhanced member of humanity's Solar branch. He saw a woman who seemed genuinely delighted by what she was about to say, and it was one of the most beautiful things he'd seen in a long, long time.

"It seems you brought everything you needed to safely return home, Lee," she said knowingly before moving through the crowd of Metalheads.

First through the door was Captain Xi Bao, who moved to Jenkins' bedside and scowled at the myriad medical devices attached to his body.

She was followed by Podsy, who clutched Jem's ruby-red cylinder to his chest. Concerningly, to Jenkins' eye, Jem's crystalline surface seemed to lack its former luster, having turned at least partially opaque at the core.

After Podsy came Styles and Colonel Moon, followed by Chief Rimmer. Lieutenant Nakamura, Private Quinn, Lieutenant 'Sargon' Benjamin, and even Lieutenant Winters were also present as Metalheads streamed in.

As the survivors of Operation Antivenom filled the cramped room, Jenkins was moved by the faces he didn't see. Colonel Li. Lieutenants Ford and Yuan. But most notable was the absence of Sergeant Major Trapper, and the briefest look to Lieutenant Podsednik saw Podsy shake his head in silence.

It had been as costly as they had all known it would be, but against all odds, they had done it.

They had saved Earth, and probably the entire Solar system, safeguarding the lives of a hundred billion fellow humans in the process.

Maybe General Akinouye would have known the right words to say as the silent, unified band of Metalheads stood around his bed following such a momentous and costly victory, but Jenkins was not Akinouye's equal. He knew with every fiber of his being that he would never measure up to the late general's high standard, so he spoke the only words that seemed appropriate under the circumstances...

"Let's go home."

21

TRUE ILLUMINATION FROM A SPARK

"I still can't believe Trapper's gone," Xi said after settling in aboard the Solarian transport. She shared a cabin with Podsy, Styles, and Quinn, with Jem silently settled across Podsy's lap.

"You should have seen him, Xi." Podsy shook his head in unmasked awe. "I've never seen anyone do what he did. A fist-sized grouping of three rounds with a fifty, from his knees, in three seconds. And those RPGs at the end..."

Podsy seemed shaken by the memory, prompting Xi to squeeze his shoulder supportively. "I thought that old bastard would outlive all of us...or at least you, Styles," she added with a lopsided grin.

"Yeah," Styles deadpanned. "Because I'm 'Mr. Dangerous' over here, always running headlong into the enemy HQ with nothing but a sidearm and a well-stuffed codpiece."

"Is that a jab at my rack?" Xi retorted, projecting outrage.

"It is what it is, Captain." Styles grinned.

"You guys are terrible." Quinn sighed, drawing laughter from the other three.

"We're like that maggot-laden cheese they used to make in Europe," Styles assured her.

"Yeah." Xi snorted. "Smelly, full of holes, and a living testament to the fact that some boundaries should never be crossed."

"Oh, come on," Podsy chided. "The way I see it, you're just talking about a little bit of extra super-fresh protein in the cheese. Sure, it may taste like ass, but that's something everyone in *this* room is familiar with after licking Drill Sergeant McMasters' boots for six weeks of Basic."

"Oh, Jesus, Podsy! I could have gone the rest of my life without thinking about her." Quinn groaned, rubbing her eyes with her hands and drawing Xi's attention to the machined nut on the woman's ring finger.

"It's not just Trapper we won't be seeing again," Xi said, casting a somber shadow over the berth. "It's funny...I was there when General Akinouye died. I saw it happen with my own eyes. It hurt, and still does, but it felt *real*. Our losses in Antivenom? They still don't feel *real*, you know?"

"I do," Podsy replied, and the others nodded. He leaned forward intently. "What's going to happen to the Legion now?"

"Kavanaugh's probably already sold us out by now." Styles snorted. "I don't know why the old man didn't boot her out years ago."

"Command is never as simple as it seems like it should be," Xi said, recalling a dozen different decisions she'd made in recent months that she knew beyond the shadow of a doubt had been less than ideal given the circumstances and available intel at the time. "General Akinouye played the hand he was dealt, just like any of us, and humanity might not have survived without him running this thing precisely the way he did. Second-guessing is one thing, but if Akinouye kept her around, Kavanaugh must have been a valuable member of the team."

"Probably," Podsy allowed. "But how can you undo an entire branch's legacy while its longest-tenured leader's body is still warm? What kind of person does that?"

"An ambitious one," Quinn suggested, drawing an approving nod from Styles.

"Not just ambitious," Xi corrected, "but *arrogant*. She didn't see the wisdom in what the old man did, which was an epic mistake. We do things a certain way for a host of reasons, some of which are obvious and others almost impossible to recognize. Akinouye didn't stand at the Legion's head for as long as he did by accident. Kavanaugh, at the very least, should have had *some* respect for his leadership."

"It doesn't matter, though." Styles sighed. "It's out of our hands at this point. I can't stop thinking about whether or not the Fleet kept our homes safe. That Jemmin gate-crasher..." He visibly shivered. "I don't even want to think about what would happen if *two* of those things came through a gate one after the other."

"It is unlikely," Jem suggested, speaking for the first time since arriving aboard the Solarian transport, "that Jemmin would have taken additional action against the Terran Republic. Jemmin is methodical, and its failure to take New America 2 will cause a radical adjustment in its priorities, but that adjustment will not manifest against your worlds for at least several of your weeks."

"How confident can you be about that?" Xi asked skeptically.

"As confident as you are that your heart will continue beating," Jem replied matter of factly. "Jemmin is vast and incorporates tremendous computational power into its matrix, but it is hardly incomprehensible. If one understands the underlying fundamentals of a thing, predicting its behavior on a macro scale is a simple if energy-intensive endeavor."

"What do you think Jemmin is doing right now, Jem?" Styles pressed.

"That depends primarily on the Vorr's current posture," Jem

said indifferently. "I was tasked by my forebears with disseminating knowledge that would be crucial to combating Jemmin. What is done with that knowledge is ultimately determined by those who receive it."

"How'd we measure up, Jem?" Podsy asked with open curiosity. "You gave *us* information crucial to humanity's survival, along with the evidence of Jem'un interaction with humanity thousands of years ago. How do you think we did with it?"

"The people of Sol were sufficiently impressed by the evidence I presented to you and which you in turn presented to them," Jem replied. "If you are asking for my opinion of 'Operation Antivenom,' I will say that you not only validated my forebears' collective expectations of your species, but you exceeded them. Jem'un life students long believed humanity to have some of the highest potential of all intelligent species. Their sole concern was whether you would survive your recklessness."

"Goddammit," Xi quipped. "First the Vorr call us unintelligent, then the Solarians call us 'aboriginal,' and now a dead race that *literally* wiped itself out with a fucking social movement calls *us* 'reckless?'"

"Consider," Jem easily riposted, "the fact that it was your species' inherent mistrust and willingness, or possibly even *eagerness* to flout authority, that led to Operation Antivenom's success. Such traits are integral to independent actors and are fundamentally incompatible with the continued progression of intelligence along the vast majority of development arcs. Even your own brains are segregated into specialized sub-components that are capable of both cooperating and actively competing with one another. These are inherently primitive traits, according to Jem'un study of life in the galaxy. Had humanity's psycho-social makeup been any *less* primitive, it is unlikely that your species would have survived Jemmin's machinations."

"Way to pull it out there at the end, Jem." Quinn smirked. "You almost made it sound like calling us 'primitive' was a compliment."

The group laughed as the intercom blared to life with a woman's voice. "We are breaking orbit in five minutes. Proceed to your flight stations."

"Earth." Styles sighed. "I never thought I'd get so close without actually setting foot on it. So close, yet so far away."

"Careful," Podsy muttered. "You wouldn't want them to learn that you'd been planning to hack the One Mind even before learning about the Jemmin conspiracy."

Xi's eyes went wide, as did Styles' and Quinn's. The ship almost certainly had ears in every compartment, given the Solarians' totalitarian approach to information, but Podsy just laughed as the same woman's voice once again came over the intercom. "The terms of your amnesty protect you from those charges, Mr. Styles...assuming you promise not to pursue such efforts in the future."

Podsy slapped his thigh while doing his utmost to hold back the tide of laughter yearning to burst past his lips as the color rapidly drained from Styles' face.

"Come now, Mr. Styles," the woman on the intercom continued. "You of all people should know that someone is always watching...as your exhaustive collection of hidden-camera pornography attests."

"You fucker!" Styles growled, chucking Podsy hard on the shoulder and causing Podsednik's pent-up, infectious laughter to fill the room. "That's not funny!" he snapped. "Now everyone in Sol knows about my collection!"

"Not *everyone*," the woman interjected. "Merely eighty-two percent of us, which is a little over eighty-two billion people."

Now it was Xi's turn to laugh. She didn't want to know how Podsy had pulled off that particular prank, but it earned top marks across the board as far as she was concerned. "Well played, Podsy." She offered a high-five, which Podsednik quickly supplied.

Even Styles grudgingly gave his approval of the pre-flight joke as the transport broke orbit and burned for the Sol 1 wormhole gate, through which a field of stars was still clearly visible when the Terran-filled vessel pulled away from Luna.

Colonel Jenkins was still in a bio-bed recovering from the wounds he had suffered at Luna One, which put Colonel Moon and Captain Xi on the transport's bridge during final approach to the Sol 1 wormhole gate. The transport, which had an alphanumeric designation of *TV-0135*, was one of the few starships Xi had been aboard that was equipped with an honest-to-God *bridge*.

With a wraparound viewing portal, the vessel's transport deck seemed like a throwback to the seafaring days of humanity's distant past when command bridges afforded the commanding officers maximum visibility. But human warships rarely, if ever, featured command decks with outside observation ports or viewing screens. And since Xi had only ever ridden warships through the void of interplanetary space, standing on an actual bridge was an experience she intended to savor.

Command and control centers or combat operations decks were well secured within fleet vessels.

The wormhole gate loomed before the ship, just close enough that she could make it out as a dull silver speck. Its magnified image was projected on the bridge's central holodisplay, and Xi noted the glittering stars on the far side of the gate where none would be if it was active.

She didn't know how the wormhole gates worked, and she

didn't much care to learn. She had been forced to study them during the battalion's earliest training sessions since they were integral to Terran Fleet operations (and since, at that time, then-Commander Jenkins' armor experiment had been under the Fleet banner and not Armor Corps'). But aside from wormholes involving a quartet of micro-black-holes, two on each 'end' of a gate pair, Xi suspected *no* member of the human race knew much of substance regarding the mysterious devices.

Somewhat alarmingly, the dormant wormhole was far from the most impressive feature on display. Xi and Colonel Moon exchanged several long, pointed glances as they beheld the most awe-inspiring sight in near-Earth space.

Stretching out in a perfect cloud formation that completely englobed the wormhole gate were four hundred Solar warships divided into penny packets and sub-fleets, some of which were individual pickets as well. The Solar Fleet was a breathtaking sight.

Xi guesstimated the fleet contained at least two hundred destroyer-class warships, a hundred cruisers, thirty battle carriers, and at least as many battleships. Several sleek, nimble-looking corvettes and cutters skirted the outer edges of the formation like hyenas stalking the perimeter of a camp in search of weakness while the heavies ignored their presence.

But one thing the Solarians lacked were rivals to the Terran Republican-class dreadnoughts. Not even the Solar battleships approached the scale of the Terran Fleet's pride and joy, However, Xi knew that while size was usually decisive, it wasn't *always* the most important factor when it came time to exchanging fire.

Still, the sight of the Solar fleet was enough to send chills down anyone's spine. The assembled firepower on display was easily several times that of the entire Terran Fleet, although it was difficult to compare the two given the lack of Solar dreadnoughts. While the Solar fleet could certainly deliver a serious punch, a Republican-class dreadnought could take the best the enemy could throw at it while continuing to pour Terran fury from its keel-mounted mass driver array.

"We are at the designated coordinates, Colonel, Captain," reported the transport's commanding officer. She lacked a formal military rank, yet she conducted herself with measures of dignity and authority rarely seen in civilian circles.

"Thank you, Captain," Colonel Moon acknowledged, turning pointedly to his junior officer. "Captain Xi, I believe it's time."

"Agreed." She nodded, activating her wrist-link and calling down to Podsy. "Lieutenant, Jem is authorized to transmit the signal."

"Confirmed, Captain," Podsednik replied. "Transmitting signal now."

The signal went out with a corresponding chime from her wrist-link. At first, nothing seemed to happen. Seconds stretched into a full minute, and nothing about the wormhole gate changed. Xi's nerves began to fray as she wondered if Jem had failed, or worse...if Jem had some ulterior motive for bringing them all to this particular point.

She trusted Jem as much as she trusted anyone who wasn't part of the Metal Legion, which was to say she didn't trust him farther than she could throw him.

But her silent skepticism was short-lived; a brilliant flash erupted from the wormhole gate. As soon as Xi turned her focus to the magnified image of the gate, she was relieved that she could no longer see stars on the other side of the ring-shaped device.

"Sol 1 wormhole is online," declared the transport's CO, and like a school of fish, the cloud of Solar warships parted and reoriented.

With maneuvers that brought some of the ships within a hundred meters of each other, the Solar fleet moved with enviable precision and coordination as twenty warships separated into a column that moved toward the now-open wormhole gate. The first group of those warships were small, a dozen corvettes and cutters proceeding ahead of two battle carriers and three battleships, with a single courier vessel bringing up the formation's rear.

Every human serviceman knew that the most dangerous period in any deployment was the moment a ship passed through the mysterious wormhole gates. Despite humanity's ongoing refinements to gate travel procedures, not a year went by without at least some human ships being destroyed while navigating the Nexus-linked transit system.

"I'll never understand," Colonel Moon muttered just loud enough for Xi to hear, "why Sol chose to position its gate so close to Earth."

Xi had wondered the same thing from a young age.

When the Illumination League had initially extended humanity the offer of provisional inclusion in the interstellar organization, Sol had been granted the benefit of choosing where to place the Sol 1 wormhole gate. Standard practice was to place the all-important terminus gate near a gas giant in a species' home star system several light-hours away from the homeworld.

Sol's government had inexplicably placed the Sol 1 gate less than two light *minutes* from Earth on an orbit that kept its position almost perfectly stationary relative to the planet. Aside from Earth's mildly eccentric orbit creating relatively minor fluctuations in the distance between the gate and humanity's birthplace, the Sol 1 gate stood constant, motionless overwatch of the blue-green planet.

As she watched the Solarian warships file toward the reactivated wormhole, Xi was suddenly struck by a haunting thought...

What if the gate's proximity to Earth was part of Jemmin's plan all along? she wondered. *What if Jemmin planned to use that proximity to expedite humanity's erasure from the face of the galaxy?*

She gritted her teeth as the first of the Solar warships disappeared over the wormhole's event horizon. The second ship followed, then the third. The fourth. The fifth. One by one, each Solarian vessel was transmitted to the Sol 2 system, where a fleet the size of Sol 1's was on constant deployment.

Xi could feel the tension throughout the sparsely-crewed bridge as the last of the warships ventured through the wormhole. She hoped Jemmin had spared the Solarians in Sol 2, rather than attempting to wipe them out as it had done to the Terrans of New America 2. Had the Terran dreadnoughts failed to unleash their full arsenal immediately upon Jemmin's arrival in New America 2, it was likely that the Jemmin gatecrasher would have succeeded in clearing that star system of Terran assets.

Which would have left New America 2 vulnerable to Jemmin attack and brought this fleet into the middle of a deadly ambush.

The minutes droned on as they awaited the courier's return. The courier was scheduled to return with news of Sol 2's status. If all was clear and the Solarian fleet stationed there was intact, the transport would move through the gate en route to the Sol 2-Nexus gate. If, however, Sol 2 was not clear, the courier would return with whatever data it could gather, and that information would inform how the Solarians proceeded.

The minutes stretched until nearly a half hour had passed with no word from beyond the gate.

Finally, the event horizon's profile changed, and the courier returned. It bore no obvious battle damage. Xi wondered about the delay.

As non-Solarians, Xi and the Metalheads weren't privy to the courier's report, but after just a few seconds, the transport's captain turned and said, "There is no active Jemmin presence in Sol 2."

"What about the Solar fleet there?" Moon pressed, but before he even finished asking the question, Xi saw the answer in the Sol 1 fleet's posture. Some of the heaviest warships in the fleet were moving toward the wormhole gate, which meant they aimed to take up new positions in defense of Sol 2 rather than remaining at their long-held posts at Sol 1.

"Guardian Fleet One is gone," replied the CO matter of factly. "Preliminary evidence points to the Vorr as the perpetrators of its destruction."

Xi's eyes went wide as saucers at hearing that. "That... I mean, that *can't* be right."

The ship's CO inclined her head fractionally. "Using information and techniques made available by the Vorr ambassador who accompanied you as well as information revealed during Jem's examination, we are skeptical of Vorr involvement. However," she added pointedly, "given that the source of both the damning and exonerating evidence is the Vorr, we are unable to reach consensus on the matter at this time."

"Jemmin is a masterful manipulator." Moon grimaced.

"That much is beyond doubt," the transport's CO agreed as the ship adjusted its orientation and moved to join the next line of ships set to pass through the Sol 1 terminus gate. "We will proceed with caution and accompany elements of Guardian Two through the gate."

Xi furrowed her brow in confusion as she turned to Colonel Moon. "Why would Jemmin kill all of the Solar ships in Sol 2, paint the Vorr as the aggressors, and then withdraw?"

Moon grunted. "The only answer I've got is that they want to sow dissent between humanity and the Vorr."

"I get that." Xi shook her head irritably. "But how the hell were the Solarians supposed to learn about Guardian One's destruction?"

Moon cocked his head contemplatively before his eyes narrowed. "I see two possibilities. First, Jemmin planned to re-open the gate at some future point when Solar enmity with the Vorr might prove useful."

"And second?" Xi asked warily.

Moon's eyes narrowed suspiciously, and he lowered his voice. "Second, that Sol has FTL communication capability, and they already knew about Guardian One's destruction before sending ships through. This whole thing," he inclined his chin toward the viewing screen, where the wormhole gate grew steadily larger as the transport fell into the back of the Solarian formation set to pass through it, "could be a bit of theater for our benefit."

The ship's CO scoffed. "Colonel Moon, your paranoia is impressive."

"Are you saying it's unwarranted?" he challenged.

"Not at all." She shrugged. "I'm merely saying that it is a remarkable trait. The amount of energy expended during Guardian Two's recent maneuvers was extraordinary. Perhaps our so-called 'Terran' cousins do not care to conserve resources, but we of Sol are conscientious of such matters."

"What do you mean, 'so-called Terran cousins?'" Moon asked.

"Terra is a dream. A myth nearly as old as human civilization," the ship's CO replied simply. "Earth is reality. Sol is reality. Humanity came from a planet called Earth, not some mystical place called Terra. We are made of stardust, not dreams."

Xi smirked victoriously. "For all your supposed enlighten-ment, you people really are dense, you know that?"

"Oh?" The other woman quirked a brow haughtily.

"Much as we wanted to," Xi's smirk grew until it was a condescending grin, "we couldn't take Earth with us. My ances-tors didn't have the luxury of bringing along the tangible roots from which they sprang, so they brought whatever they could manage as they reached for those stars you claim we came from. And you know what? Most of what they brought broke along the way, got stolen by some jackass with more brawn than brains, or was repurposed into something that made it unrecog-nizable." Judging by her expression, the ship's CO understood where Xi was heading, but Xi Bao wasn't about to let this partic-ular opportunity slip by. "The only thing they brought with them that never got broken, stolen or defaced was their dream of a better future. It's a dream that even you seem to understand is as old as human civilization. Terra isn't where we *came from*, Captain." Xi shook her head. "It's where we're *going*. And if the only way we'll find it is by building it with our bare hands, that's exactly what we'll do."

Xi turned toward the blue dot of Earth, which she regarded with both reverence and disdain for a long moment before once again facing the ship's captain.

"You can keep the reality of Earth, Captain," Xi finished passionately. "I'll take the dream of Terra over it every day of the week."

From a distance, the dormant Sol 2-Nexus gate seemed ordi-nary. Serene. Peaceful.

But closer inspection revealed the vast graveyard of broken warships surrounding it. Podsy's hand reflexively went to his mouth as he contemplated the loss of human life represented by the drifting hulks and expanding debris clouds.

"Why would Jemmin do this?" Podsy wondered aloud.

"Timetables were accelerated and contingencies activated when Jemmin was repelled at New America 2," Jem replied grimly. "Jemmin is still uncertain how the Vorr and human relationship was established, but with each passing second, its calculations bring it closer to the truth. Jemmin is powerful, but its structure is limited, and therefore so is its power. It must rely on manipulation more than brute force when it encounters unexpected obstacles."

"I'm still not clear on how that whole 'limited structure' bit works," Podsy admitted.

"Nor am I, at least not in specific terms," Jem said with surprising bluntness. "But think of Jemmin, the social system, as both the nerve center and skeleton of a great body. Bones require muscles to move, and muscles require both fuel and direction to function. Jemmin, the nerve center, would certainly be capable of nearly limitless expansion beyond its initial matrix by simply adding more bones, muscles, and internal organ mass to itself. But Jemmin, the skeleton, is fundamentally incapable of adding more than a maximum amount of musculature and supporting organs. Each loss Jemmin takes permanently diminishes it, which is partly why it does not crave conflict. To Jemmin, it is better to frame the Vorr for the destruction of Guardian One since Solar humanity would then likely take action against, or at the very least be resistant to, an alliance with the Vorr for a tactically-significant interval."

"During which interval Jemmin works to wipe the Vorr, the Zeen, and the Terran Republic from the map." Podsy nodded, thinking he understood Jemmin just a little bit better. "I'm curious," Podsy mused. "Your name is 'Jem,' and the name of your forebears' species was 'Jem'un.' What does 'Jem' mean in your language?"

"There is no direct analogy, given the differences in Jem'un and human physiology, as well as the psycho-linguistic differences in how the two species' express complex ideas," Jem said hesitantly. "But a reasonable translation for the word 'Jem' would be the English word 'mind.' 'Cognition,' 'thought,' 'abstraction,' and 'reason' would also be acceptable translations of the word 'Jem,' although they largely ignore the implied ownership of the system that 'mind' suggests."

"And the million-sovereign question," Podsy continued, "would be, what does 'un' mean in your forebears' tongue?"

"Jem'un did not have tongues, Lieutenant Podsednik," Jem said tersely. "Their equivalent to salivary glands were dual-purpose structures that secreted digestive enzymes and also ingested fluids, leaving solid food matter to be macerated in the oral cavity prior to—"

"Don't change the subject." Podsy chuckled. "What does it mean?"

"The closest English word for 'un' would be 'conscience.' 'Heart,' 'soul,' 'spirit,' and 'love' also significantly overlap to the meaning conveyed by the Jem'un word 'un.' The first syllable denotes primacy, while the second denotes final authority. Essentially, the phrase 'Jem'un' means, in simple English, 'mind before conscience, logic before heart, but no thought without love is worthwhile.' Every Jem'un considered itself to be a mind driven primarily by conscientiousness."

"Wow..." Podsy whistled appreciatively as he processed Jem's response. "Your people called themselves 'Minds of Conscience' and believed that was how they should define their existences. That's...a lot more noble-sounding than anything my ancestors agreed on."

"Yours is a predictably crude summation," Jem said witheringly, "but not wholly inaccurate."

The lieutenant gave Jem the side eye. "Talk about crude, sometimes you can be a real dick."

As the transport and its escort warships moved through the Solar fleet's debris cloud, Podsy gave voice to another concern he'd silently harbored since learning that Jem could re-open the wormhole gates. "What's to stop Jemmin from regaining control of the Nexus and all its gates?"

"My method of re-activation will interfere with every point of Jemmin control," Jem explained, "but Jemmin is intelligent and relentless. It will stop at nothing to regain control of the Nexus as soon it becomes aware that I have disrupted its control."

"When will Jemmin learn you've broken its hold? And maybe more importantly, does Jemmin know about your existence?"

"Assuming it has maintained a presence in the Nexus, which would seem to be of paramount importance given Jemmin's designs, it will be aware of my takeover as soon as the Sol 2-Nexus gate goes online," Jem replied. "While my method of interruption will make the process of regaining control difficult for Jemmin, it will certainly not be impossible. The coming weeks and months will prove instrumental in determining the nature of Nexus-linked space and the prospects of its inhabitants. I suspect that humanity will play a vital role in the future of shaping not only its own future but the future of every species with access to the Nexus."

"Great. No pressure or anything." Podsy rolled his eyes in mock dismay. The truth was, he felt proud of what they had done at Luna One, and on the Brick, and on Shiva's Wrath, and on Durgan's Folly. The Metal Legion, more than any other branch of the Terran Armed Forces, had played a pivotal role in safeguarding not just the Terran Republic but all of humanity against its neighbors' aggression.

"Humanity is a fearsome species," Jem said, an ominous note entering its voice as the transport drew ever closer to the Sol 2 Nexus wormhole gate. "Your fundamental nature makes for significant volatility, which can either be harnessed and channeled to tremendously beneficial effect...or, if left unchecked, may prove disastrous to the galaxy and everything in it."

"That's not exactly a ringing endorsement, Jem," Podsy said warily.

"It was not intended to be such," Jem replied tersely. "With a few thousand additional years of development, your species would have reached the stars on possibly the strongest footing of any race since the Jem'un, but you are dangerously primitive in many key respects. I fear your entire species will be forced to 'grow up,' as your people say, much faster than it is reasonable to expect."

"That sounds like a challenge, Jem," Podsy shot back as the transport finally reached the wormhole's event horizon. "And if I know one thing about humans, it's that we love a challenge."

The transport, following an escort of fifty Solar warships, passed through the gate and emerged into Nexus space.

Where the most epic firefight in recorded history was unfolding between Jemmin and the Vorr and Zeen battle fleets.

22

AN EPIC SHOWDOWN

Jenkins gingerly pushed his way onto the transport's bridge less than a minute before the ship transited into the Nexus system. Deep Currents accompanied him. The Vorr's enviropod had been given the run of the ship for the duration of the journey as a gesture of good faith by the Solarians. No one, including Deep Currents, spoke about where the Vorr had been after being captured by the Solarians. Deep Currents simply reappeared as if the Vorr had been there all along.

The transport moved steadily nearer to the inky surface of the event horizon, causing Jenkins' pucker factor to increase an order of magnitude, as usual for gate transit.

When the small ship emerged on the Nexus side of the gate, the transport's tactical plotters lit up like Christmas trees, doing little to alleviate Jenkins' anxiety.

"My God..." Colonel Moon breathed, his eyes wide. Jenkins and Xi looked on in silence at the unprecedented scale of the battle being waged.

Three thousand two hundred warships were engaged in two dozen distinct zones, each of which featured at least a hundred warships vying for dominance. The early returns showed that

Jemmin ships comprised roughly forty percent of the vessels present, with the rest split evenly between Vorr and Zeen forces.

It was borderline impossible to determine the total throw weight out there, but if Jenkins had to guess, he would have said that if you added up every Terran warship capable of moving under its own power, it wouldn't equal five percent of the fire-power deployed in the Nexus.

"All hands to battle stations," the ship's CO called, prompting Jenkins, Xi, and Moon to find the last three unoccu-pied couches on the bridge, where they quickly strapped in. Jenkins' eyes never wavered from the tactical plotter showing nearby space, where five hundred warships were engaged in three distinct battles.

One of those battles was in orbit of a planetoid that Jenkins had thought was still in the New America 2 system.

"The Zeen worldship?" Xi asked in surprise as the trio of grav-couches began to fill with the same shock-absorbing gel Terran ships used. In fact, the reason the Terrans were being conveyed via the thin-hulled civilian ship was that it was one of the few available craft outfitted with such grav-couches. Solar military craft required their crews to be heavily modified to permit greater flexibility during combat than would be possible with a human's natural physiology.

"You proceed on a false assumption, Captain Xi Bao," Deep Currents informed her as Jenkins put his couch's helmet on while the battle raged on the screen before them. "The Zeen have *three* worldships." Deep Currents' voice crackled in his helmet's earpieces after he had affixed it to his jaw-line.

Jenkins was uncertain how that particular revelation made him feel, but despite his sudden alarm at hearing the Zeen possessed more than one moon-sized battle-station, his attention remained fixed on the tactical readouts the ship's captain graciously forwarded to his helmet's HUD.

The Zeen ships, looking and moving unlike any spacefaring vessels Jenkins had seen prior to witnessing their devastating effectiveness in New America, tore into the Jemmin cruisers with volley after volley of missiles, though surprisingly (at least to Jenkins' mind) the Zeen seemed not to use their high-powered lasers as they had done against the Jemmin gate-crasher.

A formation of eight Jemmin cruisers squared off with twelve of their smaller, denser Vorr counterparts. Jemmin lasers lanced out, carving rents in the bulbous, round-hulled Vorr vessels. Liquid streamed from the Vorr ships' interiors, showing just how deeply the Jemmin weapons had struck.

In reply, the Vorr fired hyper-velocity missiles at the Jemmin warships. A combination of railgun and missile technology, Vorr hyper-velocity missiles were highly secretive weapons that Terran scientists had tried and failed to emulate for decades.

Each Vorr hyper-velocity missile (HVM) struck with a hundred kilotons of destructive force. Designed to penetrate even the thickest, strongest armor, the HVMs had little difficulty punching clean through the Jemmin hulls and sending cones of debris out the far side of the skewered targets.

Unfortunately, the HVMs seemed a little *too* effective at penetrating armor, since it looked to Jenkins as though more than half of their potential energy was wasted against the relatively light Jemmin warships. Piercing the Jemmin hulls, each HVM created a plume of energetic molten debris that stretched for kilometers.

The Jemmin warships seemed to pay no mind to the grievous wounds inflicted on their hulls, returning fire with mixed lasers and missiles. Two Vorr warships were bracketed in a textbook crossfire by the fleet Jemmin ships, and one of those Vorr ships suffered catastrophic drive failure.

Mere seconds after its engines shut down, the crippled Vorr exploded in a brilliant display, unlike anything Jenkins had seen. The fluid-filled interior of the Vorr warship, obeying the nearly-incomprehensible laws governing fluid dynamics in a near vacuum, propagated the ship's death throes in a visual display generally impossible in the void of space.

The near-freezing, highly-concentrated salt water required by Vorr physiology expanded in a perfect sphere as the ship that held it was annihilated by the energy released from its failed reactors. The sphere of fluid quickly turned to steam, then ice crystals that sparkled like a macabre display of fireworks before the glitter dissipated and was no longer visible to the naked eye.

As the Vorr warship died, the Solarian transport bearing the Metalheads lurched beneath Jenkins. The ship's CO took evasive action as the Solarian escort ships moved to an interdictory position between the transport and the nearest cluster of engaged Jemmin, Vorr and Zeen warships.

Her maneuvers came not a moment too soon.

Stabbing into the space where the transport had been a half-second earlier, a Jemmin laser beam swept mere meters from the transport's hull. Solarian void fighters scrambled immediately and moved to form a shield in front of the thin-hulled transport. Solar cruisers likewise moved to assume collision-close covering positions, but it would take them precious seconds to get into place.

Seconds it did not appear the Jemmin would grant them.

Another laser lanced across the transport's stern as the ship's pilot drove it toward their objective: the New America gate.

With chilling synchronicity, thirty-one Jemmin warships

spread across two separate nearby engagements turned toward the transport.

"Inbound missiles," the ship's CO barked. "Time to impact, fifteen seconds. All hands, brace for impact!"

Oh shit! Jenkins silently swore as the Jemmin warships turned their full attention on the Solar convoy. It was one thing to ride a mech into battle, even knowing that the enemy outnumbered you, since you always had the opportunity to fire back. Or, even better, to fire *first*.

But riding a grav-couch on a *civilian* Solarian ship afforded him no such opportunities. Like the helpless passenger he was, he could only look on and trust that the Solarians knew what they were doing. That hope did not grant him peace of mind. To survive one battle only to be killed in another—it was the warrior's way.

Laser beams carved into Solar cruisers and fighters alike, vaporizing the latter on contact and carving deep rents in the hulls of the former. Even in their deaths, the Solarian void fighters' debris served to block and refract a significant portion of the lasers' delivered energies.

But a weak strike on a thin-hulled ship like their transport was as bad as a direct hit on a heavily-armored warship.

The transport jerked violently beneath them, prompting the CO to call out with surprising calm, "Minor outgassing in Cargo Bay Two. Missile impact in six seconds. All hands, brace for impact! All hands, brace for impact!"

Jenkins gripped the couch's handrails as the shock-absorbing gel finally filled the compartment. The transport lurched to starboard and began a pitched, corkscrewing dive. According to the helmet's HUD, the ship pulled eight gees in that maneuver. Jenkins suspected the ship's pilot had blown a cargo bay full of gas to augment the redlined engines in creating the surprisingly effective, essentially unpredictable maneuver.

Explosions rocked the ship, but they were muted and indirect rather than direct hits.

"Outgassing in Green Four," the captain said calmly. "All personnel remain in your couches."

Solarian ships achieved the defensive shell surrounding the transport, and beam after beam carved into their armored hulls as they soaked up damage intended for the transport bearing the Metalheads. Jenkins knew that no matter how close those Solarian ships got, they could never provide full coverage. Seeming to read his thoughts, the Jemmin sent a swarm of missiles into a pair of Solarian cruisers, punching a handful of holes through each of the human warships.

The cruisers fell out of formation, and the remaining Solarian ships did what they could to close the breach. But as a fresh wave of missile and laser fire came from the Jemmin ships, Jenkins suspected they wouldn't even reach their journey's midway mark before succumbing to Jemmin fire.

Then, with a unity of purpose rarely seen in joint military exercises, nearly every Vorr and Zeen ship in nearby space moved to intercept those thirty-one Jemmin warships.

Three hundred nonhuman warships suddenly abandoned all concern for their own safety in an effort to safeguard the transport's journey back to Terran space. It was a humbling moment, but one which Jenkins was silently ashamed to realize was flavored with doubt regarding the Vorr and Zeen motives for such a seemingly selfless act.

A dozen Vorr and Zeen vessels quickly paid the ultimate price for their reorientation as their engines were expertly targeted by Jemmin fire in the seconds following the Vorr and Zeen course changes. Before those dozen nonhuman ships died, they sent a storm of ordnance at the offending Jemmin warships on an intercept course with the Solar convoy. Vorr and Zeen beams lanced out with precision, killing three Jemmin ships outright and badly damaging another two.

Vorr HVMs slammed into another four Jemmin warships, ignoring Jemmin counterfire and interceptor rockets as they tore through the void in pursuit of their targets. Zeen missiles flew in near-constant streams from their launchers, and while Jemmin counterfire sniped the majority of the inbound, the Zeen weapons that struck the mark did so with devastating effect. All told, the twelve Zeen and Vorr ships took eight of their Jemmin counterparts with them, and the twenty warships died within seconds of each other.

Then it was the rest of the three hundred warships' turn to deliver their sentiment to Jemmin.

Lasers carved into the twenty-three Jemmin warships still in pursuit of the Solarian convoy. From stem to stern, each of the Jemmin warships was sliced by at least a handful of sweeping laser beams. Like surgery conducted by psychopaths with chainsaws, the Vorr and Zeen seemed to revel in crisscrossing the Jemmin hulls with their direct energy weapons.

The Solarians added their fire to the exchange, sending railgun bolts and missiles toward their mutual enemy. The slow-moving weapons, while certainly less potent than those of the Vorr, Zeen, or Jemmin, were nonetheless devastating to already-damaged targets. And what the Solarian guns lacked in accuracy, they more than made up for in volume.

Five Jemmin warships suffered Solarian railgun strikes, with tungsten bolts piercing Jemmin hulls like nails through cardboard. Solarian fusion-powered warheads surged toward their beleaguered Jemmin targets, which intercepted all but a handful with precise counterfire long before they could impact.

But those that did reach their targets were devastating when fifty megaton warheads erupted at collision range or, in one instance, directly on a Jemmin hull.

Mini-novas of energy flared into being amid the Jemmin formations, and one by one the Jemmin ships were scrubbed from the local sector by Vorr, Zeen, and Solarian fire. Within seconds, the red specks disappeared, and the board showed green in their immediate sector.

The costs to Zeen, Vorr, and Solarian forces were high. Of the fifty warships originally tasked with escorting the transport to Terran space, only thirty-two remained. And of the three hundred Vorr and Zeen ships that had moved to intercept the Jemmin before they could kill the convoy, eighty-seven had been destroyed or crippled for their efforts.

"I hope," Deep Currents' synthesized feminine voice came over Jenkins' earpieces, "that this display of solidarity will alleviate some significant measure of the concern your people harbor regarding Vorr and Zeen intentions."

As the firefight raged for control of Nexus-linked space, with warships dying every few seconds as the engagements quickly grew farther and farther apart and the intensity rapidly dropping off as a result, Jenkins gave the only reply he knew was both the truth and the political one to give.

"So do I."

"On behalf of my people," the Vorr delegate said, "I would like to extend a formal invitation for Sol to join the Vorr-Zeen-Terran alliance."

"I can't speak for Sol, Ambassador," the ship's captain replied, "but I can say it's in my peoples' best interests to secure allies at times like this, and also that it's safe to assume we can remove the Jemmin as a potential ally given what we've learned and how they've conducted themselves here."

"Your hesitance is understandable," Deep Currents replied serenely. "Zeen Home Two, as they refer to the worldship now stationed near the gates shared by the Terran Republic and the Arh'Kel, has already secured its local space and will provide ongoing protection against Jemmin hostilities. Sol's gates are adjacent to Vorr and Finjou gates, which will require significantly greater effort to secure for obvious reasons. During this interval, Solar humanity should refrain from transit to and from the Nexus," the Vorr said in what sounded dangerously close to an order, causing Jenkins' jaw to set. "Nexus travel is too dangerous to be conducted as long as Jemmin forces maintain an antagonistic posture."

"You sound confident that the Vorr can deal with the Jemmin here," the captain challenged.

"We would not have instigated this conflict if we were uncertain of victory, Captain," Deep Currents replied with her trademark poise. "Alone, none of us can destroy Jemmin, but together we believe it is possible to do just that. Vorr and Zeen forces are more than capable of driving Jemmin from the Nexus, and that is precisely what we will do. We suggest, for your own safety, that you grant us the opportunity to complete that important task before joint operations can commence in whatever mutually agreeable capacity our species devise. We suggest you remain in your home systems until we have secured the Nexus."

Jenkins finally gave voice to his concern. "That sounds like a warning, Deep Currents."

"Then my translators are functioning as desired," the Vorr replied simply. "This war will require maximum efficiency from all involved parties. The Terran Republic has played an instrumental role in depriving Jemmin of its ability to manipulate younger races in furtherance of its agenda. Humanity will be significant in this war, but for now, your sacrifices are unnecessary. We will repel Jemmin, secure the Nexus, and then treat with your respective governments regarding future operations."

Jenkins didn't like it, but there wasn't a damned thing he could do about it. Dealing with the Vorr was well above his paygrade, so rather than sticking his foot in his mouth, he replied, "I'll relay your message to my superiors."

"Excellent," Deep Currents replied, her voice filled with satisfaction.

The hours ticked by as the Solarian convoy escaped the embattled space surrounding the Solar gates. The Terran and Arh'Kel gates were situated on the far side of the gas giant that served to anchor more than half the Nexus gates. The Solarian, Vorr, and Finjou gates stood opposite, a long transit apart.

The journey was remarkably uneventful, although Jenkins' eyes never wavered from the limited tactical display that showed the intensity of the firefights had died to a tiny fraction of the raging inferno that had greeted the Solarian convoy.

It seemed that the Vorr had timed the intense exchange specifically to cover the Solarian convoy's arrival. Although Jemmin wanted to destroy Jenkins' people before they could return to Terran space, it was equally focused on causing as much damage to the Vorr and Zeen forces as possible.

To Jenkins, that meant Jemmin was scared. Or, at the very least, not confident of victory against the combined Vorr-Zeen fleets.

As far as Jenkins was concerned, a healthy dose of fear was well-warranted after the fierce display put on by the Vorr and the Zeen.

Upon reaching the gate, Jem transmitted the same code used to unlock the Solarian gates.

But this time, traveling at the speed of light, the signal didn't unlock one gate. It unlocked *every* gate in the Nexus.

The terminus gates one step removed from the Nexus would remain shut down until Jem's code was locally transmitted to them. But like ripples on a pond spreading out from the transport's position, the Nexus wormhole gates flickered back to life one by one until they were all reactivated.

It was a development that distressed the Jemmin forces in-system. They started to fly erratically, repositioning for the expected arrival of more enemies.

Twenty minutes later, the Solar convoy moved through the gate while transmitting command codes possessed by every single Terran officer aboard the thin-hulled transport.

Fortunately, Admiral Wallace accepted the credentials instead of immediately opening fire as he had done to the Jemmin gate-crasher.

Breathing a sigh of relief, Jenkins allowed himself a few moments to collect his thoughts. It was over. They were back in Terran space.

"Now the easiest part of the whole op." He grunted, surprised to find himself believing the words as the gel inside his grav-couch slowly began to drain away. "The court-martial."

23

THE COURT-MARTIAL

"For a variety of reasons vital to the security of the Terran Republic, these normally closed-door proceedings will include a number of civilian and foreign representatives as both contributors and observers," Admiral Zhao declared to the assembled throng inside the courtroom. "But let me make myself clear: this court-martial has been convened in accordance with Terran Armed Forces regulations, and as its officiator, I will demand a certain degree of decorum in my courtroom. Now, let's be seated." Admiral Zhao's iron-hard voice cast a pall over the room as he assumed the central chair on the bench, prompting the officers flanking him to do likewise before the assembled crowd followed suit.

Jenkins and Xi exchanged brief, meaningful looks as they stood side by side before the court. It wasn't unheard of for officers to be tried simultaneously but, given the nature of the charges, Jenkins was surprised they had opted to address them jointly. Jenkins' gaze flicked to the lone empty chair on the bench. Of well-worn brown leather, with gold fittings and trim, it loomed over the proceedings like an absent parent at the dinner table.

General Akinouye's chair, Jenkins thought, feeling equal measures of pride and loss as he imagined the old man once again filling the gaping void he had left behind.

Admiral Zhao followed Jenkins' gaze and nodded approvingly. "Honor. Duty. Tradition. These words might not mean much to some, but to me, they are as vital as the air we breathe. Normally every seat on this court would be occupied by a representative from one of the Terran Armed Forces' branches, but one chair remains empty." He looked over at Akinouye's vacant chair, emphatically pausing and causing all eyes to rest upon the vacant leather seat. "Recent events have conspired to prevent one of the Republic's longest-serving branches from being formally represented at these proceedings. We will discuss those events," he said, his gaze lingering on Jenkins with the weight of a neutron star, "since they have a direct bearing on the purpose of these proceedings." He raised his voice commandingly. "Lieutenant Colonel Lee Jenkins and Captain Xi Bao have been brought before this court on charges of sedition, mutiny, dereliction of duty, willful disobedience of lawful orders, unauthorized deployment of Terran military assets in foreign space, and last, but certainly not least," he smirked, "high treason. Do you understand the nature of these charges, Colonel?"

"I do, sir," Jenkins replied firmly as all eyes swiveled in his direction.

Zhao turned his piercing gaze on Xi. "Do you understand the nature of these charges, Captain?"

"I do, Admiral," she replied unflinchingly.

"Do either of you dispute, in principle, the validity of these charges?" Zhao pressed.

Jenkins and Xi remained at stiff-spined attention while simultaneously replying, "No, sir."

"Then let's begin." Admiral Zhao gestured for them to be

seated. For a moment, all Jenkins could focus on was the spindly silver microphone before him, which seemed so very much at odds with the warm, dark-wood panels of the courtroom's interior. "Colonel Jenkins, without going into sensitive operational details, can you provide this court with a brief summary of Operation Antivenom's objectives?"

Jenkins leaned fractionally forward. "Operation Antivenom was a covert mission with the objective of deploying a virtual weapon developed by Armor Corps personnel under the direction of General Benjamin Akinouye. The purpose of the weapon was to neutralize an ongoing Jemmin infiltration of the Solar One Mind network."

"We have received sworn statements, along with substantial material evidence, from both Terran and Solar sources," Zhao gestured to the back of the room, where the Solarian delegation looked on with apparent impassivity, "corroborating that this was indeed the stated objective of Operation Antivenom. Who authorized Operation Antivenom?"

"General Akinouye was the operation's author, Admiral," Jenkins replied truthfully.

"General Benjamin Akinouye," Admiral Zhao said matter of factly, "was the ranking member of the Terran Armor Corps branch of the Terran Armed Forces, and one of the longest-serving officers this Republic has had the privilege of fielding. He had previously held the posts of Field Marshal and Grand Commander Terran Ground Forces. As such, he was afforded certain authority and latitude shared by only a handful of TAF personnel. The most relevant of these was the ability to conduct compartmentalized covert operations under his sole authority if those operations were deemed of paramount importance to Terran security. Was Operation Antivenom conducted under such authority, Colonel Jenkins?"

"Yes, sir," Jenkins acknowledged. "Operation Antivenom,

and its predecessors Operation Brick Top and Operation Shiva's Wrath, unofficially referred to as Operation Frozen Fire, were all conducted under General Akinouye's Code Black authority."

"Without going into details, were Operations Shiva's Wrath, Brick Top, and Antivenom directly related to one another?" Zhao asked.

"Yes, sir," Jenkins stated. "General Akinouye determined that each of these operations was essential to the others."

"Who else knew this operation's most sensitive details?" The admiral leaned forward, lacing his fingers together as a predatory glint flickered across his eyes.

"To my knowledge, General Mikhail Pushkin was apprised of every operational detail, as were Colonel Li, the *Dietrich Bonhoeffer*'s commanding officer, Colonel Moon, the *Bonhoeffer's* Commander Intercept Group, my XO, Captain Xi Bao," he gestured to Xi beside him, "and Chief Warrant Officer 4th Class Styles, my command's intelligence officer."

"Did you forget to mention Major General Kavanaugh, Colonel Jenkins?" Zhao arched a brow challengingly.

"No, sir." Jenkins shook his head firmly. "Major General Kavanaugh was not apprised of every operational detail, Admiral."

"Why not?" Zhao demanded coolly.

Jenkins hesitated. "I cannot comment on why General Akinouye chose not to include her in the entirety of the operation's planning phases."

"Do I have the wrong man sitting in front of me, Colonel Jenkins?" Zhao smirked. "Or are you tongue-tied from of a sense of misguided intra-branch loyalty?"

"General Akinouye made the decision who to include and who to exclude, Admiral Zhao," Jenkins explained, feeling his ears begin to burn as the admiral's confrontational style breached the thin veneer of his polished surface. "He never apprised me why he didn't include Major General Kavanaugh."

"Do you consider it possible that you, Lieutenant Colonel Jenkins, were also kept in the dark as to certain operational details regarding Antivenom's true purpose?" Zhao asked with icy disdain.

"I do, Admiral," Jenkins agreed.

"Do you also consider it possible, Colonel Jenkins," Zhao continued fiercely, "that General Akinouye's true purpose might not have been the same one he stated to you?"

"I do, Admiral." Jenkins nodded firmly.

"Do you therefore consider it possible, Colonel Jenkins, that Operation Antivenom's ultimate goal might have aligned with what some might call a 'vast Jemmin conspiracy,'" Zhao sneered contemptuously, "with the true aim of not helping humanity but of harming it?"

"I do, sir."

"Was there anything irrefutable in the collection of evidence you gathered prior to completing Operation Antivenom," Zhao pressed, "that demonstrated to your satisfaction that this was an operation that featured no tactically-significant outcome sets that might cause more harm to the Terran Republic—or, indeed, to the entire human race—than good?"

"No, sir." Jenkins shook his head, successfully fighting the urge to wince under the full fury of Zhao's inquiry.

Admiral Zhao leaned back triumphantly in his chair. "You have previously acknowledged the substantive validity of the charges brought against you—charges that carry the most severe penalties in the Terran Republic's legal codices—and now you admit that you weren't even sure that what you were doing would do more good than harm. Is that a fair characterization of your replies thus far, Lieutenant Colonel Jenkins?"

Jenkins almost felt Xi stiffen at his side, causing him to flick a sidelong glance in her direction in the hope that he could calm her down. The last thing he needed was for his hot-tempered XO to mouth off in front of the court.

Fortunately, she relaxed, and he returned his attention to Admiral Zhao. "Yes, Admiral, that would be a fair characterization of my verbal remarks in these proceedings."

"Then what in the name of God Almighty," Zhao thundered, filling the room with his roaring voice, "were you people doing making secret deals with *these* aliens?" He flicked a hand in the direction of the Vorr trio. "Fighting *obviously* unnecessary wars with *those* aliens." He gestured to the lone Finjou in the courtroom. "And then stealing Terran military assets under Candlelight conditions, which you used to besiege the most heavily-fortified military installation in *human* territory before attacking what is *easily* the most important virtual network in the history of our species!"

This was the moment. Jenkins had the chance to speak in his own defense, to plead his case to the court and the Terran people. An ambitious officer in Jenkins' position would have used the moment to grandstand, to make a passionate plea that might one day be featured in schoolbooks as an inspirational patriotic touchstone.

But Jenkins was not ambitious. Not anymore. Frankly, he was tired.

"The simplest answer I can provide, Admiral Zhao," Jenkins said, knowing that his next words might well damn him while possibly sparing those under his command, "is that I was following orders."

Xi recoiled in shock at his side, and a murmur filled the courtroom. Zhao's eyes narrowed dangerously.

"Say that again, Colonel." Zhao's voice was low and menacing.

"I was following orders, sir," Jenkins reiterated unrepentantly. "As were the men and women who carried out Operation Antivenom."

"I sincerely hope you don't intend to leave it at that, Lieutenant Colonel Jenkins," Zhao growled.

Xi shot Jenkins a furious look, and before he could try to calm her down, she turned in her chair to address the court. "Operation Antivenom was one hundred percent voluntary, Admiral Zhao. None of us were *following orders*." She glared at Jenkins. "To suggest we were is not only inaccurate, but it's also insulting."

"Captain Xi," Zhao sliced a penetrating look in the young woman's direction, "perhaps you're unfamiliar with the decorum I referenced earlier. Put simply, and in a manner you're more likely to understand, you will not speak unless spoken to."

"Admiral." Xi jutted her chin defiantly. "Not *one* of the men and women we recruited for Operation Antivenom turned down the chance to contribute to the mission, sir. We did the right thing, Admiral Zhao," she declared with conviction, "and I defy anyone on this court, in this room, or watching a 'cast to honestly claim they would have done differently under the circumstances."

Zhao leaned forward, his eyes blazing furiously. "If you sincerely thought that, Captain Xi, then why didn't you request assistance for this vital mission? Are you truly that arrogant, or are you just *stupid* enough to think it was appropriate to pin humanity's future on one battered warship and two mixed companies of armor? Which are you, Captain? Arrogant or stupid?"

Jenkins knew that Xi's tongue could dig not only her but the entire Legion a hole so deep they'd never escape it. He was ready, willing, and eager to take the heat for Antivenom if it meant the Legion could carry on its work after he was gone, but

Xi was a vital part of the Legion's future, so despite his personal preferences, he jumped in to give her some cover.

"When I said I was following orders, Admiral Zhao," Jenkins cut in, placing his hand on Xi's arm and gripping it to keep her from shrugging him off, "and that the people who followed me on Antivenom were also following orders, I meant it. But what I *didn't* say, which I think might have caused some confusion," he sent a hard look in Xi's direction, causing the fiery woman to lean fractionally back in her seat in deference, "is that I *believed* in the validity of those orders. It is my opinion that Captain Xi and the rest of Antivenom's personnel also believed in the importance of the mission." Xi nodded sharply, mercifully keeping her mouth shut as he continued, "In many respects, General Akinouye *was* the Terran Armor Corps. His peerless lifetime of service had seen him achieve victory in dozens of major engagements, some on the battlefield and some in courtrooms like this one." Jenkins gestured to the warm, wooden panels surrounding them.

"I'm not his equal, sir, and I never will be," Jenkins said, knowing beyond the shadow of a doubt that those words were true. "His death during Operation Brick Top created not only a void in Armor Corps' leadership but also uncertainty among the personnel charged with carrying out the general's secret mission. Ultimately, I decided that second-guessing one of the most decorated and valiant warriors in the Terran Armed Forces, one who served with the Joint Chiefs for longer than any officer in human history, was... Well," he quirked a lopsided grin, "it was above my paygrade, and unlikely to result in a net gain for Armor Corps specifically or humanity in general."

Zhao's piercing gaze snapped between Jenkins and Xi for several seconds before the admiral sat back in his chair. "You sound as though you disapprove of Major General Kavanaugh's decision to break the veil of compartmentalization for General Akinouye's clandestine operations."

Jenkins shook his head, deciding to skirt the fine line between half-truth and lie. "I was unaware of Major General Kavanaugh's decision to—"

"Stop right there, Colonel," Zhao interrupted. "Do you dispute that you sent Captain Chao Yun, who was assigned to the same Terra Han Colonial Guard unit that supported Operation Brick Top, to convey a clandestine message to one of the members of this court shortly before the Republic fell under Candlelight conditions?"

Jenkins hesitated. "No, Admiral, I do not dispute that."

"Who was that message's intended recipient?" Zhao asked coldly.

"You were, Admiral Zhao."

The hiss of whispers once again filled the courtroom, but Zhao ignored them as he continued. "Have you and I had any contact, direct or otherwise, since your return to Terran space, including in the lead-up to these proceedings?" the admiral pressed as the eyes of his fellow court members turned in his direction with muted surprise.

"No, Admiral, we have not." Jenkins shook his head adamantly.

"What was the substance of the message you conveyed to me via Captain Chao?" the admiral asked.

"I suggested to Captain Chao that my hand-picked Antivenom team was about to undertake a mission of vital importance to both Terran and Solar humanity," Jenkins explained, surprised at this latest turn in the inquest. "I also suggested that, as your son, he was uniquely positioned to deliver a message to you that would not be intercepted en route. That message regarded operational security concerns for Antivenom, specifically concerns related to Major General

Kavanaugh's possible declassification of Antivenom's details in an effort to increase inter-branch cooperation between Armor Corps and Fleet."

"You put it more diplomatically than I would have." Zhao snorted. "She was looking to roll Armor Corps into Fleet, just as you suggested over two years ago when you proposed the formation of a Combined Arms sub-branch of the Terran Fleet, and she thought she could curry favor with Fleet brass by opening Armor Corps' books to outside review. Does my version conflict with your understanding of the situation, Colonel?"

Jenkins winced. "No, sir. There are no contradictions."

"By doing so," Admiral Zhao continued, "she violated not just operational security, but also the chain of command by, in your words, 'second-guessing' General Akinouye while his funeral pyre's coals were still warm."

"It is not my opinion, Admiral Zhao," Jenkins objected, "that Major General Kavanaugh was knowingly violating operational integrity, nor do I think her vision for Armor Corps' induction into Fleet was sub-optimal. As you said, I pitched my experimental program to the Admiralty with precisely such an outcome in mind. I'll admit that my perspective has evolved since transferring out of Fleet and into Armor Corps, but I still firmly believe that providing tactical support in joint operations with Fleet elements, and even with other TAF branches, is the future of the Terran Armor Corps."

"Your loyalty to both General Akinouye and Major General Kavanaugh is noted, Colonel Jenkins," Zhao said smugly. "But, to be frank, the issues surrounding Major General Kavanaugh's case are..." his lips twisted into a smirk, "*well* above your paygrade. Still, since my current duties include serving in an advisory capacity to the Terran Armor Corps during this period of unprecedented transition, I can assure you that your remarks here will be given consideration during the formal review of Major General Kavanaugh's case."

"Thank you, Admiral Zhao," Jenkins said, surprised to hear those four words pass his lips.

"This court has reviewed the evidence," Zhao gestured to a stack of papers, flimsies, and data slates neatly arranged before the panel, "and has heard your testimonies here today. Do you have anything to add before we adjourn for final deliberation?"

"No, sir," Jenkins said, looking pointedly at Captain Xi, who shook her head in agreement.

"No, Admiral," Xi belatedly replied.

"Then the court is adjourned," Zhao declared, standing from his chair before sweeping the chamber with his iron-hard eyes and confidently adding, "This won't take long."

The court's members filed out of the room, causing a cacophony of commentary to erupt behind them. Jenkins turned in his chair to see hundreds of eyes looking at him, but Xi kept her back to the seated audience behind them.

"I'm sorry, Colonel—" she began to apologize.

"You did fine, Xi," he interrupted. "Zhao's an asshole, but he's also the most principled officer in the Fleet."

She gave him an incredulous look. "You sound like you admire him."

"I do," Jenkins replied solemnly. "There was a time when I looked up to that man like no other and modeled as much of my life after his as possible." He chuckled before adding, "Then I met General Akinouye."

"I don't think the feeling's mutual, sir," Xi muttered, sparing a glance over her shoulder and immediately turning back to face the empty bench. "If I had to bet the reactor, I'd say he's convincing the court to send us to the chopping block."

"You're probably right," Jenkins agreed. "What we did can't be forgiven. Even if the Solarians agree almost to the last man, woman, and child that Antivenom was warranted, we broke too many Terran laws...not to mention taking the *Bonhoeffer* and all of its attached assets." He shook his head gravely. "No military structure can persist without discipline, and we broke just about every rule in the book to carry out Antivenom. If they *don't* cut our heads off for this, they're inviting chaos into the ranks. Every jackass who thinks he knows best will hare off for some stupid reason or another... The Terran Armed Forces are too important. Too vital to the Republic's security. We *have* to go to the chopping block, but it's no worse than what ninety-four of our Metalheads suffered on Luna."

"Metal never dies," Xi intoned reverently.

Knowing he could not top that, Jenkins sat in silence at Xi's side. Ambivalent waves of pride and regret warred within him. Pride at what they had accomplished. Pride at seeing Xi Bao rise to the challenges put before her, just as the rest of the Metal Legion's people had done alongside Jenkins. Regret that they might not have done enough to safeguard the lives of their fellow Metalheads. Regret that he might have been too reckless, too aggressive, and that his recklessness might have cost unnecessary lives.

He could think of a dozen different choices he had made on Luna that had cost good men and women their lives. He knew beyond the shadow of a doubt that he was directly responsible for their deaths.

And the worst part was that he would do it all again.

He couldn't even have the common human decency to condemn himself in the silent space between his ears. And in a very meaningful, albeit narrow way, he *almost* hoped Admiral Zhao would order justice delivered via a firing squad.

Almost.

Eight minutes after they had closed, the doors to the deliberation chamber reopened, prompting everyone in the room to stand as the members of the court wordlessly returned to their seats. A pin drop would have been deafening in those seconds as the assemblage collectively leaned forward in anticipation. After the court's members were seated, Jenkins' eyes snagged once again on the lone empty chair on the bench.

General Akinouye's chair.

"Let's cut straight to it." Admiral Zhao declared as Jenkins and Xi stood at rigid attention. "Colonel Jenkins, Captain Xi, the evidence is overwhelmingly against you, and you may be dismayed to learn that this court is in unanimous agreement on all charges brought against you. You appropriated Terran military assets without authorization, including a Behemoth-class assault carrier, twenty void fighters, and two full companies of mechanized armor. You did, in fact, conduct secret negotiations with not just one but *three* nonhuman species with the intention of gaining their overt or tacit support for a mission so far-reaching and potentially self-destructive that all of humanity would be affected by its outcome. You disobeyed direct orders from a flag officer under Candlelight conditions and even ignored the chain of command within your own branch. You attacked and killed, without provocation and without a single attempt to reach a peaceful resolution, hundreds of Solar Marines and spacers. You violated the integrity of the One Mind network using a method whose reliability you admit you weren't convinced of. Do either of you dispute *any* of this?"

"No, Admiral," they replied in perfect unison.

"Then, before I deliver this court's judgment," Zhao said smugly, "I'd like to make a few comments. The first is of a personal nature, which I hope this court will indulge me in making." He looked up and down the bench, receiving muted nods of approval from his fellows.

"It may not be abundantly clear, but I'm not the easiest man to get along with," Zhao began, drawing soft snickers from the rear of the courtroom. "In fact, I've only ever called three people 'friend' in my entire life. First among these was my late wife, Melissa, who somehow managed to survive forty-two years of marriage to me before her beautiful heart gave out. Next is my son, who I still consider a friend even though we have more than the usual quotient of father-son disagreements, one of which saw him formally change his name." He snorted, drawing another round of snickers from the back of the room. "The third," Zhao finished, to the apparent surprise of everyone in the courtroom, most notably Colonel Jenkins and Captain Xi, "was Ben Akinouye."

Whispers hissed through the softly-lit chamber, and Jenkins and Xi exchanged looks of surprise. Zhao graciously allowed the chatter to persist for a few seconds before leaning forward in his chair and continuing.

"I've been told that I have a certain...*effect* on a room whenever I enter it," Admiral Zhao said with a bemused smirk. "And I won't argue with that observation, but I do understand the nature of that effect. The rank insignia is responsible for most of it, the uniform it's pinned to accounts for a little more, and the person wearing the uniform sometimes, although rarely, manages to do more than just fill that uniform out—and I'm not talking about a bulging midsection."

Nervous laughter briefly filled the room, but a stern look from Zhao silenced it.

"On Benjamin Akinouye, the insignia and uniform were like license plates on a car. They were afterthoughts or, at most, embellishments on something that required none. When Ben would walk into a room, it didn't matter who was in it," the admiral continued. "It didn't matter what insignia they wore, what office they held, or how successful they thought they were at whatever they did. One look at him could make even me feel small and insignificant. And I can assure you that the rest of my panelists reacted the exact same way to his presence."

The court's members nodded in genuine and unanimous approval.

"So when I learned that General Benjamin Akinouye had fallen in the line of duty, I knew that one of humanity's brightest stars had gone out and that we would never recover from his loss. Shortly after learning of my friend's death, the wormholes went dark, and I received a full and uncensored mission profile for Operation Antivenom, sent by Colonel Lee Jenkins and delivered by my once-estranged son," Zhao continued heavily. "Ben was a hothead. A maverick. Even a rebel." The admiral chuckled. "But despite his obvious flaws, which he wore like badges of honor instead of hiding behind an insincere veneer, I would *never* second-guess that man's strategic judgment."

In the hours and days since returning to New America, the bulk of which Jenkins had spent in a prison cell awaiting this court-martial, Jenkins had never once thought that Admiral Zhao would sound sympathetic to the Legion's cause. Forgetting the fact that he had been completely unaware of a personal relationship between Zhao and Akinouye, Jenkins' read of the admiral had led him to believe that Zhao would push as hard as he could in pursuit of justice.

But instead, it sounded like Zhao was about to unleash the biggest surprise of Jenkins' life.

"You were in an impossible situation, Colonel Jenkins and Captain Xi," Zhao said with overt sympathy, which marked the very first time in Jenkins' dealings with the man that he had manifested such emotions. "Never before in human history has so much responsibility been shouldered by so few people. And despite your charitable appraisal, Captain," he added with a pointed look in Xi's direction, "I'm not convinced that everyone on this court would have done as you did. I like to *think* we would have, but a lifetime of hard-earned experience has taught me to temper my optimism when it comes to certain facets of human nature."

Heads bobbed grimly up and down the court, surprising Jenkins and Xi as they exchanged looks of poorly-veiled bewilderment.

"The Terran Armed Forces employs a command structure," Admiral Zhao continued in a raised voice as whispers throughout the courtroom rose well above a low murmur, "that affords certain degrees of latitude and operational command authority to be vested in its officers throughout the chain of command. Those officers are selected by men and women like us," Zhao gestured to his fellow jurors, "after they have displayed their merits to their superiors. Some of those merits are technical in nature, some are social, and some are tactical, but chief among them is the ability to make hard calls in difficult situations. That's precisely what the Metal Legion did under General Benjamin Akinouye's...*unique* brand of leadership." He grinned. "And it's what I expect his beloved Legion to continue doing long after we've given him a proper send-off. There are some who will say that Operation Antivenom was an example of a good outcome despite a bad process. They'll say that the chain of command was violated by insubordinate officers, and they'd be partly right. They'll say that maintaining operational security was given dangerously high priority by those officers, and they'd be partly right about that, too. And they'll say that a more rigid system with increased transparency would have prevented the possibility of Antivenom resulting in accidental catastrophe, however well-intentioned that catastrophe's operational commanders might have been. And I'd say," Zhao silenced the room with a sharp increase in his volume, "that those people don't belong anywhere near the Terran Armed Forces."

A cheer arose from the back of the room, surprisingly bolstered by the Solarian delegation, and despite Zhao's deepening scowl, that cheer persisted for several seconds after the admiral stood from his chair. Putting his knuckles down on the bench, he glared at the assemblage and, fortunately for all involved, the cheers quickly subsided.

"As a military organization and as a society," Zhao continued, now speaking more to the crowd and the cameras than to Jenkins and Xi, "we recognized the merits of General Benjamin Akinouye, and we rewarded those merits with latitude and authority rarely vested in individual humans. It is my opinion that he correctly used those privileges on behalf of not only Terra, but also of Sol, and, I sincerely believe, on behalf of races like the Vorr and Finjou. And the two Metalheads now standing before this court, who were once General Akinouye's pupils, are among the finest examples of the Terran Armed Forces' proud legacy of honor, duty, and tradition I've ever had the pleasure and privilege of addressing." Jenkins and Xi both went slack-jawed as Admiral Zhao gestured to the ranking officers flanking him on the court, "I'm content to let my fellow jurors deliver our official verdict now. On the charges brought against Lieutenant Colonel Lee Jenkins and Captain Xi Bao, charges for which they have offered no substantive or stylistic defense, how do you find the accused?"

With a unified voice that echoed across the entire Terran Republic, the court loudly declared...

"Not guilty."

24

A NEW DIRECTION

"Colonel Jenkins," General Pushkin greeted Lee in his thick, Slavic accent. He proffered a hand as soon as Jenkins and Xi stepped through the doors of the Terran Armor Corps HQ. "Outstanding work."

Jenkins took Pushkin's hand before the general turned to Xi and shook her hand as well.

"I'm glad to see you back in public, General," Jenkins said with feeling.

"It was a nasty bit of business with Major General Kavanaugh," Pushkin replied dismissively. "But I knew you would prove Ben's faith in your team was well-founded. He saw something in you that he once told me reminded him of himself. A much younger version, of course." He chuckled.

"What's going to happen to Kavanaugh?" Jenkins pressed as the trio made their way toward HQ's central, hallowed chambers.

"It is out of my hands." Pushkin shrugged. "I made my recommendations, but Admiral Zhao is right. The public and the bureaucrats are out for blood, and Kavanaugh pushed too hard in the wrong direction. She knew the risks of her attempted coup, and while I don't think she should spend the rest of her days in a cell, I do think that her time in brown and black should come to an end," he said with finality, referring to the Corps' traditional colors.

"That's unfortunate," Jenkins said grimly. "General Akinouye entrusted her with a tremendous amount of the Legion's administrative work. Her absence will be difficult to overcome."

"No, it will not be difficult," Pushkin said sourly. "It will be *impossible*. With so many plates spinning in the air some are bound to crash, but we'll pick up the pieces as best we can and get back on track one way or another."

"What about the advisory board?" Xi asked. "Are Admirals Corbyn and Zhao staying on to oversee the Legion's restructuring?"

"Admiral Corbyn has recused himself, and Colonel Moon has temporarily replaced him on both the advisory board and as an acting member of the Legion's leadership." Pushkin smirked as they made their way to one of the longest hallways in the facility, which stretched for nearly half a kilometer and connected five separate sub-sections of the Legion's HQ. "I think that with your official court-martial in the rearview, the 'unofficial' probes into Fleet and government personnel will commence as the depths of Jemmin influence are investigated. Many careers are about to end, and the Metal Legion's list of political enemies is about to get much, much longer as a result."

"You don't think Corbyn was working with the Jemmin, do you?" Xi asked in shock.

"Of course not," Pushkin said dismissively. "Neither was Kavanaugh, but each of them represented potential failure points in the system which, given the circumstances, must be addressed with brutal finality. I don't think Kavanaugh's career will survive the inquest, but Corbyn should be back in command after a brief respite similar to the one I recently enjoyed," he added with a wan smile that made clear he had not, in fact, 'enjoyed' his house arrest.

"What about the Fleet-Legion merger?" Jenkins pressed.

"On indefinite hold." Pushkin grinned. "I have opened lines of dialogue with several key Fleet personnel, but nothing has come of it yet. I think they're still a little bitter about not being given a seat at Antivenom's table."

"So we're without transport." Jenkins grunted. "Which leaves us on the sidelines while the biggest war in Nexus history rages across the wormholes."

"Come now, Colonel." Pushkin put a dramatic hand over his heart and feigned disappointment as they reached the Legion's main conference room doors. "I may not be General Akinouye, but it is deeply hurtful to find that you think so little of me."

Jenkins, wrongfooted by Pushkin's banter, moved silently through the doors after the general opened them to reveal a small gathering already seated at the theater's main conference table.

"You already know Admiral Zhao." Pushkin gestured to the fierce-browed Fleet officer. "And his son, Captain Chao, along with Captain Guan of the *Red Hare*."

Jenkins and Xi moved to an indicated pair of chairs opposite those occupied by Zhao, Chao, and Guan, while Pushkin assumed his rightful place at the table's head. Beside Jenkins was Colonel Moon, who shook Jenkins' hand as soon as he arrived at his suggestively-angled seat.

"Yes," Jenkins agreed after shaking Moon's hand and making meaningful eye contact with the trio across the table. "In one form or another, we've been through life and death together."

"Well said," Admiral Zhao stated. "We'll make this short:

Fleet's not going to be available to taxi Legion assets for the fore-seeable future. We've got enough problems dealing with potential moles and security leaks, and like it or not, the firefight in the Nexus worlds is out of our league. We don't have the assets to spare."

"Which is why," Captain Guan interjected, confidently stroking his thigh-length beard, "after speaking with General Pushkin, my government has renewed its offer of material support. The *Red Hare* is at your immediate and ongoing disposal, although I fear it is the only drop-capable warship Terra Han can spare."

"Not just the *Red Hare*..." Pushkin grinned knowingly.

"Certainly not." Captain Guan seemed offended at the general's suggestion. "Lotus, Orchid, and Clover battalions, each at full strength, are now Armor Corps assets."

Jenkins' brow shot up in surprise, and a savage grin spread across Xi's lips that seemed to infect everyone except Admiral Zhao. "That's...outstanding," Jenkins allowed. "What's the catch?"

"No catch." Pushkin waved dismissively. "There were some...administrative details to work out, but we came to a productive and mutually beneficial agreement."

Jenkins smirked. "Terra Han still wants operational oversight."

"Which they are now fully aware they will not receive," Pushkin said matter of factly, drawing an approving nod from both Chao and Guan. "They will, however, retain tactical command of their assets, as well as direct rank transfers from the Terra Han Colonial Guard. It was a concession," Pushkin shrugged, "but one we were happy to make."

Jenkins' mind raced at the implications of that last bit as Admiral Zhao intently studied him. Jenkins knew that the rank transfers would inject captains, majors, and possibly even colonels into the Terran Armor Corps leadership. Viewed uncharitably, the rank issue could be seen as a not-so-subtle takeover attempt aimed at the Metal Legion's suddenly leadership vacuum. Even charitably, the transfers created serious administrative concerns he suspected would fill his coming days and weeks as he scrambled to come up with creative ways to retain local control of the Terran Armor Corps.

"On that front," Admiral Zhao said, seemingly satisfied by whatever he saw during Jenkins' silent contemplation, "we've drawn up a fresh round of promotions that require your approval to push through. The timing of some of these will raise eyebrows, and possibly even cause legitimate trouble within the Metal Legion's hierarchy, but the training wheels are now off for you people. It's time to step up and fill Ben's shoes or get out of the way so someone else can."

Jenkins accepted a data slate that Captain Chao slid across for his father, and after scanning it, he found himself nodding along in approval until reaching the final item on the list. "I can't—"

"You can and you will," Zhao barked unyieldingly, "because you must."

Jenkins wanted to object, but he couldn't argue with a single promotion's value to the Legion's framework going forward. Still, he thought he needed to make himself perfectly clear on one point in particular. "I didn't do any of this for personal gain. I did it because it needed to be done."

"Which is why you must accept the promotion to full colonel," Pushkin soothed. "And why Captain Xi must accept the promotion to major. You two are the new faces of the Terran Armor Corps, but the Legion doesn't just need a few pretty faces for the recruitment drives." He snorted. "It needs battle-experienced veterans with hard heads, and yours are as hard as any in the Metal Legion's history."

"In addition to the Terra Han Razorbacks," Colonel Moon interjected, "the rest of the assets you pulled together during your latest fundraising drive have arrived or are scheduled to within the week. Combined with vehicles already in the pipeline and in various states of repair, the Metal Legion now has *two* full brigades," he held up a pair of fingers, "of mechs on the roster. Given six weeks of TLC under the Legion's suddenly-swollen roster of would-be Wrenches and Monkeys, every one of them will be ready to drop."

Jenkins was pleasantly surprised to hear about the roster additions. He had known it was possible that the assets he had scrounged up during Durgan's pre-planned drive would prove vital to the Legion, but he hadn't expected them to arrive so quickly. He also hadn't thought he'd done enough work to bring the mixed mechs up to full brigade strength. Pushkin had been a busy man, and he was right. Jenkins shouldn't have thought so little of him.

"The Han Razorbacks can be dropped and retrieved by the *Red Hare* because of their uniform design," Xi ventured skeptically. "But without the *Bonhoeffer's* cans, how do we deploy all the older mixed mechs?"

"While Fleet can't lend direct support with hull reassignments," Admiral Zhao explained, "we *can* open up a few slots at the New America and New Africa shipyards to get some of your more...*classic* dropships out of mothballs in a reasonable timeframe."

"The *Mencken?*" Jenkins asked hopefully. The *HL Mencken* was a Behemoth-class assault carrier of nearly-identical design to the *Dietrich Bonhoeffer*, the sole but key difference being its lack of the *Bahamut Zero's* drop system. Along with two other derelict Behemoths, the *Mencken* was presently in the New America boneyard, where it had sat idle for forty years. It was by far the best candidate of the trio for refit, but

Admiral Zhao's irritably shaking head dashed Jenkins' sudden hopes of riding the mighty warship into battle.

"Eventually," Zhao allowed, "but that will take four to six months, even with a full refit crew and uninterrupted supplies, which will also take time to source. We can get some of the smaller ships moving under their own power and drop-capable in *weeks*, not months, so for now, the only combat-rated dropship you'll have is the *Red Hare*."

"I'd be lying if I said I wasn't disappointed." Jenkins smirked. "But the Legion has done more with less."

"That's the spirit," Zhao deadpanned before the group got down to the nuts and bolts of restructuring the Metal Legion in preparation for the greatest war humanity had ever participated in.

"Colonel Jenkins," Director Durgan greeted him in Pushkin's office six hours later, after the meeting with Zhao had concluded, "I hear congratulations are in order."

"Director," Jenkins responded graciously, "I suspect you were behind some of the recent heavy lifting."

"Some," Durgan allowed as Pushkin made his way to the minibar, where he snipped a trio of cigars and poured a round of drinks. "But not all. Mikhail is proving worthy of the big chair, as the Solar delegates suggest you are."

"I don't know how to take that, Director," Jenkins told him honestly, causing Durgan to chuckle.

"Straight as ever, Colonel." Durgan nodded approvingly. "Take it as a compliment from a society loathe to give them. You impressed them. A lot."

"The Solarians," Pushkin handed both Durgan and Jenkins cigars before lighting them in turn, "have made preliminary indications they will supply material assets to the Legion's efforts."

"Really?" Jenkins asked in surprise after drawing a long hit from the hand-wrapped stogie. It was good, with a warmth that seemed to permeate his pores, but he had never understood the infatuation with the things. "What are they offering?"

"Void fighters, primarily," Durgan replied sourly. "But they say they've got a few dozen old museum pieces they'll kick over as soon as the Nexus cools off."

"Ah." Jenkins nodded knowingly. "*That's* where the extra mechs came from."

"Indeed." Pushkin nodded. "But we don't need to talk about that right now. The three of us have something more...radical I wanted to discuss behind closed doors."

Jenkins was intrigued, as was Director Durgan, apparently. "Well, go on, Mikhail," Durgan urged. "The assassins only managed to hit me with a *near-lethal* dose of radiation back at New Ukraine three weeks ago, but it's not like my time is worthless."

Jenkins was not surprised to learn that he had suffered an assassination attempt. During their last meeting, Durgan had intimated that he might not survive the coming attempts on his life. For Jenkins' part, he was glad the business magnate was still among the living.

"It's like this," Pushkin said after taking a long, deep draw from his cigar, prompting both Durgan and Jenkins to do likewise. "With all of the fundraising we've been doing, most of which is of your design," he said in deference to Director Durgan, "and with all the positive publicity we've gotten since Antivenom, we will never again have this good a chance to take the Metal Legion semi-private."

Durgan's eyebrows rose almost as sharply as Jenkins' did, but both men gave the suggestion serious consideration for several long, smoke-filled minutes before Jenkins finally broke the silence.

"It wouldn't be the first time a Republic armed forces organization went mercenary," Jenkins mused, recalling how several aerospace forces had successfully transferred from public to private status following the first Arh'Kel attacks. Some of those organizations persisted to this day and were among the most feared and celebrated Terran paramilitary organizations in the Republic.

"I'm not talking full mercenary. I'm thinking more along the lines of establishing parallel structures, one public, and the other...not so public," Pushkin clarified with a mischievous grin before turning serious. "How much material support have we received from the Republic's bureaucrats in the last ten, twenty, or even thirty years? Frozen Fire, Brick Top, Antivenom...*none* of them were possible because of the limited funding we receive from the government coffers. They were accomplished almost entirely because of private donations made by businessmen like you." He made meaningful eye contact with Durgan. "If Fleet had gotten its way, it would have swallowed every single fusion core and capacitor you quietly slipped to us, and we wouldn't have had *half* the battle-ready mechs we needed for Brick Top and Antivenom."

"Things are different, Mikhail," Durgan replied pointedly. "The last thing you want to do is spoil your branch's ascent by an ill-timed shift just when things are changing in your favor."

"Nothing ever changes." Pushkin snorted. "Admiral Zhao is a good man, but the only reason he could convince Fleet to give us access to those shipyards is that we are at an all-time-high in public approval. Have you seen the unsolicited enlistment submissions pouring into TAC's servers?" Pushkin snorted derisively. "Armor Corps has received two hundred thousand applications since the court-martial was aired. I've had to ask the administrative staff to work double-shifts to process the paper-work before the applicants move on. Probably ten percent of the applicants would make good Metalheads or support staff, and *all* Metalheads would make good spacers."

"I'm not sure, General," Jenkins said skeptically. "It seems...cold."

Pushkin held up his hand calmingly. "I'm not even suggesting it's what we should do. I'm just saying that I've spent an entire career watching those fuck-sticks carve little pieces off this branch year after year. I'm telling you both," he fixed them with a hard look, "this is the best opportunity I have ever seen for the Metal Legion to widen its stance and shore up its base. I will continue to quietly make preparations, but I will not act without your input," he added, settling his heavy gaze on Jenkins.

"Why mine?" Jenkins asked warily.

"Because you *are* this branch," Pushkin replied. "I am its past. I will not make decisions you disagree with or set courses you cannot hold after my hand is gone. I am an old man who has remained here out of loyalty to a dear friend who is no longer with us. My days are numbered, both in the Legion and in the universe." He chuckled. "But I will do everything I can to help you take the Metal Legion in whatever direction you think appropriate. Ben trusted you. You gave him hope, and in doing so, you have given me purpose."

Jenkins shook his head in disbelief. "I...don't know what to say."

"Say nothing." Pushkin grunted. "Just give my suggestion as much consideration as you can."

"I don't think I'm ready to make those kinds of decisions," Jenkins said bluntly, drawing a smirk from Durgan and a belly laugh from Pushkin.

"No one ever is, Colonel." General Pushkin smiled. "You do

the best you can, second to second and day to day, in the ultimately futile hope that you can keep it all from crashing down around you as you work to stay ahead of the mother of all bitches: entropy. Every second of life is a struggle for survival. Why should a second in the Legion be any different? It was how we worked under Ben, and it's how we'll continue to work after we hold his funeral tomorrow."

"I'm unconvinced of the mercenary option on the whole," Durgan said into the growing silence that followed the mention of Akinouye's funeral. "But you're a smart man. You'll come up with a winning strategy, and I'll continue to support it even if I end up lashed to the wheel of government."

"You are doing well in the polls, no?" Pushkin laughed.

"Well enough," Durgan allowed. "But there's still a lot of time between now and the general election."

"Well, a better candidate for President I could not imagine," General Pushkin said with feeling. "Especially given the circumstances. You will have my support."

"I appreciate that, Mikhail." Durgan nodded, turning to Jenkins. "I've got a courier to catch, but I wanted to look you in the eye and offer my congratulations. You did well, Colonel, and considering the magnitude of the operation, that's quite a feat."

"Thank you, Director," Jenkins replied.

The trio parted company and Jenkins made his way to the quarters assigned him at Armor Corps HQ. Once there, he hit the sack and didn't move for fourteen hours.

EPILOGUE: A NEW BEGINNING

"That was quite a moving service, Major," Sarah Samuels said after Xi Bao sat down in the chair opposite the annoyingly beautiful reporter.

"Fifty-three guns was nowhere near enough for a proper salute to General Akinouye's career," Xi retorted, referring to the number of guns fired at Terran military funeral services. Fifty-three was the original number of colonies, most of which had been snuffed out when the wormholes had first collapsed. "But it's tradition," she added, "and as much as he supported individual expression, the old man cared a *lot* about tradition."

"The musical performances blended a bit of both, no? A ten-hour medley of tracks performed solely by Armor Corps personnel was certainly a feast for the ears. On that note," Samuels veritably purred, "I had no idea you were such a talented guitarist, Major."

"I can pick a little," Xi said dismissively. "But it was Podsy's drum work that really shined. And if you weren't impressed by Blinky's upper vocal register during his interpretation of *Number of the Beast* or *Soulforged*, there's something very, *very* wrong with you."

"That would be Lieutenant Staubach?" Samuels clarified.

"He may be Lieutenant Staubach to you," Xi cracked a wry grin, "but he'll always be Blinky to me."

"There's that razor-sharp tongue again." The reporter flashed a winning smile. "Are all Metalheads as quick-witted as you, Major Xi Bao?"

"Iron sharpens iron." Xi shrugged. "You try living for weeks on end in a sweaty metal box with someone who, on a good day, smells like they crawled out of a high school football team's soiled laundry bin and see if *you* don't develop a prickly demeanor."

Samuels' lips twisted into a faint smirk. "You may have forgotten that I *did*, in fact, spend several weeks aboard your mech on Shiva's Wrath?"

"Sharing a space with you for a month isn't the kind of thing someone quickly forgets," Xi quipped. "But you were already prickly before you came aboard."

"Coming from you, I'll take that as a compliment." The blond reporter laughed.

"That'd be the safe play," Xi agreed with a bemused grin.

"So how does it feel being the youngest major in Terran Armed Forces history?" Samuels switched gears with the maddening ease all professional reporters seemed to possess.

"I don't think about it." Xi shrugged. "It just is. I do everything I can, day after day, to be worthy of the trust my fellow Metalheads give me."

"Did you earn their trust on Luna?"

"You'd have to ask them," Xi said steadily, still unsettled by the events of Operation Antivenom. She had no doubt she would eventually overcome the losses, both from a professional perspective and a personal one, but just now those wounds were too fresh to ignore. "What I'll say without hesitation is that they validated mine in them."

"My, my." Samuels cocked her head curiously. "Did saving Solar humanity blunt some of that sharp edge you've become famous for?"

"We lost a lot of people on Luna, Ms. Samuels," Xi said tightly. "Both Terra and Sol lost sons, daughters, brothers, sisters, fathers, and mothers. We'll *never* recover from that loss. All we can do is move on and keep the torch as high as possible while we keep putting one foot in front of the other."

"Just six months ago, the Terran Armor Corps was considered a vestige of the Terran military." Samuels shifted gears again. "But today it enjoys a popularity that surpasses even the universally-beloved Terran Fleet. What do you think about that?"

"I think people appreciate results," Xi said carefully, "and it's natural to support victory. I think the Metal Legion has a brighter future than its detractors care to admit, and I think the Terran people see that more clearly now than ever."

"That sounded awfully diplomatic," Samuels observed. "Can we expect to see Xi Bao on a political ballot in the near future?"

"Not likely." Xi scoffed. "Besides, aren't Tier One felons prevented from voting or holding public office for twenty years?"

"I'm glad you mentioned that," the reporter said neutrally, causing Xi's mouth to suddenly go dry in anticipation of a purely antagonistic line of inquiry. "There's a lot of conversation going on about how the Metal Legion's active roster features an inordinately high ratio of prisoners and general ne'er-do-wells. Much has been made of whether it was a fluke that you came together to pull off some of the most difficult operations in human history, or whether maybe we've collectively misjudged who can and can't contribute to society."

"I think society always has blind spots," Xi said measuredly, knowing that this particular line of questioning could lead her straight into a political minefield. The last thing she wanted to do was hurt the Legion just as its momentum started moving in the right direction. "I don't think anyone can be faulted for missing out on opportunities, and I don't think societies should feel all that bad about implementing and continuing practices that later turn out to be problematic. But I *do* think that once there's evidence in hand to suggest those practices could use revision, society owes it to itself and its individual constituents to make the appropriate adjustments. Nobody can know everything. Humans are *terrible* at predicting the future. Maybe we're not actually all that smart," she allowed, recalling the Vorr's consistent remarks along those lines, "but we're pretty good at using evidence to revise our beliefs and practices...when we want to be. You and I will probably never be friends," she added, "but I respect the job you do, and I think a large part of that job is at least as noble as anything I'll ever do. Your role, certainly more than mine, is to help expose the blind spots that end up hurting society. I can offer my opinion and perspective, but in the end, I'm just a girl who likes playing with big guns."

Samuels' grin spread into a genuine-looking one. "If there was one thing you could say to every Terran, what would it be?"

Xi considered the question for a long moment before leaning forward and meeting the other woman's eyes. "The Metal Legion did something extraordinary on Luna, but we didn't do it alone. We had the support of many people, from wealthy businessmen to factory workers who made sure our ordnance was up to standards by caring deeply about doing their jobs to the best of their ability. For example, Antivenom was the first time in my career that my crew didn't have a single cartridge jam or a pack of supplies fail. That *means* something to me," she said passionately. "It means that even though I might be out on a cold, dead rock somewhere way beyond the line, there are literally *thousands* of people working various jobs in the Republic who've got my back. The military is just the tip of the spear, Ms. Samuels. A spear-tip by itself is unwieldy, poorly-balanced, and more likely to harm its wielder than the enemy. But with the shaft of society behind it, that spear-tip becomes part of a devastating system. We Metalheads will keep charging forward because, frankly, it's what warriors do. It's the only way we know how to be. We *want* to be on the line doing our part to keep society safe."

"Hearing you say that," Samuels mused, "I think I actually believe it. It runs in such stark contrast to some of the sentiment we see expressed in the media, with distressed servicemen coming home and struggling to rejoin society."

"Everyone faces different challenges," Xi said heavily. "I can't speak to theirs. I *can* speak for the rest of the Metalheads when I say we'll keep our eyes on the enemy for as long as we can, but we can't do it alone." She shook her head with dramatic emphasis. "We need everyone *behind* us to do their part. Humanity's horizons have never been broader and the sky over our heads has never been darker than they are at this very moment. Right now, all-out war rages between nearly every single intelligent species in Nexus space, and both Terra and Sol have choices to make about how we will contribute to that conflict. If we're not careful, humanity will end up as a footnote in some non-human archeological record when they pick over our long-dead bones thousands of years from now. I, for one, will not stand by while my fate is decided by strangers from distant stars."

She stood from the chair, and for a moment she thought Samuels looked more than just interested in her surprisingly-impassioned speech. The reporter actually looked *convinced* by Xi's words.

"I'm going back to HQ, Ms. Samuels, where the rest of my

Metalheads are getting ready for the next fight. And the next. And the one after that," Xi said with conviction, smartly donning her beret. "The Metal Legion is ready to play its part in shaping humanity's future. It's my sincerest hope that *every* human, both Terran and Solarian, feels the same." Xi took one step away before stopping and turning back. "Never forget, Ms. Samuels: metal never dies."

The End

Metal Legion, Book 4

If you like this book, please leave a review. This is a new series, so the only way I can decide whether to commit more time to it is by getting feedback from you, the readers. Your opinion matters to me. Continue or not? I have only so much time to craft new stories. Help me invest that time wisely. Plus, reviews buoy my spirits and stoke the fires of creativity.

Don't stop now! Keep turning the pages as Craig talks about his thoughts on this book and the overall project called Metal Legion.

You are still reading! Thank you so much. It doesn't get much better than that.

What a fabulous end to the first arc before the Metal Legion drops onto new planets in prohibited space against old and new enemies. As the Marine Corps of today knows, it takes fighters to control the sky, but it takes boots on the ground to win the war.

That's what Jenkins and Xi bring to the fore—the will to win against a determined enemy. How about that court-martial? I love the respect that people can show their fellows. I also claim very few friends. It's not the quantity that matters but the quality.

I had the great fortune of spending Christmas in Hawaii, New Year's in Australia, and a few days after that in Bali. The weather in all three places was incredible, maybe a little toasty down under, maybe a little too humid in Indonesia, but that was all good compared to what we came home to. It was -38F when we landed in Fairbanks. From when we got up earlier that day for our flights home, the temperature had changed 123 degrees. It was quite the shock to the system.

We had turned the thermostats down in our house, but even 64F felt warm after spending ten seconds outside. I turned the pellet stove on and the thermostats up. It took a while, but soon we were able to snag a few hours of sleep. Sleeping on a plane messes with me, and it took nearly a full week to get back into the groove.

It could have also been the extreme cold. It hit -44F this morning. Poor Phyllis the Arctic Dog! She is very efficient at these temperatures, but it's still hard on her.

What is next in the worlds where I live?

I love the *Metal Legion*, so look for the next four books in that story arc. I think Book 5 may hit around the middle of February. That would be way cool:) Then we're going to do a new series in the same universe, but completely standalone. *Battleship Leviathan*. I'll let the series name work its magic. A ship. Alone in space. Fighting the battles that others can't. Or won't. Space combat amid the majesty of the universe.

I have Executioner 5 to write. *Slave Trade* is off and

running, but with so many projects ongoing, I'm working like a fiend to stay caught up. By the time you read this, *Mystically Engineered 1 – Dragon Invasion* (with Valerie Emerson doing the heavy lifting in that series) will be published along with *End Days 1 – Blue Apocalypse* (E.E. Isherwood is doing the lion's share of the work). Those two books hold great potential, even though they are on different ends of the genre spectrum. One is dragons in space. The other is a post-apocalyptic adventure. Both are great stories and great series.

Monster Case Files is a passion project that could be a huge hit. Think of Scooby Doo meets Nancy Drew. That is what's called the Young Adult Cozy Mystery genre. I have four books already in hand and need to crank out a short prequel that we'll give away for free to show current and potential future readers what it's all about. Take a look for yourself if you'd like. I don't expect my hardcore military science fiction readers will be into this, but I love mil sci-fi and also Scooby Doo... You can get Real Ghosts, Monster Case Files, Book 0 for FREE – just join the email list - BookHip.com/CRCPXK

Back to the grind. No rest for the weary, as they say.

Peace, fellow humans.

***

Please join my Newsletter (www.craigmartelle.com – please, please, please sign up!), or you can follow me on Facebook since you'll get the same opportunity to pick up the books for only 99 cents on the first Saturday after they get published.

If you liked this story, you might like some of my other books. You can join my mailing list by dropping by my website **www.craigmartelle.com** or if you have any comments, shoot me a note at craig@craigmartelle.com. I am always happy to hear from people who've read my work. I try to answer every email I receive.

If you liked the story, please write a short review for me on Amazon. I greatly appreciate any kind words, even one or two sentences go a long way. The number of reviews an ebook receives greatly improves how well an ebook does on Amazon.

Amazon – www.amazon.com/author/craigmartelle

BookBub – https://www.bookbub.com/authors/craig-martelle

Facebook – www.facebook.com/authorcraigmartelle

My web page – www.craigmartelle.com

That's it—break's over, back to writing the next book.

BOOKS BY CRAIG MARTELLE

Craig Martelle's other books (listed by series)

Terry Henry Walton Chronicles (co-written with Michael Anderle) – a post-apocalyptic paranormal adventure

Gateway to the Universe (co-written with Justin Sloan & Michael Anderle) – this book transitions the characters from the Terry Henry Walton Chronicles to The Bad Company

The Bad Company (co-written with Michael Anderle) – a military science fiction space opera

End Times Alaska (also available in audio) – a Permuted Press publication – a post-apocalyptic survivalist adventure

The Free Trader – a Young Adult Science Fiction Action Adventure

Cygnus Space Opera – A Young Adult Space Opera (set in the Free Trader universe)

Darklanding (co-written with Scott Moon) – a Space Western

Rick Banik – Spy & Terrorism Action Adventure

Become a Successful Indie Author – a non-fiction work

Enemy of my Enemy (co-written with Tim Marquitz) – a galactic alien military space opera

Superdreadnought (co-written with Tim Marquitz) – a military space opera

Metal Legion (co-written with Caleb Wachter) - a military space opera

End Days (co-written with E.E. Isherwood) – a post-apocalyptic adventure

Mystically Engineered (co-written with Valerie Emerson) – dragons in space

Monster Case Files (co-written with Kathryn Hearst) – a young-adult cozy mystery series

For a complete list of books from Craig, please see www. craigmartelle.com